UNPROFESSIONALLY YOURS

EVE STERLING

ISBN-13: 979-8-88627-586-5

Cover design by: Eve Sterling
Cover Photo: Depositphotos
Edited By: Dee's Notes

Printed in the United States of America

For my friends and family that believed I could...
And never stopped telling me that.

PLAYLIST

"Never Be the Same (Acoustic Version)" by Jonah Baker

"There's No Way (feat. Julia Michaels)" by Lauv

"Mine" by Taylor Swift

"If You Love Her (feat. Meghan Trainor)" by Forest Blakk

"You and Me" by Lifehouse

"Today Was A Fairytale (Taylor's Version)" by Taylor Swift

"Little Did I Know" by Julia Michaels

"Because of You" by Kelly Clarkson

"That Don't Impress Me Much" by HAIM

"For You" by Daniel Josefson

"One Woman Man" by John Legend

"No One – Acoustic" by Alicia Keys

"Heaven – Acoustic" by Kane Brown

"Halo" by Beyonce

"Out of My League" by Stephen Speaks

"She Will Be Loved" by Maroon 5

"Best of You" by Foo Fighters

"Take A Bow" by Rihanna

"Speechless" by Dan + Shay

"Angel" by Florida Georgia Line

ONE

HOLLIE

Clack Clack Clack

The receptionist, whose desk fills the center of the spacious marble and glass lobby, continues typing away while I nervously glance at the time on my phone for what must be the hundredth time in the past five minutes. Occasionally, she raises her head of perfectly coiffed hair and eyes me suspiciously. I'm sure she's wondering what I'm doing here as much as I am.

I'm perfectly out of place in my best—and only—black pencil skirt, white blouse, herringbone blazer, and 3-inch heels I borrowed from my much more stylish roommate, Bianca. It's unfortunate that said heels are about two sizes too small and pinch my toes cruelly.

This is my sixth job interview in the past month. I sent my resume out to at least one hundred companies and six interviews was all I had to show for it. How many call backs had I gotten from those interviews? Exactly zero.

Everyone wanted someone with experience for their marketing department. The problem was that I couldn't get anyone to hire me to *give* me that experience. I felt like I was stuck in a perpetual catch 22.

The only reason I was sitting here in the executive lobby of Clarke Hotels' executive offices was because Bianca's father had called in a favor. Apparently, he and the CEO, Archer Clarke, have done some business together in the past and were friends. Mr. Clarke has agreed to give me an interview, but I would have to earn the job on my own.

At 10 a.m. on the dot, the receptionist clears her throat and narrows her eyes on me. "Ms. Simmons, Mr. Clarke, will see you now. Follow the hall on the left and it will be the office at the end." She quickly diverts her eyes back to the computer screen, effectively dismissing me.

I hop up, trying not to wince as the borrowed shoes scrape across the backs of my heels. I was definitely going to have blisters. "Thanks," I choke out, adding a little wave that the receptionist doesn't acknowledge and make my way down the hallway.

As I proceed across the lobby, I nervously smooth my skirt over my full thighs. This was the most professional outfit I could put together from the meager offerings in my closet. I *had* to get this job. My family back home was counting on me. They needed any money I could send them. My mother isn't exactly what you would call a nurturing provider. In fact, I was pretty sure she blamed me for every problem in her life. Mostly because that was what she told me when she was wasted. Which was often.

Mom made it clear that she blamed me for coming along unexpectedly and my father taking off. He didn't provide any support while I was growing up, even though he was well off and a major player in the Seattle business scene. Mom did the best she could, working retail and waitressing jobs, but when my half-sister came along and she didn't even know who her father was, the drinking got worse. Like it often does, the drinking eventually led to drugs and soon she couldn't keep even the simplest jobs.

Throughout high school, I had to step up to make sure that the house stayed in order and the bills were getting paid. I wasn't so much worried for my mother as I was for my half-sister, Paige, who was now in her junior year of high school. Since I'd been gone for the past four years at Branson College, they needed all the help they could get.

I didn't spend four years acing every class and completely neglecting my social life to sit around unemployed. I was going to get this job and send money home. Everything would fall into place.

Keep telling yourself that, Hollie.

I turned left and swiftly made my way down the long hallway lined with artwork that probably cost more than I could ever make in a year. There was a buzz in the air as I walked by offices filled with people working away. Every person I passed seemed to move at high speeds, like they had somewhere very important to be.

Approaching the office at the end, I notice the

conspicuously empty desk in front of Mr. Clarke's giant door where an assistant would normally sit. Maybe they're on a break? Releasing a shaky breath and gathering my courage, I knock on the wooden door. From within I hear a deep, masculine voice bark, "Enter."

Pulling open the door, I step inside an office that's almost as large as the lobby downstairs. There's an impressive wall of floor to ceiling windows that look out on the downtown Seattle skyline and the waterfront beyond.

Glancing around the room, I spot who I can only assume is Mr. Clarke. His head is down, staring at documents on his desk, and he appears to be making notations on them with a red inked pen. His desk and leather chair are huge, but that seems only to be to accommodate the enormous expanse of his shoulders in what looks like a bespoke gray suit. It had to be custom, right? No off the rack suit would fit those shoulders.

Sitting down in the plush chair stationed in front of the mahogany desk, I hold my head high, ready to make my best first impression. I can't see his face as he reads the document centered in front of him but note his dark brown hair that's cut shorter on the sides than it is on the top. He still hasn't looked up at me or said a word. After about a minute, I grow more anxious and fidget in my chair.

He knew I was here, right? I mean, he had to. He told me to come in. Was he expecting me to say something? "Excuse me, Mr. Clarke—"

"Just a moment." His deep voice washes over me and makes my stomach do a tiny flip. This is ridiculous. No guy's voice has ever made me nervous before. That's what the flip was, right? Nerves. I take a deep breath and try to steady myself while studying his masculine, yet somehow elegant, hands as he marks up his paperwork.

After what feels like an eternity, he sets aside the pen and lifts his gaze to mine. I suck in a quick breath as whiskey-colored eyes meet my own.

Man, he's pretty. Wait, can a man be pretty? He's gorgeous. Of course I researched him online before coming here and it was obvious the man was good-looking. However, those pictures didn't do the man justice.

In the flesh, Archer Clarke is more than good-looking. He radiates an energy of strength and power that only the most confident of men could possess. I've met men with this kind of presence before and they were always bad news.

There's that stomach flip again, only larger this time. Nerves. That's what it was. His eyes flash an emotion that I can't quite read before he schools his features and stares at me steadily. "Miss. Simmons, it appears you are here for a job."

"Y-yes, sir," I stammer slightly.

Get it together, Hollie. This is just another guy in a suit.

I suck in another breath and straighten my shoulders, steadily meeting his eyes. "Thank you for taking the time to meet with me."

"I'm sure you realize I don't make it a normal practice to meet with prospective entry-level employees," he says icily. "Dante Moreno asked to give you a shot, and he's been a good friend and business associate to me over the years. That doesn't mean you have the job yet."

There's an almost hostile vibe coming off him. Of course he wouldn't normally interview someone like me. In fact, I hadn't expected him to. I was sure he would pass me off to some lower-level employee. It wasn't my fault that he took the interview himself.

"Of course, Mr. Clarke. I'm very grateful to Mr. Moreno for putting in a good word for me, but would never expect you to just hand me a job. I'm a hard worker and believe I can be an asset to your company."

He purses his lips and hums at me slightly, diverting his eyes to the computer screen next to him. With a few clicks of the mouse, he brings up a document I can't see.

"Your resume says you recently graduated from Branson College with a degree in marketing and that you're looking for a place on a marketing team."

"Yes sir, I graduated Summa Cum Laude."

"It doesn't appear you have much experience in marketing and none in the hotel industry."

"That's correct, sir." I nervously smooth out my skirt once again. This has been the crux of the problem in all my previous interviews. "While attending school, I worked for a local independent bookstore and helped them with some small marketing campaigns that saw a five hundred and seventeen percent ROI and a thirteen percent up-tick in business. I can assure you, I'm a hard worker and a quick learner. If you give me a chance, you won't regret it."

"Hmmm…" There's that hum again. I wonder what it means. He continues assessing me with those deep brown eyes and I meet his gaze as confidently as I can while my hands shake slightly in my lap. I twine my fingers together, hoping to steady them. After a few moments of silence, he turns his eyes away from me to glance back at his computer screen, where my resume apparently sits.

"Well, Miss. Simmons, we don't currently have any openings in our marketing department and even if we did, I don't believe you have the experience that would qualify you." My shoulders slump in defeat. I came all the way here for this? If he didn't have an open position, he should have just told Mr. Moreno and saved us both the trouble.

"However." His eyes dart back to me, only lower this time. Is he staring at my lips? An unwelcome blush heats my cheeks, and I involuntarily wet my bottom lip with my tongue in response. That seems to bring his eyes right back up to mine. "I lost my latest assistant this morning and I'm going to need someone right away. If you can start on Monday, the job's yours. I think you'll find that the salary and benefits are more than fair. You'll receive a salary of seventy-five thousand and full health benefits, including a 401k with an employer match."

My eyes bug out as I hear the number. Seventy-five thousand dollars? Most entry level marketing positions start below fifty thousand dollars. There has to be some kind of catch. "You *lost* your assistant?" I ask, unable to keep the skepticism out of my voice.

"That is what I said, Miss. Simmons," he practically snaps back at me.

Ooookay. While the money is certainly tempting, I worked my butt off the past four years to be in marketing, not someone's errand girl. Especially not a sexy arrogant grouch like this man.

"What about the marketing position?"

He leans back in his chair, steepling his hands in front of his chest. The corner of his mouth lifts a fraction in what looks like it could be a smirk one day if it tried *really* hard. "You can learn the business while working for me and if you want to transfer to the marketing department after a period of time, I'm willing to consider it."

What choice did I have? This job would pay better than a marketing position and it's not like any of those offers were rolling in anyway. I could work for him, learn the business, and then move to a marketing job. I could make this work. Paige needs school supplies, and I'm sure that my mother is behind on her rent again. Yeah, there's no other logical choice.

"In that case, Mr. Clarke," I stand, reaching my hand across his desk to give him my most professional handshake, "I accept. I look forward to working with you." He raises out of his chair, and I'm suddenly made aware of exactly how tall he is. I'm five-foot-four and he's almost a foot taller than me. I tip my head way back to look him in the eye while his large hand engulfs mine. A shock immediately runs up my arm, through my chest, and down to my center. With a tiny gasp, I pull my hand back from his and avert my eyes so he can't see my reaction. I squeeze my thighs together to lessen the ache that's settled there.

What the hell was that, Hollie? We don't get all gooey for boys. Especially not a grouchy one in a suit who is going to be our boss. But Archer Clarke isn't a boy at all. He's most definitely a man and I don't have any experience with men. Hell, I don't have very much experience with boys.

"I'll see you Monday at nine sharp, Miss. Simmons. Not a minute later." Not daring to speak in case he changes his mind, I simply jerk my chin down in a quick nod, turn on my heel, and swiftly exit his office. I can feel the weight of his eyes on me until I close the heavy wooden door and sag against it with relief.

Stepping into the typically gloomy Seattle morning, I can't hide the wide smile on my face. After months of searching, I finally have a job! Sure, it's not the job I was expecting, but it is something. Plus, my salary is more than I could have hoped for. If Archer Clarke needs someone to answer his phone and make him coffee, that's fine by me. I'd be happy to do that for $75,000 a year.

Of course, he wasn't very forthcoming about how he "lost" his last assistant, but I'm sure I can handle anything he throws at me. I'll be the best damn assistant he's ever had. Then he'll have no choice but to move me to the marketing department. It is a start, and that is all that matters.

As I make my way down the street to the nearby parking structure where I left my decades old Toyota Camry, my phone buzzes in the bottom of my purse. I step out of the foot traffic and lean against a building while I dig in my bag, looking for the insistent cell phone.

I grab it triumphantly, but my smile falters a bit when I see who is calling. Mom. I should make her ringtone the theme for the Wicked Witch of the West so that I have fair warning. Anxiety pools in the pit of my stomach. I don't know why she's calling, but you can bet it isn't for anything good. Shaking my head at myself for being unkind to the woman who raised me, I accept the call and hold it up to my ear.

"Hi, Mom," I say while continuing down the street to my car.

"Were you planning on calling me?" Her words are slightly slurred, and I heave a sigh when I see that it's only 10:45 in the morning. She's starting with the liquor early today. Either that or she's high. Hell, it's probably both. "Of course, Mom, I just left my interview and I'm walking to my car right now."

"And?" she clips out at me. My hand tightens around the plastic of my phone. If I squeeze it any harder, I'm afraid I'll crack the plastic. When she's drinking, she is not the most cordial person to speak to. I mean, our conversations are never great, but they are exponentially worse when she has some vodka in her.

My voice is tight as I say, "I got a job, Mom. I'm starting on Monday and should be able to send you and Paige money real soon." I know that's all she really cares about. She couldn't care less about my career. I definitely wasn't telling her how much money I will be making. She would expect all of it.

"So, I guess that fancy degree in marketing was worth it. Surprise, surprise," she slurs at me. I want to chuck the phone at the wall now. She's never been supportive of me going to college. She considered my leaving an act of abandonment, equal to that of my father's. If she had her way, I'd still be in our small town of Milford in eastern Washington, working a job waiting tables and taking care of her.

"It's actually not a marketing job. I don't have enough experience yet for that. I'll be working as the Personal Assistant to the owner of Clarke Hotels, Archer Clarke. It's a great opportunity for me to learn the ropes of the hotel business and could lead to me transferring to the marketing department eventually."

I can hear her snort in my ear. "Oh. A *Personal Assistant*," she practically sneers at me. "That's the way those rich men operate. They just want a pretty little thing to warm their beds and hang on their arms. Then he'll dump you and leave you all alone with a kid and nothing else to show for it. Believe me, I know."

I sigh into the phone. She's talking about herself again. I've heard this rant about successful men many times in my life. My father was one of those men and he left her high and dry. But not every successful businessman was like that. Right? Besides, it doesn't matter. I have zero intention of letting anything inappropriate happen between Archer Clarke and me. Plus, let's be honest, I'm not exactly his type.

"It's not like that, Mom. I'm just his personal assistant, that's it. There's no way I'm sleeping with him. You taught me better than that." Maybe complimenting her horrible parenting will get her to stop this line of conversation.

"Your sister needs some more books for her English class and there's a fee for her upcoming school trip, so we'll need you to send some money right away."

"Of course, Mom, I'll make sure Paige has everything she needs." I really don't want to ask the next question, but I do anyway. "How's the rent? Is it up to date?" I reach my old and dented sedan and lean up against it, waiting for her response.

"Well, it's a little behind. You know how it goes. There's always some unexpected expense that comes up."

I squeeze my eyes shut, letting my head thump against the roof of my car. "Yeah, Mom, I get it. No problem. When I get my first paycheck, I'll send you guys as much as I can."

"Thanks honey, I gotta go. Jeff is coming over." Ah yes, the loser boyfriend, Jeff. I'm pretty sure that this one doesn't even have a job, or if he does, it's as her dealer. That he's coming over in the middle of the day on a Friday speaks volumes. She sure knows how to pick 'em.

"Bye, Mom," I say, but the line is already dead. Of course. I toss the phone back into my purse, unlock the door, and slide into the driver's seat. I won't let her get to me. Paige needs me and despite everything, my mother is basically my only parent. I can't abandon either of them.

Pulling out into the congested downtown Seattle traffic, I head for home, hoping my two roommates aren't there yet. I absolutely adore them, but I need some time to shake off the fog my mom's call has left me in. As I turn onto the highway, it starts to rain.

TWO

ARCHER

What. The. Fuck.

My eyes are still glued to the door she's escaped through. I shake my head, trying to get my thoughts in order. Reaching down to adjust the hard length in my slacks, I let out a low groan. I've never had this kind of reaction to a woman before. Certainly not from merely being in her presence.

The moment Hollie Simmons opened the door and stepped into my office, I was hit with the intoxicating smell of honeysuckles. It reminded me of summer vacations and sunshine. The fragrance had clouded my mind, made my heart rate pick up and my dick twitch. I had to keep my eyes down on my paperwork while trying to get control of my emotions. I even tried ignoring her for a time while I got a grip on myself.

Once I had that moment of insanity smoothed over, I looked up and saw the most beautiful woman I have ever seen. My dick was at attention. Again. *Fuck.*

Her honey blonde hair was pulled up into a neat bun on the top of her head. My fingers itched to reach across the desk and pull the pins out so that I could see the hair fall around her shoulders. I wonder how long it is. I knew it would feel as soft as silk in my hands. She was in a professional but prim outfit of a blazer, skirt, and blouse. Her white blouse was buttoned up to the tantalizing hollow of her throat, covering her completely. That didn't stop me from imagining what her obviously curvy body would look like out of it, preferably spread out wide on my desk. I was certain her breasts would overfill my hands. The demure outfit was more tantalizing to my imagination than if she had walked in with a miniskirt and breasts hanging out. Not that I would mind seeing that either.

There was so much blood in the lower half of my body that my head spun. Women didn't do this to me. I had way too much control for that. Of course I appreciated a beautiful woman and occasionally took them to bed, but this kind of feral reaction is unheard of for me.

What the fuck was I thinking? I shouldn't have hired her as my assistant. She is going to be far too distracting. I should have created a job in the marketing department for her. I'm sure that Claire could use the help. Or better yet, I should have just told her that there was nothing here for her and sent her on her way. But I truly was in a bind with no personal assistant.

My latest PA, Jeremy I think, had quit first thing this morning, which was really quite rude of him. If he had told me last night, I could have gotten a temp for the day. People say that I am demanding, unreasonable, and intolerant. I think those people are lazy. I merely have exacting standards for not only myself, but for everyone that works for me. There is nothing wrong with that. I pay well and if I can work a fourteen-hour day, so can they.

With any luck, Miss. Hollie Simmons would crash and burn within the first few weeks, just like the rest of them. I am working on the most important deal of my career and can't afford any distractions right now. Especially not a blonde, curvy distraction that I absolutely cannot touch. Besides the fact that she is most likely ten years younger than me, she is also now my employee. I am many things, but I won't be the creepy boss hitting on his young secretary.

There is a knock at my door and for a second, hope blooms in my chest that Hollie has come back. Perhaps she has forgotten something? I push the feeling down and tell the knocker to come in.

The door opens and my CFO, Richard Osman, swiftly enters the room. Richard had been working at Clarke Hotels when my father ran the company before his death and I find his council invaluable. However, at the moment, I am annoyed he has interrupted my thoughts of Hollie. *Get it together, man!*

Richard settles into the seat that was recently vacated by Miss. Simmons. "How is the Santa Cruz deal coming along?" he asks. Yes, the Santa Cruz deal. I've had my eye on that piece of property for years and it is finally up for sale. At this point, it is almost an obsession. I want that land and I want to build a Clarke Hotel Luxury Resort there. It would be a flagship hotel for us. It is the start of a new venture for Clarke Hotels, breaking out of the boutique hotel business and into that of vacation resorts.

"It's going well. I've been moving around some of our resources for the purchase of the land and the subsequent building of the hotel. As you well know."

He leans forward in his chair, bracing his forearms on his legs, and gives me an assessing stare. I've been exceedingly careful to keep this deal hush hush. Only a select few employees and the members of the board know about it. They were reluctant at first to commit so many of our resources to this venture, but I had convinced them this is the best direction for us. I am staking not only the company, but my reputation on this deal.

"You didn't come in here just to ask me how the deal is going. You're the CFO. If something happened, you would probably be the one telling me. Why are you really here?" I ask, wanting to get straight to the point so I can go back to fantasizing about Hollie bent over my desk, wet and eager for me.

"We need to keep in close contact with Caroline DuPont." He's leaning back in his seat now, grinning at me. "Perhaps you could use some of that charm on her you're known for."

My jaw drops into what I'm sure is an appalled expression. "I don't think anyone has ever accused me of having charm before, Richard."

He barks out a laugh and shakes his head. "You're right, but maybe you could try it this time. Mrs. DuPont isn't the kind of CEO you're used to dealing with. She seems a bit more sentimental. This is her family's land after all, not some faceless company's."

I stare back at him incredulously. "She's a businesswoman like everyone else. I'm sure she'll find our offer more than generous and be happy to sell to Clarke Hotels."

"Of course, you're right Archer, but it couldn't hurt to smooth talk her a bit. I know how important this property is to you, and I don't want to see it slip out of your grasp."

I school the features on my face and give him a hard stare. "Of course, this property is important to me. This marks a new chapter for Clarke Hotels. We'll be a vacation destination, not just somewhere to stay."

"You can sell that line to the board all day long, but you and I both know it's more than that. You can lie to them, but don't lie to me or yourself. This property means everything to you."

I won't even dignify that with an answer.

"Was there anything else that you needed?" I ask him before turning my focus back on my computer screen that's still displaying Hollie's resume.

"Actually, yes, I noticed Josh isn't at his desk, so I assume he's quit as well? Or did you outright fire this one?"

My brows furrow in confusion. "Who the fuck is Josh?"

Richard lets out a genuine guffaw at that. "Your most recent assistant. You didn't even know this one's name?"

"I thought it was Jeremy," I grumble, not wanting to admit that I absolutely did not remember his name. "He abruptly quit this morning saying something about me being unreasonable and him not being able to sleep at night. As if his sleep is somehow my problem." Honestly,

I didn't pay much attention to what *Josh* was saying. I was busy preparing for my 9 am conference call with some of our hotels' general managers.

"I suppose I'll have to have Greg in HR send you the latest batch of resumes. You can't go too long without an assistant. It's a good thing we always keep them on file, considering how often we need them." He goes to stand from his chair, but I wave my hand at him dismissively.

"There's no need. I've already hired a replacement." I avert my eyes and begin straightening the paperwork on my desk. Richard can read me better than anyone and I don't want to hear what he has to say about my impulsive hire of the young Miss. Simmons.

Richard's eyebrows shoot up, almost reaching his hairline. "How did you manage that already? He quit this morning. Did you just grab someone off the street?" His teasing tone of voice has me getting defensive. That's okay, getting defensive is better than him finding out I'm attracted to my new beautiful young assistant.

"Actually, she was a referral from Dante Moreno. She came in for a marketing position, but since there is nothing available right now and I need the help, I figured it would be a good match."

He's eyeing me incredulously, seeming to think before he asks, "And why would Dante refer someone to work here? He owns a construction company, not a staffing service."

I narrow my eyes at him. Why he feels the need to tell me things I already know, I don't have a clue. "Yes, but this was a favor to him. I guess she's a friend of his daughter's and is looking to get her foot in the door since she's a recent graduate."

"Recent graduate," he mumbles to himself.

"Yes, is there a parrot in the room I'm not aware of? She graduated from Branson, Summa Cum Laude." There's a hint of pride in my voice. Why I would be proud of someone I don't even know is beyond me, but it is what it is.

"Archer, does she even have any experience as a personal assistant? Let alone as one to a CEO of a Fortune 500 company?"

Here comes that defensive feeling again. "No, she doesn't have experience in this particular position, but we've hired dozens of assistants with stellar credentials over the past year and they have all been sub-par. Maybe somebody fresh will finally be able to hack it."

Richard leans back in his chair and stretches out his legs in front of him. He's looking at me with a knowing stare I don't appreciate one bit. "Is she pretty?"

I scoff at that question and try to sound offended. "I didn't notice, Richard. When have you ever known me to dally with employees? I mean, she's not hideous. Villagers wouldn't come after her with pitchforks, if that's what you're asking." I cross my arms and settle back into my chair.

"Riiiiight," he says, stretching out the word like he knows my game. He's just too loyal to say anything. Besides, I don't play games, and if I did, I would win. No question.

"Good luck with that. Hopefully, this one sticks around for more than a few weeks. Just—" It looks like he's not sure if he should say what comes out of his mouth next. "Be careful Archer, this is no time to give the board any reason to question you with the Santa Cruz deal so close."

"You have nothing to worry about, Richard," I deftly brush off his concerns. He, above all others, should realize that I'd never do anything to jeopardize this deal. This isn't just business, it's personal. Hollie Simmons may be the loveliest creature I've ever set eyes on, but there's no way I'll let her or anyone else interfere with this deal.

THREE

HOLLIE

Once I'm home, I change into my pajama shorts and tank top before collapsing on the couch. The first thing I'm doing once I get paid—besides sending money to mom and Paige—is buying some better work clothes along with shoes that actually fit. I briefly consider soaking my aching feet before I pick up the remote and surf Netflix, trying to find something to watch that will let my brain veg out for a while. However, my brain doesn't seem to be on the same page. My thoughts keep drifting back to Archer Clarke and those piercing brown eyes. It's almost like I can still feel them on me.

I'm being silly. There is no way a man like him would find a girl like me attractive. Don't get me wrong, I love myself and all my glorious short curviness, but men like Archer Clarke simply don't date girls like me. In fact, I know he doesn't. When I was researching for this interview, I saw pictures of him with dozens of women and they were all tall, thin, and perfectly poised. I'm pretty sure some of them were actual models. That's the type of girl Archer dates. Not a girl with a few too many curves and who is just starting out in life.

Not that I want to date him. He's my boss. This is strictly professional, even if he makes my body tingle all over with only a handshake. It's not a problem, I just won't touch him. Even if I wanted to, my mother's reminder of being a rich man's personal plaything was more than enough to put me off the idea. I settle back into the couch and start up a trashy TV show featuring housewives in California and prepare to space out when the front door bursts open.

In comes my roommate Bianca, known by everyone, except her parents, as B. She comes rushing in like the glorious storm she is, all color and excitement. She's an artist and is currently working at a small gallery downtown. I can't imagine her sitting down to do an office job every day. It's not in her DNA. She needs fresh air and freedom to express herself.

Following closely behind Bianca is my other roommate, Violet. If Bianca is a summer storm, then Violet is a quiet December snowfall. These two could not be more opposite. The three of us have been roommates for years and while Bianca and I have graduated and moved into the workforce, Violet stayed and is getting her master's degree in Comparative Literature. That girl enjoys nothing more than an evening sitting quietly with a book and a glass of wine. I love both of them to death.

"Hollie!" Bianca shouts, even though I'm sitting about five feet from her. "Well?" She has an expectant look on her face and the energy is practically radiating off of her. I think she may actually be bouncing on the balls of her feet.

"Well, what?" I play stupid, trying to hide my smile. I love to rile Bianca up. She says it's the Italian blood running through her that gives her personality that touch of spice.

"Don't you start with me, Hollie Simmons! 'Well', the job? Did you get it?"

My face breaks out into a huge grin as I confirm for them both that I did indeed land a job. They both rush over to me and the next thing I know, I'm being smothered to death with hugs.

"I'm so happy for you, Hollie," Violet says, being the first to extract herself from the pile of hugging arms and legs on the sofa. "I knew you would get something eventually. You're too smart and talented not to."

I give her a grin and squeeze her hand. Violet is definitely the sweet one of the group. "Actually," I say, straightening my top from where it's ridden up on my stomach from our impromptu mosh pit, "it's not a marketing job. There weren't any openings." Bianca's face falls immediately, so I'm quick to add, "but I got a job as Archer Clarke's personal assistant and it's even more money than the marketing job. Plus, he said I could transfer over after I learned the ropes of the business."

Bianca lets out a squeal. "That's even better! Plus, you get to work with that hot piece of ass, Archer Clarke!"

"B, he's my boss, you can't say that!"

"Why not? He is, you can't deny it." She turns to Violet and lifts her eyebrow.

"Totally hot," Violet confirms with a small smile touching her lips.

The blush on my cheeks runs down my chest, giving away my unease. "I don't know what you're talking about. I hadn't noticed. He's just a guy like any other. I'm concentrating on the work." *Thou doth protest too much, Hollie.*

"Sure," she says, not buying it for a second. "I'm sure you'll be running that place in no time." She nods her head like it's all set. Bianca has proclaimed it, so it shall be done.

I laugh and shake my head at her. "I'm not so sure about that, but I'm excited. My mom called and she's behind on the rent again and Paige needs some school supplies, so I should be able to send them money as soon as my first paycheck comes in."

Bianca's face turns serious and even Violet is sporting a tiny frown. I let out a sigh. Here we go.

"Hollie, you can't do everything for your mom," Bianca says, as if it's that easy. "You don't owe her anything. The fact she's still guilt tripping you is ridiculous."

Violet chimes in with, "She's right, Hollie. I mean, it's great to help take care of Paige and I'm not saying you shouldn't, but your mother might be taking advantage of you."

This is nothing I haven't heard from either of them before. I know how they feel, but they know my stance on this as well. "Come on you two, what happens if I don't help with the rent? It won't just be my mom out on the street, it will be Paige too."

Bianca crosses her arms over her ample chest, "I'm just saying—" I hold up a hand, stopping her from going on. I'm not in the mood to hear this again. Sure, my mom is probably asking too much of me, but what am I supposed to do? She's my mom.

"Enough about my mom." The only way out of this conversation is to change the subject. "What's going on this weekend? You realize it's my last one before I'm a real working woman?" Bianca reaches into her bag and pulls out a baguette and a bottle of white wine, presenting them to me like they are the Crown Jewels.

"Tonight," she exclaims happily, "we feast on wine, bread, and cheese to celebrate your new gainful employment. Oh also, I'm having brunch with my dad on Sunday and he wants you guys to join us."

"Of course," I say without hesitation. I owe Mr. Moreno for getting me the interview, and I can't wait to thank him. Plus, he's let us stay in this house, one of his rental properties, for years, free of charge. Frankly, without his help, I would have tucked my tail and run back to Milford a long time ago. There's no way l could have survived here on what I made working at the bookstore part-time. I'm also acutely aware that living here rent free isn't something that I can count on forever. Mr. Moreno could change his mind at any moment and we would be out of a place to live. This is a fantastic house in a safe neighborhood. Why wouldn't he want to collect rent on it? It's not like we have a lease or anything.

We both glance over at Violet, whose eyes are focused on the floor. She looks up and I notice a slight redness in her cheeks. I hope she's not getting sick. She has a ton of work to do for her graduate program. "No problem, I'll be there," she states quietly.

"How about we open up that wine and get down to business?" I grab the bottle from Bianca's hand and head over to the kitchen to grab a corkscrew and three glasses.

We spend the rest of the evening watching bad TV shows, gorging on cheese, and drinking a bit too much wine.

The weekend passes in a blur of cleaning, laundry, and stressing about my new job. Before I know it, it's Sunday morning and the three of us are seated at the Singing Lark for brunch, waiting for Mr. Moreno, who is running a few minutes late. It's one of the nicer restaurants in the area and I feel guilty because he always insists on picking up the tab.

We're sitting around, drinking bottomless mimosas, and chatting about life, when Bianca jumps up and waves her arms. "Dad! We're over here!" Dante Moreno comes sauntering over to us with a bright smile on his face and scoops Bianca into a bear hug. "Hey Bianca, how was your week?" he asks. They are chatting with each other while moving to their chairs across from Violet and me, and I can't help assuage the stab of jealousy inside.

I don't begrudge Bianca the relationship with her father. After her parents divorced when Bianca was two, her dad tried to keep in touch with her even though they lived hours apart. Since she's moved back to Seattle, he's done everything he could to become an active participant in her life. Unlike my father.

They get together for brunch practically every Sunday, and we were almost always invited. He was supportive of her moving into the art field and never pressured her to try something "more practical" like a lot of her friends in the Branson arts program.

Meanwhile, I hadn't spoken to my father in four years and that last time was not pleasant. I'm not proud that I basically had to blackmail my own father in order for him to pay for college. The man has barely given anything to my mother or myself over the years and he runs, from what I can gather, a very successful business. I ambushed him at his offices and merely asked him if he wanted all his fancy friends and business associates to know that he had a daughter out there that he basically abandoned.

Apparently, that's the way to get the man to open his wallet. Threaten his reputation. If I had any other way to pay for college, I would have done it. Since he is listed on my birth certificate, it looked like I had way too much money to receive any financial assistance. I absolutely hated asking that man for a single thing. That moment four years ago was the last time I'd spoken with him. However, his checks arrived at the Bursar's office every semester like clockwork. That's all that really mattered. Now I was out completely on my own and was relieved to not have to rely on him any longer.

As they both settled into their seats, Mr. Moreno turns his grin to me and asks, "How did the interview go, Hollie?"

"It was amazing. Thank you so much for getting me the interview."

He gives me a smile and peruses the menu in front of

him. "That's great to hear," he says.

"I wasn't expecting to meet with Mr. Clarke himself. That was a bit of a surprise. But I got a job as his personal assistant, so I'm pretty ecstatic. I never would have gotten it without your help."

The corners of his mouth turn down, and he sets the menu aside. "You're working directly for Archer?" I nod in confirmation. "Shit, I thought he would have something for you on his marketing team. I'm really sorry."

"There's no need to apologize. I'm honestly thrilled. The job starts tomorrow, so this is a great send off into the working world." I put on my biggest smile so he knows that I'm truly happy about this, even if it wasn't the job I was expecting.

"Just don't take anything he says too personally, Hollie," he says with a reassuring tone in his voice.

"What do you mean?"

"Archer Clarke isn't exactly known for his... graciousness. He's a bit of a hard ass. In fact, I'm not sure I've ever spoken to the same assistant twice when I've called his office."

My eyes grow large and I'm suddenly about ten times more anxious about tomorrow than I was a few moments ago. Does Archer Clarke really go through assistants like tissue paper? I mean, I met the man and I could tell that he was going to be tough to work for, but I had also expected him to give me half a chance.

Seeing my worry, he reaches across the table and gives my hand a fatherly tap of reassurance. "Don't worry Hollie, I'm sure you'll do great. Like I said, don't let him get to you."

I nod my head and turn back to my menu while the conversation at the table turns to the new collection that's going to be displayed at Bianca's gallery and Violet's classes.

What have I gotten myself into?

FOUR

ARCHER

It's Monday morning and I'm walking into the office at my normal time of eight thirty. To my surprise, Hollie is already sitting at her desk with Greg from HR next to her, filling in paperwork. I told her she didn't have to show up until nine. Perhaps this is a sign of good things to come.

Does Greg need to be sitting with her while she fills out all the required employment forms? And does he have to be sitting that close? Shaking my head at myself, I continue to make my way down the long hallway. I spent most of the weekend pointedly *not* thinking about Hollie Simmons. I didn't think about her at my business lunch, or while working out with my trainer, or while I laid awake staring at the ceiling at night. And I certainly didn't think of her in the shower this morning. *Twice.* This was not going well.

Young, naive girls like Hollie were looking for a relationship. That's not something I had to give, even if she wasn't an employee. Relationships aren't for me. I am married to this company and any woman that I may briefly encounter is merely a side piece. My preferred companions understood that and were looking for the same thing themselves. We both get pleasure out of the time we spend together and then are on our way.

Sure, sometimes I saw the same woman more than once, but the second I thought she might expect anything more from me, I was quick to cut her loose. There is no way I could do that with someone who was working for me. That and the potential sexual harassment lawsuits were keeping me far away from her.

"Good morning, Miss. Simmons. Greg," I greet them both coldly, masking my attraction to her while also hoping that Greg will make his way back to Human Resources where he belongs.

He jumps up from his chair, practically knocking it over. "Good morning, Mr. Clarke. I trust you had a good weekend." I simply give him a small nod and focus my attention on Hollie. She's wearing a pencil skirt again and a white blouse, this time sans blazer. Her shirt isn't quite buttoned up to her throat today. The very top button is undone.

Is that for me or for Greg?

I almost laugh at myself for that thought. If a woman is trying to attract a man, she certainly doesn't leave her top button undone to entice him. That is apparently just my kink.

"Miss. Simmons, when you're done with your paperwork, please come into my office and see me. Also, I'd like a coffee. One cream, one sugar."

"Yes, Mr. Clarke," she chirps at me and gives me a smile that I don't return.

I quickly stride past them both, entering my office and closing the solid door behind me. I let out the breath I didn't realize I was holding and take a seat at my desk, determined to concentrate on all that needs to be done today. The San Diego hotel is having staffing issues because of some immigration regulations. It must be bad if it's made its way up to me. I'll need to talk to the manager ASAP.

I bring up my email and note the staggering number that has accumulated between when I left the house and now. There are too many. I'm glad I'm not going through another day without an assistant.

I concentrate on returning one email after another for the next fifteen minutes until I hear a knock at my door. "Enter."

Hollie walks in with a confident stride and her head held high. She has a notebook and pen in one hand, coffee in the other. She gingerly sets the coffee down on my desk and then remains standing in front of me with an expectant expression on her face.

My eyes sweep from the top of her blonde bun down to the tips of her high heels. Every dirty secretary fantasy I've ever had is running through my head.

"Have a seat."

She quickly plants her butt into the same chair she sat in on Friday and opens her notebook to the first fresh page, pen poised to take notes on whatever task I assign her. It would amaze you at how many of my previous assistants have walked in here with nothing to take notes on. They're usually gone by the end of the day.

"I assume you've taken care of all of your HR paperwork?"

"Yes, sir."

Heat shoots through my body. Damn, I like it when she calls me 'Sir'. It would be even better if she was on her knees in front of me while she did it. It would probably be inappropriate to add that to her to-do list.

"I'll expect you here every morning before me so that you can prepare to brief me on my schedule for the day. In fact, if I'm here, I'll expect you to be here as well. That means your day isn't over until mine is." I pause for a moment to see her reaction to that. This is the point where the weak ones usually hem and haw about other responsibilities or places they need to be in the evenings, as if I should care. Hollie merely nods, pen poised over her pad of paper.

"I'll also require my coffee to be on my desk when I arrive. It should never be cold. Understand?" I know I'm being rather short with her, but I need to get her out of my office and back to her desk. Plus, I don't plan on treating her differently than any other assistant I've had, even if she did star in my fantasies this weekend.

"You got it, Mr. Clarke." She's studiously making notes in her notebook, her tongue poking out the corner of her mouth as she concentrates on what she's writing. Jesus Christ.

I clear my throat, and she brings her hazel eyes up to mine. "You'll have access to my calendar and scheduling my appointments. You'll also be screening my emails. If there is something that you can take care of, do it. I don't need to see requests for appointments, just handle it. If there is anything that I should see, forward it to me." I don't even give her a moment to finish writing before I continue rapid-firing information at her. "There should be a list in your desk of people that should be put through to me immediately if they call and those that need to go straight to my voicemail. There's only so much time in a day and I don't want it wasted."

"Of course."

I glance at the white gold Patek Philippe on my wrist and realize that I'll barely make my nine a.m. video conference with the board. "I need to speak with the General Manager of our San Diego hotel. Notify me when you have him on the line. That will be all for now, Miss. Simmons."

I dismiss her with no room for discussion, and she closes her notepad. Before she makes it out of my office, she stops and turns back to me. My eyes haven't left her once.

"Oh, Mr. Clarke?"

My eyes remain on her, staring, while waiting for what she has to say.

"Thank you again for the job. I can promise you won't regret it."

"The best way for you to thank me is by doing your job," I say gruffly. She nods and is quickly out the door, closing it behind her. I'm once again left alone wondering what I've done by hiring her. I was hoping when I showed up today I would find that my reaction on Friday had been a mistake. A fluke. That she wasn't as beautiful as I remembered, that her curves weren't quite as soft and grabbable. If anything, my memory had underestimated her appeal.

Letting out a sigh, I log into our secure site for my conference call. As the screen populates with boxes of other board members in their offices, I wait impatiently for the meeting to start. If it's not one thing, it's another with these people.

I see the box pop onto my screen that contains the rounded and reddened face of my Uncle Gilbert. Once upon a time, after my parents died when I was sixteen, Uncle Gilbert took over the operations of Clarke Hotels. It had not been a great time for us as a company. He was more interested in partying than he was in the business, and things slowly started trending downhill.

I couldn't let my father's legacy be run into the ground. I graduated from Stanford with a degree in business in three short years and at twenty-one, I took the reins of Clarke Hotels. It was my father's wish that I take over as CEO and while some of the board members resisted, most could see the writing on the wall with my uncle at the helm of this ship. When I took over, Uncle Gilbert maintained his position on the board. I can't imagine he was thrilled about giving up his job to a kid just out of school, but he didn't really have a choice.

Over the next twelve years, I not only righted the ship, but expanded operations, taking the company to a whole other level. Suddenly, a company with boutique hotels exclusively in Washington state had grown outwards until we were blanketing the western United States. What was once a multi-million dollar company was now a billion dollar one.

I am planning on opening a New York City hotel

within the next three years. In the meantime, we are going to up our status and value considerably once we open the resort in Santa Cruz. While no one could complain about the job I've done, a few board members are still worried about what putting so much of our resources into the Santa Cruz property would do if it failed.

They don't realize that I won't allow that to happen. This resort is going to be my crowning achievement. I just have to get Caroline DuPont to sell it to me. I know she is entertaining bids from several developers, but I'm confident that we'll offer her the most enticing deal.

Richard clears his throat over the speakers and begins the meeting. About thirty excruciating minutes later, everyone is logging off and my internal intercom buzzes. I hit the button to answer and Hollie's sweet voice comes out of the speaker at me.

"Mr. Clarke, I have a Mr. Rivera from The Clarke, San Diego on the line for you."

"Send him through." I glance at my watch, noting that the morning is slipping by me. There's a soft click in my ear as Hollie drops off the line and connects me to San Diego. I'm not looking forward to hearing Rivera complain about staffing problems. This should be something he can handle on his own. This is a general manager issue, not mine. However, I didn't make this company successful by keeping my hands clean.

I'm not sure I'll have time for lunch today with how things are going. It's not even ten, and I'm already woefully behind.

There isn't a chance to leave my office for the rest of the morning, so I haven't seen Hollie. She's begun forwarding me emails she thinks are relevant and most of the time she's correct. I also notice her forwarding emails that don't require my attention to the correct department. She is turning out to be at least competent. She has initiative. Perhaps this will work out better than I thought. I just have to stop thinking about her hair... and her lips... and her breasts.

At about two, there's a knock on the door and once I give permission to enter, Hollie pokes her head in. "I'm sorry to bother you, Mr. Clarke. I noticed it was getting late and you haven't had lunch yet. Can I order you something?"

Yes, this was definitely going better than I had hoped.

I let out a sigh and run my fingers through my hair. "Actually, yes, that would be great. All my regular orders are saved with the delivery service, along with the payment information. Order yourself something as well."

"Oh no," she says while shaking her head. "I brought a muffin and granola bar from home and had that a while ago. I just wanted to make sure you were taken care of."

Somehow, I'm both warmed and slightly annoyed at the same time. This girl wants to make sure that I'm taken care of. Sure, I have people doing things for me constantly but not things that I haven't ordered them to do. She went out of her way and came in here to make sure I was fed. Yet, she somehow thinks a muffin and a granola bar is an appropriate lunch. Someone obviously needs to be taking care of this girl. My mind wonders if there is someone at home that should be doing the job. Does she have a boyfriend? Now I'm truly getting angry. If she has a boyfriend, he should make sure that she eats better than that.

"A muffin and a granola bar are not a lunch. They are a snack. They're a breakfast at best. Make sure you order yourself something. If you're not hungry, take it home." My irrational anger at her maybe boyfriend not taking care of her, is leaching into my voice but I couldn't care less.

"Ummm, okay. I will, thanks." Her eyes are narrowed at me and I can tell that she doesn't appreciate my tone or my high-handed manner. Too bad, I'm the boss.

"Order us something from Emilio's." She doesn't answer, but closes the door a little harder than necessary. Well, now she's annoyed. Welcome to the club, sweetheart.

I get back to work and barely notice when she enters the room and slides my lunch onto my desk and leaves. Good. This is how it should be. Minimal conversation, not caring what my assistant eats, working efficiently together but apart.

Six p.m. quickly rolls around, so I gather up what I'll be taking home to work on for the next two or three hours before I exhaust myself enough to sleep. I step out of my office and see Hollie still stationed at her desk.

"You can leave for the day, Miss. Simmons. I'll see you in the morning." I don't wait for her answer as I stride to the elevator. With any luck, at home where I have some distance from her, I'll be able to get her out of my head.

FIVE

HOLLIE

The two weeks I've been working at Clarke Hotels have passed in a blur of phones, emails, and a hot as sin CEO with a bad attitude. The tasks aren't that complicated, but Archer's timelines and specifications are. He must have thought he hired a magician as his assistant. Still, I've managed to cram everything into the day. Sleep is for people with disposable incomes.

Archer has become a puzzle for me to figure out. The man is gorgeous but also the biggest grump I've ever met. If I was as rich as him, I'd smile every once in a while. I do my best to anticipate his needs and get him what he wants before he even needs to ask. Actually, "ask" is generous. Archer Clarke doesn't ask, he orders. In the entirety of my two weeks as his assistant, the man has never said please or thank you. Not once.

There are stories and rumors everywhere about what happened to his previous assistants. I don't know how much is made up and how much is true, but I get the impression they aren't being exaggerated. If rumors are to be believed, he's let go of assistants for everything from coming in late because of a sick pet to making a dinner reservation at the wrong restaurant.

Every day I'm expecting to be tossed out on my cushioned ass, but I'm surprised every time he walks out the door without handing me a pink slip.

I've made friends with Carl, the security guard downstairs. Now he texts me when Archer is on his way up every morning so that I can get his coffee on his desk while it's still hot. Lord knows what he would do if he arrived to cold coffee. The man might burst a blood vessel.

Every morning I stand in front of his desk and give him the breakdown of the day's schedule. He rarely even bothers looking up at me and answers most of my questions with grunts and head shakes. He's not exactly a dazzling conversationalist.

For some reason, the grumpiest man I've ever met insists on buying me lunch every day. For the first few days, I brought lunch from home and tried to turn him down. After the third time that I told him I didn't need him to buy my lunch, he put his foot down and told me that anytime I was ordering food for him, he expected me to order something for myself as well. No exceptions. I've stopped bothering to bring a lunch now since it would just go to waste.

There hasn't been much time to socialize with other employees, but I've met the other assistants on the executive floor. They seem to have a substantial amount of sympathy towards me for putting up with "that man." Then they usually go on a detailed analysis of his good looks. As if I hadn't noticed. I've gotten pretty good at artfully dodging those conversations. The last thing that needs to get around the office is that I think my boss is hot.

Unfortunately, he lives rent free in my head anyway. Archer Clarke has starred in my fantasies every night for weeks. If he knew, I would die from embarrassment. I keep everything extremely professional and try not to give off any hint that I think anything about him at all, let alone that I think about what's under those bespoke suits. Just the thought sends me into a blush and shame spiral.

We haven't touched again since that first day when we shook hands and while I'm sure it's a good thing, I'm also a bit disappointed. I want to see if touching him again would give me that thrill that ran through my body like last time. The man could make a nun ditch her habit after only a handshake.

I'm sitting at my desk after finishing my Turkey sandwich from the deli down the street and looking over the fresh batch of emails that came in. Archer got a rare roast beef sandwich. No onions. The one time his food arrived with an onion on it, he threw it in the trash and told me to call the place and have them send a replacement. Imagine not being able to pick the onions off a cheeseburger and needing a new one. Since then I always check his food before I send it in to him. Yesterday, there were onions on his Greek salad, so I quickly picked them off and added them to my own so he wouldn't toss it into the trash again. Never shall an onion touch this man's plate again on my watch. I'm sure if he knew I had picked them off and still served it to him, he would be horrified.

Someone clears their throat in front of me and I glance up to find a young man that looks to be in his mid to late twenties. His blond hair, blue eyes, and relaxed smile remind me of a California surfer.

"Hi," I say. "How can I help you?"

"Hey there, you're the new assistant for Mr. Clarke, right? I'm Lucas Brody." He flashes his very white teeth at me and I'm suddenly wondering if our dental plan covers that kind of whitening.

"Hollie Simmons, nice to meet you." He pops his hip and leans it against the edge of my desk. It looks like he's settling in for a chat. While he seems nice enough, I have a ton of emails to get through and Archer will be back from his meeting any minute. I glance down at his hand and notice he's clutching a large foam chord board. "Is that for me?"

He pulls the board up to chest level and flips it around so I can see what's printed on it. There's a large drawing of a hotel by the beach. It's absolutely stunning. I can picture myself staying there and laying out on that beach under the tiny blue umbrellas depicted in the drawing.

"I work down on six in architecture. My boss wanted me to bring Mr. Clarke the latest rendering for the Santa Cruz property." He flashes me another blinding smile and lowers the board back to his side.

"It's beautiful. We're going to have a hotel in Santa Cruz?" I've been studying the company and I definitely don't remember seeing Santa Cruz on the list of hotels or properties we own.

"Yeah, I guess Mr. Clarke and Mr. Osman are working on the final negotiations to buy some land there. I think we've revised this thing at least ten times and we don't even have the property yet."

"That's a lot of work for something that's not a sure thing."

He shrugs at me and says, "You know how it is, what Mr. Clarke wants, Mr. Clarke gets." I give him a tight-lipped smile. The last thing I want to do is discuss my boss, even if this guy seems pretty nice. "So anyway," he continues when I don't chime in, "since it's Friday night, some of us are getting together and going down to the Radiator Whiskey after work, get a few drinks, unwind. You up for some fun tonight?"

"Actually, I'm not sure what time Mr. Clarke is leaving tonight and I have to stay here until he leaves. Another time?"

"Oh, come on, Hollie." He stands up and looks at me straight on. He's giving me his best puppy dog face and I can't help but let out a giggle. Lucas is a bit of a charmer. "You've got to meet some new people," he says. "I bet you haven't even been off this floor yet. Come with us and I'll introduce you to some people in my department. Plus, I think there'll be some people from marketing there too."

That piques my interest. It can't hurt to make some connections in the marketing department, since that's where I want to end up eventually. Plus, Lucas seems nice. He looks like a bit of a playboy, but a girl can never have too many friends. I'm about to tell him I'll try to make it when I hear a deep voice from behind him.

"Excuse me. Don't you both have some work you should be doing?" Lucas turns and we both stare at Archer, who is now standing directly behind Lucas, arms crossed in front of his chest. I'm not sure how tall Lucas is, but Archer towers over him, making him seem small.

Before I can say anything, Lucas jumps to my rescue. "Mr. Clarke, I'm just here to bring you the latest rendering of the Santa Cruz property." He yanks up the poster board and shows it to Archer, who doesn't even bother glancing at it before plucking it from his hands.

He pins his cold and assessing gaze on Lucas even as he addresses me. "Miss. Simmons, I'm going to need you to stay late tonight. I've had some things come up that we need to handle before the weekend."

"Sure, Mr. Clarke." What else can I say? That it's Friday night and I want to go out drinking with his other employees? Somehow, I don't think that's going to fly with him. He remains fixed where he is, his eyes never leaving Lucas.

"So, I guess I'll be going," Lucas says as he makes his way towards the elevator before looking over his shoulder at me. "Rain check, Hollie? I'll shoot you an email." Did he just give me a wink?

The expression on Archer's face turns almost murderous. If his eyes were lasers, Lucas would be cut in half, bleeding out on the expensive carpeting. "Sure," I mumble as my gaze bounces back and forth between the two of them. Once Lucas is out of sight, Archer turns his attention to me.

"Miss. Simmons, my office." He strides past me, and I quickly grab my notepad and jump up to follow after him. I guess his meeting didn't go well.

I trail behind him into his office and perch on the edge of my usual chair, ready to jot down notes on whatever takeaways he has from his meeting.

"Miss. Simmons, you signed all the paperwork that was given to you by Human Resources, correct?"

"Of course." I wonder where this is going. I lay the pen across my notebook and wait for him to continue.

"Then I'm sure you read and made note of our company's no fraternization clause."

My head rears back slightly. No fraternization clause? Thoughts quickly go flying through my head.

What no fraternization clause?

Why is he bringing this up?

Did he hear Lucas ask me to happy hour?

Does he think I'm running around "fraternizing" with a bunch of his employees?

"I don't recall seeing that in the handbook."

"Then I suggest you pay closer attention to what you're signing in the future. What would your boyfriend think if he heard the conversation you were having?"

Wait. What? Why is he asking about my boyfriend? This conversation has taken a distinctly unprofessional turn. Is he fishing for information? He wants to know if I have a boyfriend?

Of course not, Hollie! He's probably concerned about a sexual harassment lawsuit. His eyebrow is raised, and he's silently leaning back in his chair, his gaze unwavering. Apparently, he actually expects me to answer that.

"I don't have a boyfriend," I admit, feeling a blush stain my cheeks and travel down my chest. I'm sure he thinks I'm a loser for not having a boyfriend. Just as quickly as the embarrassment starts, it turns to annoyance. My personal life is none of this man's business.

"Well," he clears his throat and leans forward, "I want to make sure you're concentrating on what I need and not with the little boys wandering the building."

"Mr. Clarke, he was only here to drop off *your* building schematics. The conversation took two minutes, tops. I'm aware of my job and have no plans on shirking my duties to you or this company." I raise my head up, practically begging him to challenge my work ethic again.

He quickly changes the topic of this very uncomfortable conversation, almost giving me whiplash. "As I mentioned, we'll be working late tonight. Order my usual from Emilio's for dinner and order yourself dinner as well. That will be all for now."

I've apparently been dismissed. I give a small nod and walk towards the door.

"Miss. Simmons?" I stop in my tracks and turn to see what this man could possibly want now. He doesn't even look up from his computer as he says, "I'm going to need another coffee."

That's it. I'm done. His attitude over the past few weeks, plus this entire insane conversation, may have pushed me over the edge. For a second, I completely forget how desperately I need this job.

"Please." I practically spit out the word at him. He jerks his head up and widens his eyes at me in surprise before narrowing them again.

"Excuse me?"

In for a penny, in for a pound. "You're excused. I'm going to need another coffee, *please.*" Giving him the sweetest smile I can muster, I remain planted on the spot. I can practically hear his teeth grinding as a vein I've never noticed before jumps out at his temple. I hope I haven't given him a stroke.

"Please." He grits out, eyes not leaving mine for even a second.

My smile widens even more as I say, "Of course, Mr. Clarke, I'd be happy to." Before he can say anything else to me, particularly the words "you're fired", I turn and make my way to the break room to fetch his highness's coffee.

SIX

ARCHER

What the fuck was that?

I run my hand over my face repeatedly, trying to wipe away some of my frustration. When I was returning to my office from the main conference room on the other side of the floor and spotted that kid leaning on Hollie's desk, I immediately felt a bolt of jealousy run through me. With no forethought, my pace quickened until I stopped behind him and could hear their conversation.

He was asking her to go with him to a happy hour? Didn't he know she's mine? Well, my assistant anyway.

Mine.

The thought seemed to warm me from the inside out and before I can stop myself, I was interrupting their conversation and making up some work that simply had to get done tonight. It didn't matter that I had planned to leave at six and go straight to my home gym to work out the week's tension on the punching bag. There was plenty to get done around here. I'd find something for her to do.

I sent the boy on his way. Hollie shouldn't be playing around with boys. She needs a man. My mind wandered back to thinking about her maybe boyfriend again and before I could stop myself, I was calling her into my office.

The question about her boyfriend was pure fishing on my part. I couldn't stand not knowing any longer and I didn't understand the sense of relief that swept through my entire being when she said she didn't have a one. Acting on this outrageous attraction was still out of the question. I just wanted to know if she was leaving me at night and going home to someone who was making her happy. Sue me.

I'm not sure if I covered it up well. Actually, considering how annoyed she got with me, I'm positive I didn't. And who was that who just left my office? Hollie is normally exceedingly polite and rather subdued, always taking my orders with a "yes, sir" or "of course." Today she was having none of it. Apparently, underneath that quiet exterior is a spitfire waiting to be unleashed.

The sweet smile on her face as she cut me down for my lack of manners sent a thrill through my body, and I was immediately as hard as steel. Didn't she understand I kept things short and formal between us so that I wouldn't bend her over my desk and slide my cock into her warm, tight pussy?

I groan as I adjust my length in my pants for the

thousandth time since she's come to work for me. This woman does things to me that no one ever has before. I need to keep my eye on the ball and off of her curvy ass. I would fire her, but she's the best assistant that I've ever had, anticipating what I need before I ask and executing tasks she's given with precision and speed. If anything has been proven to me over the past few years, it's that competent assistants are hard to find.

Hollie comes back into the room, setting the fresh coffee on my desk. Fighting the urge to thank her for bringing the coffee, I pointedly ignore her and pretend to concentrate on my screen.

"Mr. Osman is here for his appointment," she says in her sweetest voice. She's probably worried I'm going to fire her. Good.

"Send him in." Richard barges in and is pacing back and forth in front of my desk before I even have time to greet him. This doesn't seem like it's going to go well. Before I can ask him what's wrong, he collapses into the chair and levels his gaze at me.

"Shaw," he says without bothering to add anything else.

"What about that prick?" Just his name has me tensing up.

"I hear he's sniffing around the Santa Cruz property."

"What?!" I practically shout at him. "How is that fucking possible? I made sure that this deal didn't leave the walls of this building."

If I had an arch nemesis, it would be Patrick Shaw. The man is my own personal Dr. Evil. He is the founder and CEO of Shaw Capital, a company that developed land into strip malls and cheap housing. The man has no scruples and even less personality.

We have been fighting over properties for years. When I was younger, I would resoundingly beat him out for top properties in the western United States. I wasn't very gracious about it either. Not to his face and not to his investors. What can I say? I was a snot-nosed kid that was proud of beating one of the best in the field.

For the past few years, he seems to have gotten the upper hand. He's been taking properties out from underneath me by giving last-minute offers marginally higher than my own and purchasing the properties before I even realize he's looking at them. Not this time. Not this property.

"I honestly don't know how he found out. I got a call from Caroline DuPont and she pointedly told me that Patrick Shaw was asking about property specs. She also said that he had some not very nice things to say about you."

Shit. "Of course he didn't. That man is the biggest pain in my ass. We need to find out who has been blabbing their mouth, and either shut them up or fire them."

Richard is leaning forward, elbows on his knees, head down, deep in thought. "We need to do damage control on this," he says. "We'll get a meeting between you and Mrs. DuPont on the books. I'll get your schedule from Hollie and set it up in the next few weeks, if possible."

Nodding my head, I try to hide my dismay. It doesn't matter what I've done, Patrick Shaw could really fuck this up for me. This property is my dream. I have the board tentatively behind me because everything I've ever pitched them has always turned into a cash cow for us.

They are already worried about building a resort in a small beach town on the California coast. I know in my gut it's the right move, but I need to show them results.

"Why is he interested in this property anyway?" I ask. "It's land on the beach. Not exactly the best location for cheap housing or a shitty mini mall. It's way out of his normal price range."

Richard shakes his head. "It doesn't make sense to me either. It's possible he's still upset about Selene."

Selene, I had almost forgotten about her. Those two had been off and on for years. Back when I was rubbing his face in his defeats, Shaw's little plaything had hit on me during one of their off times. I gave her the fuck of her life, and I made sure he knew about it. It wasn't my finest hour.

"But that was years ago," I protest. "He couldn't still be angry over some girl, could he?"

Richard's giving me a look like I might be a little touched in the head. "You mean Selene *Shaw*?" he asks.

Well, fuck. "He married that gold digger? I genuinely thought he was smarter than that."

"Apparently, he loves her... or her family connections. You need to pay closer attention to these things," he chastises.

I wave my hand in the air dismissively. "I'm too busy for that kind of shit. We're going to need to go back over everything about that property and make sure there isn't anything I'm missing. We've got to make sure we're giving the best offer we can. I don't need any of his sneaking in at the last minute and one-upping me. This is too important."

His face is full of sympathy, but thankfully, he keeps

his thoughts to himself. I'm not in the mood to psychoanalyze my need to make this hotel happen.

"Hollie and I are working late," I tell him. "I'll have her do some additional research while I run the numbers again. If there's anything I've missed, we'll find it."

"It's Friday," he states, raising his eyebrow at me questioningly.

"Since when is that an excuse not to work?"

"You know, you could always go out and have some fun. You could try to meet someone."

I roll my eyes at him, "Thanks, but I don't need a mother asking me when I'm going to give her grandchildren, Rich. Go home to Flora while I handle the heavy lifting," I tease him. I realize that he's just looking out for me. He's the only person who I can count on to always have my back. Usually Uncle Gilbert's too wrapped up in himself to know or care about what's going on. He certainly never had that paternal instinct.

We come up with a tentative plan for reworking the quotes and meeting with Caroline DuPont before he heads out for the evening.

I don't pull my head out of my work again until I notice that the light outside my floor to ceiling windows has begun to fade. Hollie knocks and walks in with my meal from Emilio's, setting it down on my desk.

"Grab your food. We'll eat together so I can go over what needs to be done tonight."

She heads back to her desk to grab whatever she's ordered while I take the lid off the container holding my Chicken Parmigiana. I always get the same thing from Emilio's and the Chicken Parmigiana never disappoints. She takes a seat, setting her meal down on the desk while

I head over to the wet bar I keep at the back of my office. It's been a long week and even though the meal calls for wine, I need a bourbon, especially if I'm going to be spending the evening with my sexy as hell assistant.

"Can I get you a glass of wine?" I ask her, pulling out two glasses.

"Sure," she looks over her shoulder and gives me a small smile. "White, if you have it."

I reach down to the small wine fridge and pull out a local Pinot Grigio to fill her a glass. Carrying both drinks back to my desk, I sit down and hand her the glass of wine.

"Thanks," she says. As she takes the glass from me, our fingers touch and desire shoots through my body. I guess my reaction to our handshake on the day we met wasn't a fluke. I'm pretty sure my dick has been hard more than it's been soft since I met her.

She jerks her hand back from me, almost allowing the wine to slosh out of her glass. Looking into her eyes, I can see that they are a touch glassy. Could it be possible that she feels this connection between us as well? I certainly fucking hope not. That might tear away the last shred of restraint that I've been holding on to.

Clearing her throat, she looks at me with a hint of a smile on her pink lips, "I emailed Greg and had him send me a copy of the employee handbook."

I'm not exactly sure where she's going with this, so I cut into my chicken while she swirls her fork in what looks like some kind of seafood pasta. Thank God. I'm sick of going out with women who order a piece of lettuce and a glass of water and call it a meal. There's something intrinsically sexy about a woman who isn't afraid to eat in front of another person. Lord knows our society says it shouldn't be done. Hollie's soft curves need actual food to be maintained. It would be a shame if she tried to get rid of them.

"I read through the entire thing this afternoon, and there's only one spot that spoke about employee fraternization."

Well shit. I didn't expect her to look it up. Does she want to go on a date with that boy from downstairs that badly? Irritation bubbles up inside me as I take a large swallow of the bourbon in my glass. "You don't say."

"Yes, and it says that only supervisors and their direct reports are subject to the non-fraternization clause. It doesn't pertain to other employees. I thought I should let you know. After all, you are the CEO. I want to make sure you're up to date on your own policies." There's a twinkle in her eye that says she's teasing me and, while I shouldn't, I absolutely love it. When was the last time someone challenged me?

"It's been a while since I've read the handbook. There must have been a change." I avert my gaze, eager to move on from this topic. "Let's go over what we need to work on this evening."

She again smiles, like she knows what it does to me, and nods. I shovel a bite of pasta into my mouth, giving me a moment to collect my thoughts before I continue. "So, you've heard about the Santa Cruz property that we'll be purchasing?" I gesture to the mockup that I brought into my office after our hallway encounter this afternoon.

"Sure, but as I understand it, we haven't purchased the land yet. It's not a done deal, is it?"

"It will be," I answer confidently. She doesn't know me well enough yet, but if I say we're getting the property, it's as good as done, even if there is now a tiny nagging doubt in the back of my head named Patrick Shaw.

"I want to review everything we've done and all the information we've gotten on the property so far. We need to make sure we haven't missed anything. I'm going to re-run all the numbers and I'd like you to review the information we've gathered. Geographical surveys, local and visitor demographics, all of it. Go into city, county, and state records and compare anything you find to what we already have on file. See if you can find any discrepancies."

"No problem." She sips her wine, and a drop lingers on her plump bottom lip a moment before her tongue darts out to capture it. I shift uncomfortably in my seat, trying not to replay one of the thousands of fantasies I have about that tongue.

"All the data is housed on my personal drive. You have all the login info for that, but let me know if you have a problem accessing it."

We take a little longer to finish our meals and we spend that time pleasantly chatting about inconsequential things like the courses she took while attending Branson and the plethora of odd jobs she's worked over the years while I tell her a bit about my time at Stanford and the triathlon I competed in last year.

It's one of the better evenings I've spent in recent memory, which I find a little disturbing. I enjoy Hollie's easy company. I wouldn't think that a woman as young as her could hold my interest outside of the bedroom.

Eventually, she grabs both of our containers, tossing

them into the trash while I refill our glasses. If we're going to be working, it might as well be as pleasurable as possible. We both start on our own projects for the evening and before I know it, almost two hours have passed.

Hollie calls out to me from her desk, breaking the laser-like focus I have on this spreadsheet. "Have you seen this article?"

I stare up at the ceiling, trying to recall if I've come across any articles that would apply to the land in question. Realizing I have absolutely no idea what she's talking about, I ask, "What article?"

She hits some keys on her keyboard and then scurries out of my sight without a word. When she returns, she practically jogs up to me and slams the papers she's printed in the middle of my desk. "This article," she says triumphantly.

I pick up the printout and start to examine it. "What am I looking at?" It's a blog post from something called "Sustainable Santa Cruz" but I'm not sure why she thinks it's relevant.

"It's an interview with Caroline DuPont. Check out the third paragraph." She reaches across the desk and points out her discovery. I read aloud, waiting to see what she's getting at.

Caroline DuPont, long time Santa Cruz resident and business owner, speaks to us about the legacy she wants to leave the city. "I want to assure my fellow residents of Santa Cruz that even though I'm selling this parcel of land on our shore, I will always have your best interests at heart. My team and I are carefully screening all potential buyers to make sure that they also understand the needs of our unique city and are committed to enriching our community and citizens. Santa Cruz is my home, and I would expect nothing less from any other landowner here."

My eyes grow wide as I glance up at Hollie's face, that's shining with pride. "Where did you find this?" I ask. I've never seen this before. Richard certainly never brought this to my attention. Though he mentioned Caroline DuPont wasn't like just any other business person I've dealt with. This could be the key to securing the property away from Patrick Shaw. If this article is any indication, she certainly won't want to add a strip mall to the city's center.

"I ran a bunch of google searches on anything related to the address or anyone in the file and this came up. All you have to do is convince her you'll be enriching the fabric of the city by adding a Clarke Hotel."

She practically claps her hands together in excitement. Fuck, she's cute. A new thought enters my mind and I sigh. "This actually might not be good for us."

That puts a damper on her premature celebrations. "Why not?"

"I don't think Caroline DuPont is the kind of person who thinks leveling her land to build a luxury resort is going to be very 'enriching' to its residents."

"But it's going to bring in so much more money for local businesses," she argues with a pout.

You're preaching to the choir, sweetheart. I need to put some thought into this, get Richard's take on it. It's possible we could make this work for us.

"You're right. I'm sure we can convince her. Besides, my hotel will certainly be better for the community than anything Shaw Capital will put in."

As I'm talking, the color seems to drain from Hollie's face and she lists a little to the left, like she might collapse. I jump up out of my chair and rush over to her before she can fall to the floor, grabbing her elbow and steadying her. I barely even notice the flesh on flesh contact, which is a testament to how much her sudden malady has affected me.

"Hollie, what's wrong? Are you ill?" I know my voice sounds slightly frantic, but I can't help it. I'm worried. I've never seen her like this before. My gaze moves up and down her body, searching her for some sign of what might be wrong.

"I'm sorry," she rushes out, "I'm fine. I had an interview there before I got this job, that's all."

She still seems a little unsteady, so I maintain my grip on her elbow, worried she's going to take a tumble. "That must have been some interview," I mumble while watching her closely.

"It... wasn't great," she shares while reaching out to put a steadying hand on my chest. Even though there is a layer of cotton between us, her hand's burning my skin as if she's touching my bare chest. I suck in a breath, suddenly feeling like I can't get enough air.

"I always knew Patrick Shaw was an idiot, but that seals it. If they didn't hire you, the entire company is incompetent." She looks up at me through her eyelashes. The color returns to her face in full force.

Like a magnet is pulling me in, I take another step forward until I'm definitely invading her personal space.

I don't care. This is the closest I have ever been to her, and all I can think about is pulling her into my arms.

My gaze travels over the planes of her face and I notice her pupils are dilated, covering much of the green and gold of her eyes. Are those tiny freckles across her nose? A shiver runs through her body that I'm pretty sure is not from her little scare a moment ago. I'm looking into her eyes and can see my own desire reflected there. If I wanted her, I could have her.

Both of our breaths are labored and all it would take for my lips to be on hers is for either of us to make a slight movement forward. I can practically taste her mouth. Holding back any longer isn't an option.

I'm lowering my head when I hear the doorknob rattle and quickly take a large step back, releasing her elbow from my hold. Hollie almost falls forward now that she is no longer using my chest to hold her up, but catches herself just in time.

"I hope I'm not interrupting..." Uncle Gilbert says cautiously. Of course, who else would walk in here, unannounced, like he owns the place?

"If you were so worried about it, then why didn't you knock?" I growl. My tone isn't helping to smooth over this awkward situation, but I couldn't care less. I almost had her.

Hollie seems to have come back to her senses, even if her cheeks are still a bright pink. "If you'll both excuse me, it's late and I have to be getting home." Before I can say anything to her, she flees my office, closing the door behind her, leaving me alone with my uncle, who is most certainly not welcome at the moment.

I move back behind my desk before he notices the

large bulge in my pants that's been there for weeks. "What do you need, Gilbert?"

"Yes, sorry," he mumbles. The man is probably two sheets to the wind at this time on a Friday night. "I came to see if you set up a meeting with Caroline DuPont yet. The board has been breathing down my neck on when we're going to get this deal signed."

I almost laugh at that. I'm sure no one on the board expects Gilbert Clarke to do a damn thing. He did nothing when he was CEO and he certainly isn't doing anything now. I'm sure he's just inserting himself into board gossip.

"I'm working on it. If people would stop barging into my office, I might be further along."

He has the good sense to look abashed. "Well, if you need anything at all, my boy, you know I'm here for you. All you need to do is ask."

"Thanks, but I've got everything under control."

At that, he narrows his eyes. "I hope you do."

He takes his leave and I'm left in my office. Alone.

Running my hands through my hair, I try to get my emotions and my body under control. That was too close. It's obvious that we're both attracted to each other, but, as my uncle reminded me, the board's watching my every move right now. If they caught me kissing, or God forbid fucking, my assistant in my office, that would be it. Goodbye, Santa Cruz. Goodbye, job.

I'm more resolute than ever to stay far away from Hollie Simmons. Messing with her would bring me nothing but trouble, and no woman is worth that. A voice inside my head whispers...

But what if she is?

SEVEN

HOLLIE

I walk through my front door half an hour after I left Archer's office. Did I almost kiss him? Did he almost kiss me? This cannot be happening. What if I just threw myself at my boss? Is he going to fire me? God, it would be even worse if he thought he had to let me down easy. The naive, young, full figured girl who thinks she could date a man like him.

I shake my head at myself. No, I'm almost positive he was about to kiss me. I can't let that kind of negative thinking enter my head, even if this entire situation is crazy.

"Is everything okay?"

Apparently, I've been standing in the doorway for a

little too long, which has prompted Bianca to turn from her place on the couch and question me. "I'm fine."

There's an open bottle of wine sitting on the table and even though I already had two glasses at the office, I could certainly use another. "I'm gonna need a glass of that." I make my way into the kitchen and pull out a stemless wine glass from the cupboard. Stemless wine glasses are the single greatest thing to happen to wine drinkers like me in the past ten years. Some of us speak with our hands when we get tipsy, and when hands go flying so do glasses that are teetering on stems.

I approach the couch and let Bianca fill up my glass. Violet exits the hallway into the living room and takes a seat next to Bianca, popping a grape into her mouth. "Are we all home tonight?" I ask.

"Sure are," Bianca confirms, while still eyeing me. "I want to work on some pieces for the show the gallery is putting on next month, and Vi here says she needs to study." Always a woman of few words, Violet only nods her head in confirmation. "What is going on with you, Hollie? You look like you've seen a ghost."

Before answering Bianca, I down half the glass of wine she poured for me and squeeze in between both of them on the couch. Do I really want to talk about this? I've been hiding my attraction to my crazy hot boss for weeks. I've never hidden anything from them before. These girls are like my sisters. Besides, I could use another opinion or two on what the hell is happening.

I take a deep breath and then spill my guts. Everything from the instant attraction during my interview right up until the moment where his uncle walked in the door of his office tonight. As I finish my tale, the room is silent.

"Ho—ly. Shit," Bianca practically squeals. "I knew you were going to land that hot piece of man meat."

I bury my head in my hands. "Did you hear any of what I just said? I made a fool of myself in front of my boss. How am I supposed to face him on Monday?"

"I don't know," Violet interjects. "It sounds like he was just as into it as you. What was that whole thing about basically asking if you have a boyfriend?"

"Right?" Bianca shouts. I can tell she's getting tipsy because when Bianca gets tipsy, she gets loud. "And telling you there's a policy against employees dating? He was jealous! That man wants you, girl. You should totally hit that!"

"Oh my god, I can't hit that! He's my boss. I can't lose this job, my family is counting on me. Besides, as I found out, a supervisor can't have a relationship with a direct report. Even if he is interested, and I'm not saying he is, we would both get fired."

"He can't get fired. His name is on the building. Like, it's on EVERY building that company has," Bianca protests.

"He certainly can get fired," Violet answers her for me. "There is a board of directors and while he may own the majority share of the company, that doesn't mean that they have to keep him in the CEO position."

"I thought you were a comparative literature major." Bianca eyes Violet, who simply shrugs as if this is something that everyone knows. Bianca switches gears, making my head spin. "Whatever, let's have girls' night and forget about men. We are smart, beautiful, independent women and we don't need men to complete us." And now we're having a girl power moment.

I finish my glass of wine and reach for the bottle, realizing it's now empty. "Is there any more wine?" Bianca jumps up, rushing into the kitchen. I assume to get more wine. I look over and smile at Violet, who merely rolls her eyes. Bianca always gets like this when she's overindulged a bit. She re-enters the room with a bottle of wine in her arms, along with pretzels, bread, cheese, and almonds.

"I wish we had something sweet," she mutters as she plops back down onto the couch, the bag of almonds slipping from her grip and onto the floor.

"Should I make cookies?" Violet asks us.

Bianca and I both freeze in place. Before I can open my mouth, Bianca is already telling her, "We are trying to get her mind off her super hot boss, Vi. Not poison the poor girl."

Violet sticks out her lower lip in a pout but doesn't seem truly offended. This isn't something she hasn't heard before. "Come on you guys, my baking isn't *that* bad."

Bianca settles everything she's hauled in from the kitchen onto the coffee table before turning to Violet. "Honey, we love you, you are amazing. But your baking is atrocious. Now dig in and I'll buy you a donut for breakfast."

"It better be pink with sprinkles," Violet grumbles before popping another grape in her mouth and winking at me.

That's how the three of us spend the rest of the evening. Drinking, eating, and laughing together while we watch trashy television. While it doesn't completely take my mind off of the events of this evening, it certainly pushes them to the background as I enjoy the company of my best friends. I'm so lucky to have them both, especially since I don't have parents I can exactly count on.

Around one a.m. we all head to our separate rooms and I'm once again alone with my thoughts. Laying in bed, I can't help but replay the 'moment' Archer and I had this evening. His lips were so close to mine that I could feel his breath on my face. All I had to do was lift onto my tiptoes and place my lips against his.

I wasn't even thinking when I placed my hand on his chest. I was a little dizzy and needed to steady myself. Immediately, anything else that was in my head was completely erased. All I could think about was Archer's solid chest underneath my palm. He mentioned earlier tonight that he had done a triathlon last year. I believe him. That man is pure muscle, and I had wanted to lean into him and press my soft body against his hard one.

I can feel myself getting wet just replaying tonight's events in my head. I've only had sex with my high school boyfriend and it was nothing to write home about. It was always awkward and fast. I certainly never had an orgasm with him. The entire experience was rather disappointing and I haven't understood the need to meet someone else and repeat it. However, I suspect there would be no room for disappointment after a night with Archer.

I glide my hand down the swell of my stomach, past the trimmed patch of hair to my dripping wet center. While I slowly play with my hardening clit, I bring my other hand under my top to pinch my nipple and let out a quiet groan. I think about what would have happened if

I had kissed him tonight and moan as the hand in my panties moves more quickly. I think about Archer bending me over that enormous mahogany desk and roughly shoving my skirt over my hips before sinking into me. My fingers slide inside my drenched opening while I move my hand to my other breast and pinch that nipple as well. I picture him slamming himself into me, grabbing my hair, taking his pleasure from me. The mental images send me over the edge and flood my body with warmth as I come hard against my fingers. I'm panting at this point, unsure if I've ever come this hard before.

Readjusting my sleep shorts and tank top, I roll over onto my side and close my eyes. I try not to think about Archer Clarke but fail miserably as I drift off to sleep.

Saturday seems to drag as I'm plagued with thoughts of our late night work session. I've almost convinced myself quitting is the right thing to do. Not only am I embarrassed that I basically tripped and almost fell onto my boss's mouth, but I'm not sure it's a good idea if I work for a man that I'm so incredibly attracted to.

If I gave into my attraction to him, he would chew my tender heart up and spit it back out. Men like Archer Clarke don't mess with naive girls like me. They take what they want and move on, and I wouldn't be able to handle that. I've barely touched him and I already know that any kind of flirtation with Archer would ruin me for anyone else.

Besides, do I really want to end up like my mother? She fell for the charms of a rich man once upon a time. He left her with nothing but a baby and a deep-seated bitterness that persists to this day. I can barely help my mom and sister as it is. The thought of trying to do it with a baby is terrifying.

Pushing those thoughts aside, I fold laundry in my bedroom. I would never be so stupid and he would never go for it. But, there's no denying that this electricity I feel between us is becoming a problem for me. I need to put some distance between us and make sure our relationship remains nothing but completely and undeniably professional.

I'll speak to Lucas on Monday about going out for that happy hour. I'm not interested in dating him, or anyone else really, but it would be good for me to make some more friends in the office. That way, my daily interactions aren't limited to my boss.

As I'm putting a pile of panties in my drawer, I hear the musical tinkling of my phone. I grab it off my bed and see my sister's name and picture across the display. Smiling, I click to accept the call and hold it up to my ear. "Hey Paige! How's it going?"

"Hi Hollie! I miss you!"

"I miss you too! You should come up for a visit over your next break. B and Violet would love to see you, and we could explore the city a bit."

"That sounds great," she says before trailing off into a heavy silence.

"Paige, is there something wrong? Is Mom okay?" A trickle of fear enters my stomach. My mom is always a wild card. She could be at home making my sister lunch or she could be sitting in jail. Once again, I'm filled with guilt for not being in Milford to watch out for them both.

"I'm sure she's fine, Holls. It's just... she didn't come home last night, but you know how that goes." I glance at the clock. It's three in the afternoon. It's not like I'm surprised. There were plenty of times when I was living there that Mom would disappear for days and show up when she had come down from her high. "I hate to bother you about this, but I was wondering if you sent her some money."

"I sent some last week. She told me she got it. What's going on?"

When she speaks again, there's a hiccup in her voice and I know she's crying. "We got an eviction notice, so I was hoping she just hadn't gotten the money to pay it yet."

Goddamnit. There should have been more than enough money to catch up on the rent. Paige shouldn't be the one that has to handle this. It should be my mother talking to me about getting evicted, not my sixteen-year-old sister. She needs to be thinking about her future, not surviving. What happened to the money? I hope Mom didn't shoot it all up or give it to her boyfriend, but I wouldn't put it past her. She's done it before. I'm going to have to contact the building manager and send the money to him directly.

"Don't worry about it," I assure my baby sister. "I'll call the building Monday morning and take care of the rent. She probably just forgot to pay it." I hear her hiccup again on the other end of the line and I'm so pissed at my mother I want to scream. "Enough about that. Tell me how school is going. How are your classes?" I hope the change of subject calms her down a bit. She hates this as much as I do. I've asked Paige to leave Milford and come live with me more than once, but she doesn't want to leave her friends and I know she's worried about leaving Mom to her own devices. I would feel better if she was here, with someone that would actually watch after her instead of the other way around.

"Everything is going pretty good. I think my Calculus teacher hates me though." I laugh at that. No one hates Paige.

"Not possible. You're amazing. You're probably just so smart she doesn't know what to do with you." I hear her giggle and it lifts a weight off of my chest.

"There's also the homecoming dance coming up that my friends are all going to..." Her voice trails off and I prompt her to continue. "It's just that I don't have a dress. I'm hoping one of my friends can lend me one."

The weight comes back, twice as heavy this time. She shouldn't have to worry about not going to a dance. I never got to go to one. I didn't have anything to wear. Prom wasn't even an option for me because I couldn't afford it and my boyfriend at the time was cheap as hell.

"Don't worry about it. We'll get you a dress," I reassure her.

"Oh, no! That's not why I told you Hollie, I don't need you to get me a dress."

"I don't have to do anything. I *want* to. Besides, after you wear it, maybe I can borrow it for a night out," I tease her. She knows as well as I do that I would never fit into any dress she could wear. While I'm all curves, boobs, and ass, Paige is tall and willowy. In fact, she looks a little like those models that Archer has on his arm in photos.

Ugh, can I not think about him for five minutes?

We chat for a while longer, then get off the line so we can both go about our day. I'm going to have to crunch some numbers and see how much money I can afford to give her since most of my first paycheck is already gone. I'll also need to call the apartment manager and find out how much Mom owes and then tuck away at least one hundred bucks for Paige's dress. With another hundred, I might be able to buy her some new shoes too. I can't even imagine the last time she got a new pair.

I log into the banking account on my phone and sigh at the dismal number that's staring back at me. It doesn't look like I'll be quitting my job any time soon. I'll just need to control my urge to climb Archer Clarke like a tree.

EIGHT

ARCHER

I'm at my desk Monday morning and my eyes feel like they have sand in them. I barely got any sleep this weekend. Unlike most nights, thoughts of Hollie weren't the only thing that kept me from sleeping. Ever since this Santa Cruz deal has been on the table, I've been thinking about my parents more and more. I usually kept them in a nice, neat box in the back of my mind. Sure, I thought about them often, but not *that night*. I'm dreaming about it again, which I haven't done in about five years. Between the dreams and thoughts of my curvy little assistant, I was dogged at every turn.

When I left the office on Friday night, I was resolved to not think about that minx for the rest of the weekend.

Our relationship was purely professional and would remain that way. I kept up that way of thinking until I was in the shower that night. I stroked my hard as steel cock while thinking about her little pink mouth. Her lips against mine. Her lips wrapped around my cock while she was on her knees. I let my head fall back and rest on the cold tile while she invaded my mind. When I shot my seed against the shower wall, it was the strongest orgasm I'd had in recent memory. Not that it did anything to abate my lust.

After getting out of the shower, I sat on my bed, scrolling through my contacts. I thought about calling up one of the women that previously shared my bed with no strings attached. I obviously needed a good fuck or else this girl wouldn't have me tied in knots. Ultimately, I tossed the phone on the bed and leaned back against my headboard. That incredible orgasm that rolled all the way through my body was proof that nothing but Hollie would satisfy my needs. If I came that hard from my own hand while merely thinking about her, I can't imagine what it would feel like to sink into her tight, wet pussy.

I filled the rest of the weekend with working out, business calls, and jerking off by myself. Maybe I could fuck her and get her out of my system. I never wanted any one woman more than a few times, anyway. However, I suspected it wouldn't be like that with her. I worried that once I had a taste of her, I wouldn't be able to stop. I couldn't afford that. Not with everything I want so close within my grasp.

I picked up the coffee that Hollie left on my desk this morning and took a long drink. How was it still hot? I had showed up twenty minutes later than usual this morning, so the coffee should have been sitting here cold. Maybe she really was magical. Laughing at my flight of fancy, I took another sip from the cup. I needed to wipe the cobwebs from my brain. There is too much to do today and first on the list is talking to Richard about the article Hollie found. We need to work on a new strategy to make sure I am the most attractive buyer for The Village at Santa Cruz.

I had been worried that Hollie would bring up what almost happened Friday night. I didn't need this girl trying to cling to me. Or worse, she could threaten to take what didn't quite happen to HR. There were plenty of women who could see a potential payday in that evening. I was almost positive she wasn't one of those women, but it wasn't worth the risk.

However, as soon as I got in, it was apparent that I didn't have to worry. She didn't even glance up from her computer when I walked by, bidding me good morning without a glance. The easy camaraderie that we had established over dinner on Friday night was gone. That was fine. It was better than fine. It was exactly what I wanted. Then why am I so pissed off?

In the afternoon, my intercom buzzes, showing that Hollie is on the line. She's probably going to ask what I want for lunch. It was past the normal time we ate. Thai food would hit the spot right now. When I pick up the extension, all I hear is ice in her voice. "Mr. Clarke, your girlfriend is here to see you."

What is she talking about? Has the girl lost her mind?

"I don't have a girlfriend," I respond immediately, feeling the unreasonable need to correct her misconception.

Before she can reply, my door bursts open and the whirlwind that is Julia Kellogg comes bustling in. Her perfume is so cloyingly sweet that I can smell it all the way across the office, making my eyes sting.

"Darling!" she calls out as she comes striding over to my desk. Behind her, Hollie is standing in the doorway with an unreadable expression on her face.

"I'm sorry, Mr. Clarke. I asked for her name, but she insisted on coming in."

I want Hollie away from Julia as quickly as possible. Not only do I not want Hollie to overhear anything she might say, I also don't want Julia to get any idea of my desire for my young assistant. She's the kind of woman that can smell blood in the water and wouldn't be afraid to lash out at her.

"It's fine, Miss. Simmons," I reassure her. "I have a few minutes for Miss. Kellogg."

She silently slips out of the door, closing it behind her, and I'm left with Julia.

"Why are you telling people you're my girlfriend?" I ask coldly.

She laughs dismissively at my question. "Oh darling, you know it's inevitable. Besides, we've been seeing each other for months."

I look at her as if she has two heads. "What are you talking about? We went out three times and we haven't spoken in months. We're not dating, we were barely fucking."

I notice a flash of anger in her eyes before she's able to smooth over her features, giving me a placating smile. "Archer, don't be silly. You and I are so good together. Can you imagine the power couple we would make?

Every time that we're together, our pictures always end up all over social media."

She says that like it's a good thing. I'm wondering if this woman has lost her mind. Julia and I have traveled in the same social circles for years. While she isn't a big player on the Seattle business scene, her father is. Julia has what I would consider a "vanity career" as an interior designer. Meaning she's basically given jobs by her parents' friends that she would never get on her own. Julia Kellogg is nothing more than a glorified debutante.

We slept together a few times about four months ago, but I don't think I've spoken to her on the phone in the past three. There was obviously nothing between us other than two people looking for a night of release. The thought of falling into bed with her again has absolutely no appeal. Especially after she's barged into my office, proclaiming that we're in some sort of relationship.

She's clothed in designer couture from head to toe, with a Hermès bag hooked on her arm. She has a thick layer of expensive makeup on her face that I'm pretty sure would leave a stain on my white shirt if I gave her the opportunity to get close enough. Everything about her presence is practiced. She has a poise that I once would have called elegant, but now seems wooden. Was I really ever attracted to this woman?

She's basically the exact opposite of Hollie, who wears simple clothes that show off her curves without revealing too much and only a light smattering of makeup to enhance her natural beauty. Frankly, Julia looks like she could use something to eat. How I didn't hurt myself on her bony frame is beyond me.

"Archer," she pouts at me while moving closer. God,

even her voice is grating. What the fuck was I thinking?

She doesn't seem like she's getting my subtle hints, so I decide to lay it out for her. "Look Julia, I thought after months of no contact, you understood that our brief entanglement was over. I didn't realize that I would have to spell it out for you so plainly. I'm not interested and frankly, I don't have the time at the moment."

"Excuse me?" She practically shrieks at me while her head rears back like I've slapped her.

"Come now, Julia, let's be adults about this. There's no reason for hard feelings. I'm sure we'll run into each other from time to time. Let's not make this awkward."

"You know what, Archer? Fuck you." Now she's dropped all pretense, her voice no longer in that sing-song tone she had when she entered.

"I believe you already have, *darling.*"

I guess she didn't appreciate that. Snatching the closest thing to her, which happens to be a Mont Blanc pen, she throws it at my head, which I deftly dodge.

This woman needs to get out of here. Now. I was blessed she'd been off my radar so long. Apparently, she's seeking some attention for one reason or another. Perhaps her father has tightened his purse strings again.

"Julia, are you going to leave now, or do I need to call security?"

A rage fills her face that she doesn't bother to hide. For a moment I'm worried she might actually come over the desk at me.

"You don't deserve me, Archer Clarke. You'll be crawling back to me and I won't give you a second chance." She makes her way out the door and I'm certain she would have slammed it if the mechanism hadn't caught it, bringing it to a gentle close. I'm sure that pissed her off even more. This day just keeps getting better.

I try to go back to work, but my heart isn't in it. I'm going to be taking off early to meet my friend Reed, anyway. I might as well get out of here.

Reed and I met during freshman orientation at Stanford, bonding over the fact that we both came from high-profile families and both of us had lost our parents. We were close throughout our college careers and remained that way until this day. While I immediately moved back to Seattle after college, he spent some time in San Francisco practicing law, before also making his way up here and opening his own firm, which has quickly taken off. There aren't many people I can sit down and have a drink with, but Reed is one of them.

I gather up my things and head out the door. I'm about to tell Hollie I'm leaving for the day and to forward any important calls when I notice that she's not at her desk. It's not completely out of the ordinary for her to step away, but I guess I'm used to her always being here when I need her. The woman is making me soft. I've never relied on an assistant as much as I rely on her.

I pull out my phone and shoot her a text message. Even though I'm not expecting a response to my simple instructions, I'm still a little disappointed when one doesn't come through. I notice that I've been hanging around her desk for the past five minutes and decide to take off before someone notices that I'm standing here waiting for her like a teenage boy about to ask out his crush.

Determined to wipe the temptress from my thoughts, I slide my phone into the side pocket of my coat, but not before I glance at the screen one more time. Just in case. There's still no response from her. She's probably using the restroom.

I take off down the hallway towards the elevator and am only mildly annoyed when I don't run into her on the way to my car.

NINE

HOLLIE

As soon as Archer dismisses me from his office to be left alone with his girlfriend, I march over to the break room to pour myself some coffee. I don't want to sit there at my desk and listen to him have an afternoon quickie.

Grabbing my mug, I yank the coffee pot from its holder, almost spilling the contents all over me. I can't help it. I'm pissed, even though I know I shouldn't be. Archer never said that he *didn't* have a girlfriend. I just kind of assumed. And who wouldn't? He almost kissed me last week! Or I almost kissed him... whatever. It doesn't matter. The fact is, he's had a girlfriend this whole time and hasn't even brought her up.

Sure, there was no way I was ever going to do

anything about my attraction to him, but that's not the point. I'm so angry at myself that I forget to add any sugar or cream into my drink before I head out of the break room but gulp down the bitter brew anyway.

Haven't I been telling myself to stay far away from Archer Clarke? Even my mother warned me! Men like him can't be trusted. They are too used to getting what they want without regard to anyone else's feelings. He probably thought it was funny hitting on his young, naive assistant with the crush on him. I'm sure he and his uncle had a good laugh over it after I ran off Friday evening. It would serve him right if I stop *Miss. Kellogg* on the way out of the office and tell her what kind of man he really is.

As I approach my desk, I see that his office door is still closed. I'm not sitting over there waiting for them to be done with whatever they're doing in there. I head over to the elevator without a thought of where I'm going and get on, needing to put some distance between myself and them.

God, that woman was gorgeous. She was everything that I'm not. Tall, thin, and elegant. She practically reeked of money. Honesty, that perfume that overwhelmed my senses and almost made me sneeze, was most likely worth more than every item I currently had on my body. That was the kind of woman that Archer Clarke was supposed to be with. Not some frumpy secretary, fresh out of school, supporting her teenage sister and addict mother.

Tears gather in my eyes and I quickly blink them away. I will not cry over some man. Especially one I'm not even involved with. He should be so lucky. I jut my chin out and press the button for the sixth floor before I even realize what I'm doing. Architecture is on sixth.

It's time for me to make some friends here so my focus won't solely be on him. I'm not exactly sure where Lucas sits, so I slowly make my way through the twisting lines of cubicles and offices. Some people give me curious glances while others stare at their screens, completely ignoring me.

After a few minutes, I hear my name being called and look to the left. I see Lucas standing up in a cubicle as he waves, "Hollie! Over here."

I make my way over to him as a smile settles on my face. It's nice to have someone here that's actually happy to see me for a change. "Hey Lucas, I was looking for you."

"What?" He questions in mock surprise, "You mean, you don't usually wander the floors with your coffee?" I laugh and set my cup down on his desk, taking the seat he's directing me to. When he settles into his chair, he asks, "To what do I owe this visit?"

"I hoped you were having another happy hour. I know I couldn't go last week, but I'd love to meet some other people that work here. It's kind of lonely up on the top floor."

"I'll bet." He gives me a smile and a wink. This boy is too charming for his own good. I want to make it clear I'm not interested in anything more than friendship with him, though. It wouldn't be fair to lead him on.

"I could really use some more friends around the office, you know?" I hope he gets what I'm trying to convey. Flirting is probably just second nature to him, so I don't want him to think I'm reading too much into it.

I'm not in the mood to embarrass myself any more than I already have here.

"Of course. I'm not sure if anyone is going out tonight, but let's ask around and check. There's usually a group of people that are down for drinks after work."

There's a buzzing in the pocket of my skirt—yes, it has pockets!—and reach down to pull out my phone. Annoyance shoots through my body when I see it's a message from Archer.

Archer: Leaving for the day and won't be back. If any important calls come in, forward them to my cell.

I can't help but wonder if they had sex in the office and now he's taking off to spend the rest of the day with her.

Whatever, it works for me. This way he won't be able to make me work late and I can go out to network with my new coworkers.

"Everything alright?" Lucas asks, genuine concern on his face. I realize I must have been scowling at my phone and work to relax my features back into a smile.

"Of course. It's nothing. The boss is going home for the day, which means I'm free for the evening."

"Awesome. Let's hit up some people and see who's up for drinks." Lucas leads me through the maze of cubicles and stops to introduce me to several of his coworkers. Everyone seems friendly and there's a decent sized group of people forming for drinks tonight. I'm excited about getting out and letting loose a bit. I make my way back upstairs to my desk while Lucas emails a few other people about this evening. We plan to meet in the lobby at six so that we can ride together to the bar.

When I make it back up to my station, I see that Archer's office is unsurprisingly empty. There's a brief pang in my chest when I'm reminded he's left with his girlfriend. I hate that it bothers me. I need to get this man out of my system.

I sit and concentrate on the stack of emails that has come in since I stepped away and try to think about the fun that I'll hopefully have this evening.

This is good for me. I'm glad I found out that he's like every other rich businessman, just like I always suspected. On to bigger and better things.

When six o'clock comes around, I head to the lobby and spot Lucas amongst a group of people in business casual wear. Some of them I recognize from introductions with Lucas this afternoon. I stride over to them and he introduces me to those I haven't met yet. We divide up into groups and decide to take ride shares to the bar. That way, we won't need a designated driver to get back to the office.

I'm squished in the back of a Kia Forte between a girl from marketing and a middle-aged man—Thomas maybe?—that I met this afternoon. We pull up to Radiator Whiskey and file inside.

The bar is decorated with warm tones, wood, couches, and comfy looking chairs. I've never been here before, but it looks like a wonderful place to shed the work stress.

Getting the bartender's attention, I order a Moscow Mule. A double. I rarely drink hard alcohol, but after that shit show with Arthur and his girlfriend this afternoon, I need this drink to hit my system fast. Out of the corner of my eye, I see a well-dressed woman with beautiful caramel skin sidle up to the bar next to me.

"Hi," she says, flashing me a bright smile. "You must be Hollie. I'm Claire from marketing." She reaches her hand out and I quickly shake it. I don't know why, but I have a good feeling about her. Plus, she works in the marketing department, which is where I want to be. It can't hurt to make some connections there.

"It's nice to meet you." I tell her, gripping her hand. We both wait on our drink orders and make small talk.

"So, how do you like working for Archer?" she asks me. I raise my eyebrow a bit. People rarely refer to him by his first name. Even though I've never heard him tell anyone *not* to call him Archer, it seems like something no one dares to do.

"It's good," I reply. "He's very..." I search for a word in my vocabulary to describe him that doesn't begin with 'jack' and end in 'ass' "... professional," I spit out. At that, Claire lets out a bright laugh, but I don't get the sense that she's laughing *at* me.

"You're too nice. Archer Clarke is a pain in the ass." I'm reaching across the bar for my drink and almost spill it at her comment. I glance over at her, not sure what I should say. Should I admit he is indeed the biggest pain in the ass I've ever met, or should I make the boss look good? "It's alright," she quickly interrupts my thoughts. "You don't have to agree with me. I already know he is.

I've been working with the man for seven years and I don't think it ever gets any easier."

"You work with him directly?" I ask, now curious about what this woman does.

"Yup, I'm in charge of the marketing department."

My eyes widen as my mind searches for the bit of information that I'm seeking.

"Claire... Keating," I state, looking up at her in awe. I recognize the name from Archer's emails, but I always pictured a much older and stuffier woman.

"That would be me." She laughs. "I see my reputation precedes me."

"I'm so sorry. I should have put two and two together when you said you work in the marketing department. It's nice to meet you in person."

She takes a large gulp of whatever orange cocktail she has in her hand and pats my shoulder warmly. "Don't worry about it. I'm glad to put a face to the emails."

"I actually have a degree in marketing," I admit to her. "I came here to interview for a marketing job, but Mr. Clarke told me that there weren't currently any openings."

"Then we should definitely get to know each other." She raises her glass in a little salute. "He's right. We don't currently have any openings, but you never know when that is going to change. Here, let me introduce you to my team." She leads me over to another group that is stepping through the door and makes introductions.

Over the next hour, any nerves I had about going out with new people are wiped away. I'm not sure if that's because of how nice and welcoming everyone is to me or if it's the fact that I'm on my third double cocktail.

Drinking this much isn't a great idea. Especially when I'm out with new people I work with on a Monday night, but it's been so long since I put all my worries to the back of my mind and just relaxed. My mom, Paige, Archer... none of them seem so important right now.

Lucas comes over to the table with a tray of shots. "Come on, everyone," he shouts. "I've got shots to celebrate our new friend and coworker, Hollie. May she survive Archer Clarke!" A cheer goes up as he passes out the shots of clear liquid and I can feel my cheeks heat. I hate having everyone's attention on me. That's one of the reasons that I hang out with Bianca. She's always the center of attention, which lets me hang back on the sideline where I'm more comfortable.

I don't think it's wise to take a shot with how much liquor I've already consumed, but they're toasting me, so what choice do I have? I grab a glass and join in with them. Tipping the shot glass back, the clear liquid burns all the way down my throat and settles into my stomach. I sputter as Lucas whacks my back, trying to make sure I don't choke.

"What the hell was that?" I ask him, eyeing the remaining shot glasses on the tray warily.

"Bacardi 151. It'll put some hair on your chest." He winks at me.

What's with this dude and winking? Does he have something in his eye?

I take another sip of my Moscow Mule to wash the gasoline taste out of my mouth. At this point, I'm feeling a little dizzy. I should head out soon before I do something embarrassing that has me the talk of the break room tomorrow. I excuse myself to use the restroom but nobody seems to hear me. As soon as I stand, I know I'm in trouble. I'm not just a little dizzy, the entire bar seems to sway around me. I slowly make my way to the back of the bar, trying my best not to trip over my own two feet. These heels are definitely not helping matters.

I groan as I realize that I'm going to have to take an Uber home. There's no way I'll be sober enough to drive home once we get back to the office where my car is waiting for me.

As I stumble for the second—or maybe it's the third—time, an arm snakes around my waist from behind. My entire body stiffens at the unexpected contact and an unfamiliar voice in my ear says, "You need some help there, babe?"

I pull out of his grasp and turn to see a middle-aged man dressed in a cheap suit. He seems a little unsteady on his feet and the look in his eyes has me glad I've run into him in this crowded bar and not in some dark alley.

"I'm fine, thanks. No help required." I try to head for the bathroom, but he's grabbing my upper arm now, holding it tightly.

"I don't know babe, it looks like you might need something that I can give ya." He gives me a smile that I'm sure he thinks is charming, but in reality, it's just creepy.

"There's nothing you have that I need," I spit out at him as I try removing his hand from my arm. Unfortunately, he doesn't seem too inclined to let go.

"Why don't you come over here and sit that nice fat ass right in my lap?"

Great, one of these assholes. I yank my arm back once again, but his grip is like a vice. I'm thinking about my options for getting out of here when his hand disappears from its hold on my arm. Confused, I look around before spotting the man huddled on the floor. There's another person towering over the creep while he holds a hand to his face like he's in pain. I look up at my rescuer and a lump forms in my throat.

Archer.

TEN

ARCHER

An evening hanging out with Reed, a couple drinks, and a few rounds of billiards have me feeling like a new man. I put all the problems of today to the back of my mind while we reminisced about old times and laughed at each other's shitty jokes. I don't have many friends, but the ones I have, I value immensely.

We're heading out of the darkened, upscale bar and I'm hit with the frigid evening air.

"This city is too fucking cold," Reed grumbles behind me. Pulling my coat closer to my body, I nod in agreement. Though it's not currently raining, it obviously did while we were inside. Even the air in Seattle seems wet.

"I'm parked down the street," he says, pointing in the direction where I also managed to find a space. We take off down the street and continue our easy banter from inside the bar.

As we're walking, suddenly the hairs on the back of my neck stand up. I stop in my tracks and scan my surroundings. Noticing that I'm no longer at his side, Reed also stops and turns around, looking at me questioningly. "What's up?"

I take a moment to search the empty street but don't see any reason I would have this unsettled feeling. I'm about to shrug it off and head to my car when I catch movement out of the corner of my eye.

Across the street is a bar that's lit up like the Fourth of July and with noise spilling out into the street. The front of the bar is covered in enormous windows, affording me an unfettered view inside. A girl in a dark gray skirt, blue blouse, and heels catches my attention with her long blonde hair. My breath catches and I forget to breathe for a moment. The girl turns her head and smiles at the person next to her, giving me a glimpse of her face.

Hollie.

My breathing starts again. Now I'm greedily gulping in air.

"Archer?"

Reed. Right. "You know what? I have a call I forgot to make. Thanks for this evening. It was fun. I'll catch up with you later."

He looks like he's about to argue but then shrugs his shoulders, wishes me good night, and heads off down the street towards both of our cars. I wait another moment, then step off the curb, jaywalking across the street until I'm in the shadows next to the very last window. From here, I've got a perfect view of her.

Hollie is talking and laughing with a group of people that look vaguely familiar to me. Her blonde hair is falling down against her shoulders in silky waves that I'd love to run my fingers through right before I clench it in my fist and guide those plump lips to my cock. I shake my head, trying to rid myself of the completely inappropriate thoughts, but it doesn't help the semi I'm now sporting in my pants.

She always has her hair up in that prim bun at the office and seeing her like this, I realize that's an excellent thing indeed. I observe the crowd she's with and it only takes me a moment before I spot the guy she was speaking to on Friday.

Anger runs through me. Didn't she understand she wasn't supposed to go out with him? I know that I'm thinking like a mental patient, but I can't seem to stop. Irrational jealousy is apparently my new thing. Hell, I'm standing outside in the dark and cold, spying on this girl. She's turned me into a fucking stalker.

Even though I'm definitely acting like a crazy person, I stay put. I'm only going to watch for a few minutes. I just want to make sure she's okay...

The entire group lifts their glasses and downs a shot of something. I see Hollie's shoulders shake and can tell that she's coughing. Whatever was in the shot glass was apparently a little stronger than she expected. The kid from six swiftly moves to her side and is patting her on the back.

My fists clench at my sides and I'm ready to march inside and tear him away from her. I barely manage to stop myself. These are obviously all people that work for me. I can't go barging in there like a madman, pulling that kid off her. The gossip would be everywhere before I even made it to my car.

I'm about to tear myself away from the entire scene and leave when Hollie pulls away from the group and starts heading towards the rear of the bar. She looks completely unsteady on her feet and I'm a little worried she's going to fall. I'm stuck in my spot, watching her weave through the crowd, when she suddenly trips and heads towards the floor.

I'm striding to the door before I even realize I'm moving when I see a man grab a hold of her from behind. This guy wasn't from the group she was with and by the way Hollie's body has stiffened, I can tell she doesn't know him. She certainly doesn't look like she wants his arm wrapped around her. I sprint the rest of the distance to the door and head inside, luckily avoiding any of my employees.

Approaching Hollie and the stranger, I get a better look at him. He's shorter than me but a good thirty pounds heavier. Luckily, it looks like none of that weight is muscle. He's wearing a cheap and wrinkled suit that screams middle management and his expression says he's completely wasted. I'm about five steps away when I hear Hollie tell him to let her go and see her trying to pry his fingers off her arm.

I'll kill him. White hot rage thunders through me. Before I even realize what I'm doing, I grab the collar of his shirt, pull my arm back, and swiftly punch him in the face. The man crumples to the floor like all of his bones were just removed from his body.

I immediately turn to Hollie and start checking her for injuries. The girl looks white as a ghost and I'm not sure if it's because of fear from this creep or the fact that she just watched me punch someone.

"Archer?" she squeaks at me. I ignore her questioning voice for a moment and finish my assessment of her for injuries. It doesn't seem like she's hurt too badly. There are some marks on her upper arm that will probably turn into bruises but no permanent damage and she shouldn't need a doctor.

I force my eyes from her arm up into her eyes. It's like a punch to the gut. All the anger inside me turns into an icy fear. What if I wasn't here? What would she have done? Sure, it is a crowded bar, but I didn't see anyone coming to her aid. The fear makes my voice come out more harshly than I intend as I tell her, "We're leaving." Before I take her out of here, I give the man, who's still sitting on the floor holding his face, a sharp kick in the side for good measure. Maybe next time he'll remember to keep his hands off what's mine.

I'm careful not to touch her injured arm and settle my hand into the small of her back to guide her towards the front of the building. She doesn't offer me any resistance and I'm worried she's really shaken up if she's not making a scene right now.

There are so many mixed emotions running through me, I don't bother speaking to her as I guide her down the sidewalk towards my car. I glance over and she looks as lost in thought as I am, though she's obviously a bit more wobbly than me. I could strangle her for going out and getting so drunk that someone almost took advantage of her. It's really not her fault, but that doesn't seem to matter to me at the moment.

We approach my Maserati and I unlock the car with my fob before steering her towards the passenger side. I pull open the door and she sits in the seat without a word. I'm getting a little worried about her silence. Perhaps she's in shock?

I grab the seat belt and stretch it across her body, locking it into place before closing the door. Even though I'm careful not to brush up against her body, it doesn't mean that her scent doesn't wrap itself around me, teasing me, practically begging me to lean in and kiss her.

Heading around the front of the car, I slide into the driver's seat and press the start button. I flip the heat on full blast, hoping to thaw out my body while simultaneously bringing Hollie out of the stupor she's in.

"What are you doing?" she asks. She's talking, that's a good sign.

"Taking you home." I say in a voice carefully devoid of all emotion. I can't let anything slip right now. Lord only knows what would come out. I don't want to tell her how scared I was, how that man could have done anything to her. I'll stick to my ice cold front instead.

"Oh, I can get a ride share. My car's at the office." She pulls her phone out of her purse and almost drops it several times before she has a firm enough grip to scroll through her apps. I grab it out of her drunken hands and slip it safely into my pocket. Before she can protest, I lock eyes with her.

"Do you really think you should be in a car with a stranger right now? You're drunk, Hollie. You're so drunk you almost got hurt. If I wasn't there, what would have happened? Have you thought about that?" The words are practically spit from my mouth. Yes, I'm taking all of my worries out on her, but I don't care at this moment. This can't happen again.

Sinking back into the leather seat, she says quietly, "I know, thank you." A few seconds of silence pass between us before she continues on. "How are you here?"

I'm not about to tell her I was standing outside watching her, so I simply say, "I was passing by. The important thing is you're okay. Now give me your address so I can take you home."

That seems to bring her back to life. Her voice has its normal strength back, even if it is a little slurred, as she says, "No! My roommates can't see you dropping me off. No way. I promise I'm sober enough to take a share ride. Just let me out here." She practically begs, making like she's going to open the door and hop out.

I don't know what the big deal is about her roommates seeing me, but I'm too tired to question it at this point. Plus, the fewer people that see us together, the better. Before she can get out, I check over my shoulder and pull the Maserati out into the Seattle evening traffic, weaving my way through the cars, heading east. The only sound in the car is that of the low playing radio until she asks, "Where are we going?"

"To my house."

"What?!"

"Miss. Simmons, you won't give me your address and I'm not leaving you alone in some stranger's car, so this is the only option we have left."

She lets out a little *humph* and settles back into her seat. "It's always Miss. Simmons with you," she bursts out, taking me by surprise with the change of subject. I thought for sure she would have more protests for me about bringing her home. "Miss. Simmons, this. Miss. Simmons, that." She's lowered her voice, and it's apparent she's trying to imitate me. Quite poorly, might I add. "Miss. Simmons, my coffee must never be cold. Miss. Simmons, nary an onion shall ever touch my plate."

At that, I almost let out a laugh. Almost. Instead, I turn to scowl at her. "I have a name, you know," she says.

"I'm aware."

"You can use it. I don't mind."

I remain staring forward and don't bother responding to that. I've been calling her Miss. Simmons to maintain the professional distance we have. Getting too familiar with her would be a disaster of epic proportions. However, it does seem kind of silly to call her that at this point. I can use her name. "Only if you call me Archer."

She doesn't respond, so I glance over at her. She's passed out in the passenger seat. Her honey colored hair is spread out across the seat and reminds me of a halo. She looks like an angel. My fingers twitch to reach over and smooth the strands away from her face when she lets out a loud snore, almost startling me.

I can feel my lips turn up in an involuntary smile.

Adorable.

Well, shit. Hollie has always been someone that I'm attracted to. A woman that I want to fuck. I haven't thought of her as adorable before. In fact, I can't remember the last time I thought anyone was adorable. This can't be good.

I continue driving in silence, lost in thought, until I pull into the driveway to my house in Madison Park. As I approach, the garage door opens and I park the car in the empty bay next to my Land Rover.

"Hollie, we're here." My gentle voice doesn't stir her from her slumber, so I try again a bit more forcefully. "Hollie."

Her eyes shoot open and she looks around in confusion, like she can't remember where she is.

"Come on, let's go inside."

"This is your house?"

"I certainly hope so, or else we have a lot of explaining to do to the owner. Come on, let's get you some water."

"Wait, what's that?" She points to the far end of the garage where there's a bit of blue paint peeking out from under a cover.

"A car." I roll my eyes and try to get her to follow me into the house. It's no use, her interest has been piqued. She's moving towards the car and chattering on about having too many cars. I'm not paying as much attention as I should be because all my focus is on her wide hips swaying back and forth as she moves in front of me. Once she reaches the car, she swiftly yanks the cover off to the floor with no preamble. "It's so pretty!" she squeals in excitement.

I have to laugh at that. I'm not sure anyone has ever called the 1963 Corvette Convertible pretty before, but what do I know?

"It was my dad's." Catching hold of her elbow, I try to guide her back towards the entrance of the house, but she stops and places her hand on my chest.

I'm thrown back to memories of us. God, was that really only three days ago that we were back in my office, my hands on her body, close enough to kiss?

"I'm sorry about your parents, Archer." Her voice is so soft and her eyes so earnest I can't even be annoyed at her for bringing up a topic I rarely cover with anybody, not even my uncle.

I'm not surprised that she knows my parents are dead, since my job makes me rather high profile, it's pretty much common knowledge. Even so, I don't like to talk about my parents. It's a painful topic. People always say that you'll "get over it." Well, I never got over my parents' death. I feel their absence every day. I just choose to go on and do the best I can to honor them and their legacy. It's one of the reasons I'm so completely devoted to Clarke Hotels. I'd like to think my father would be proud of how much I've accomplished. I'm also pretty sure my mother would be hounding me for grandchildren by now.

"Thanks. It was a long time ago. I—" Hollie's lips are on top of mine in an instant, removing all memory of what I was going to say next. For a moment, my entire being relaxes and my arms wrap around her, pulling her into me. However, I quickly come to my senses and instead of drawing her in, I slowly push her away.

I'd like to say that I broke off the kiss because I wasn't interested in her or because she is my assistant, and it wouldn't be proper. That there aren't shivers running up and down my body. Really, the only reason I stopped is because Hollie is drunk. If she was sober and kissed me like that, none of those other excuses would have mattered. I'd have her up against the wall and moaning my name right now.

"Hollie, honey, no," I tell her while taking a step away. My breath is coming in and out of my lungs in big gasps as I try to get my body back under control. It's the most chaste kiss I've had since I was twelve years old, but somehow, it's still the hottest.

She sticks out her bottom lip at me in a pout and I have to stop myself from grabbing her again, nibbling on that lip myself.

"How come you never drive it?"

Uhhhh, what? "Excuse me?"

"The pretty car," she points over her shoulder, taking me completely off guard and changing the subject like she didn't just completely blow my mind with a peck on the lips.

I involuntarily let out a laugh at the absurdity that is tonight. There is zero chance that she's remembering any of this in the morning. Thank God for that. "It's a 1963 Corvette. It's not *pretty.*" I try to scowl but am positive I'm not pulling it off.

"Looks pretty to me," she harrumphs at me.

"It's a convertible and we live in Seattle, one of the rainiest places in the Northwest," I remind her.

"We should go for a drive," she tells me enthusiastically.

"We should get water and go to bed." At that, she jerks her head up and focuses on me. "Go to bed in different rooms," I explain lamely before she can question my motives. I don't want her to get the wrong idea after all. This is all completely innocent. I would have brought any employee to my home that was too impaired to drive.

Keep telling yourself that, you idiot.

With no further questions, she follows me into the main house from the garage and we make our way to the foyer. I glance around and try to see the place through Hollie's eyes. Some would find the furnishing slightly out of date, but when I inherited this place from my parents, I didn't have the heart to change much of anything. I've switched out a few pieces of furniture over the years and updated the electronics, but it's still the home I've always known and loved.

Nothing is of poor quality or even shabby, but it lacks the sleek modern ambience of most of the homes of my friends and colleagues. They all have bachelor pads filled with steel and glass. While those places radiate wealth and status, I find this immensely more comfortable. The place screams "family home" but you never know, it's possible someday there will be a family running around the large open concept living room we're walking through. Of course, now that I'm older, I realize it could use a bit of updating, but who has the time?

I steal a glance at Hollie, who is unabashedly looking around with wide eyes. "Come on, the kitchen is through here." I lead her through the great room and into the open kitchen, opening the refrigerator and pulling out a bottle of water while Hollie jumps up to precariously perch on the edge of one of my island barstools. "Here, drink this." I tell her, handing her the bottle. "Do you want something to eat?"

"Nope," she says, popping the P sound then giving me a giggle. There she goes, being adorable again. I realize I'm smiling like an idiot, but who cares? She probably won't remember much of tonight anyway. "Thanks for taking me home. You really didn't have to."

"That's where you're wrong." She doesn't answer that and instead gulps down the water I've given her. I stop to remove my suit coat and tie, feeling her eyes on me without having to look at her, I roll the sleeves of my shirt to my elbows.

"I'm really sorry if this causes a problem for you with your girlfriend. She doesn't have anything to worry about from me."

"I told you I don't have a girlfriend," I bite out, not bothering to mention that if I had a girlfriend, she most certainly would have something to worry about where my curvy little assistant was concerned. "Let's drop it."

"I've only had sex with one person before." I glance up and Hollie has slapped her hand over her mouth, eyes widening in shock as if she didn't mean for that little piece of information to slip out. This is a new direction for our conversations. Apparently, drunk Hollie has no filter.

My eyes rove over her body, taking in her halo of curls, disheveled blouse that's come untucked from her skirt, and her bare feet. She must have kicked her heels off under the counter. "I mean, we had sex a few times, but I didn't think it was very good. Maybe I was bad at it."

A sound suspiciously close to a growl exits my chest. "You can't say shit like that to me, Hollie."

"Why not?" Her eyes are full of innocence, and I want nothing more than to drag her upstairs right now and take her to my bedroom.

"Because when you say shit like that, it makes me want to fuck you until you can't even remember that other man. There's no way you're bad at it, angel."

Her pink lips form a little O of surprise and now all I can think of is sliding my cock in between those lips and feeling her tongue run over me. I'm so hard at this point that a spurt of pre-cum leaks out of my cock and wets my boxer briefs. It's time to get her out of my sight before I lose control.

She doesn't appear opposed to my suggestion, but there's no way I'm fucking her now while she's drunk. She looks like she's about to speak and before she can say something to make this situation even more painful, I usher her out of the kitchen and towards the stairs.

"I can sleep on the couch," she offers, heading towards the aforementioned piece of furniture before almost taking a nose dive down the short steps into the sunken room.

"Angel, I have a guest room. Several, in fact. You'll sleep in one of them." I grab her hand and redirect her to the stairs. She doesn't quite clear the first step and catches herself on the stairs.

"Whoops." She laughs, spinning to sit her ass down on the stairs. This obviously isn't working. The girl is too drunk to make it up the stairs. I reach down, put one hand under her knees and the other at her back before scooping her up into my arms. She lets out a little shriek of surprise and wraps her arms around my neck to stabilize herself as I head to the second floor. I try not to notice how soft she is, how good she feels in my arms. I passed appropriate about forty-five minutes ago and am firmly in dangerous territory.

She sighs contentedly against my chest and mumbles, "You're warm," before tucking her head under my chin and passing back out. I studiously do *not* think about how right this is, how she fits into my arms like a missing piece of a puzzle. Before I can stop myself, I'm taking a deep breath of her scent that's surrounding me. It's honeysuckle again, just like that first day, plus something else that's distinctly Hollie.

I maneuver the door to the guest room open without waking the sleeping beauty in my arms and place her down in the middle of the king-size bed. My fantasies of Hollie have all been restricted to the office. I never imagined her spread out on a bed in my home. That is my mistake. I'm not sure she's ever looked more beautiful. Her hair is around her in small tangles, bare feet, and long lashes resting against her porcelain cheeks.

Before I can stop myself, I reach down and smooth back a strand of hair that's fallen onto her face. I need to get out of here now. She's going to have to sleep in her clothes. There's no way I'm undressing her, even if I want to.

Pulling the throw blanket at the bottom of the bed over her body, I turn away from my slumbering temptation and leave the room. Firmly closing the door behind me. Letting out a shaky breath, I rub my hand over my face. I need to get my shit together. This can't happen. I've already crossed so many lines with her. Instead of sitting in the room and watching my angel sleep like I want to, I head to my home office. A few hours of work will hopefully exhaust me enough where I can actually sleep while Hollie is under my roof.

ELEVEN

HOLLIE

The light spilling in from the window falls on my face, waking me from what feels like the sleep of the dead. Disoriented, I open my eyes and stare at the ceiling. Something doesn't seem right. My room never gets morning sun. My head is pounding like Fred Astaire spent all night tap dancing on it. I sit up slowly, careful not to jostle my tender head too much, when I notice that I'm not in my bedroom.

Where the fuck am I? This isn't Bianca's or Violet's room either. It's not unheard of, one of us waking up in the other's room after an evening out. It's decorated tastefully in a Cape Cod style. The walls are a gentle blue-gray hue that serves to enhance the view out of the large bay windows. Is that Lake Washington? I definitely don't know anyone with a place on the lake. The bed is the softest I've ever had the pleasure of sleeping in and it's decorated with a fluffy comforter and a boatload of pillows which scream expensive.

Lifting the blanket that's covering me, I note that I'm still wearing yesterday's clothes, thank god. At least I know I didn't do anything I'll regret too much.

Reaching over to the nightstand where my phone is resting, I notice a twinge in my bicep. I inspect the ache and notice what looks like bruises in the distinct shape of fingers. My thoughts are pulled back to the scene from the bar last night. Bits and pieces of the evening come back to me in flashes, almost like I'm watching a movie montage.

I was having fun meeting new people. I drank too much. Some man grabbed my arm and wouldn't let go. The thought sends a wave of nausea through me. Why didn't anyone try to help me? A vision of Archer's face, filled with fury, clouds my mind. Archer was there. He punched the man and took me outside. Oh my god, I wouldn't let him take me home so he took me to his house. I'm in Archer's house? That would make sense because I can't imagine that I know anyone else who could afford this kind of view. Nothing else is coming to me beyond that. This is not good.

I grab my phone and check it for messages. Luckily, there is nothing from my roommates. They were probably too involved in their own lives to notice I never made it home. Or maybe they think I finally bagged Archer. Groaning, I note that it's almost seven. I have to get moving.

On the nightstand, next to my phone, is a glass of water, two ibuprofen, and a t-shirt and boxers, with my heels stacked on top of them. Archer must have left these for me. Warmth fills my body at how thoughtful he is before it's swiftly pushed aside by a crushing embarrassment. I can't believe he had to deal with me in that state.

I never drink like that. god only knows what came over me. Wait, I do know. Archer's girlfriend. Oh my god, what if she's here too? I was ready to die of embarrassment when I thought it was only Archer who saw me at my worst. I can't imagine what his girlfriend thinks about me. Are they talking about me right now? Laughing at me?

Tears sting my eyes, but I quickly blink them back. This is nobody's fault but my own, and I need to own it like the adult that I am.

God, I hope he doesn't fire me.

Clutching the tee and boxers, I make my way to the en suite bathroom. It's larger than my bedroom at home. There's a walk-in shower and a huge soaking tub. I would give my left boob to sit in that tub and soak for the next two hours, but I don't have that kind of time. Turning on the shower, I wait for the water to heat before I step under the spray. The heavy water pressure soothes some of the stiffness out of my muscles. I let the scalding water wash away the alcohol that's practically seeping out of my pores.

After the five minutes I let myself indulge in the water pouring over me, I step out of the shower and wrap a plush towel around myself before digging through the myriad of cabinets and drawers looking for a hair dryer.

Score! It's one of those Dyson ones that I'm pretty sure works via magic.

My hair is mostly dry when I slip on the t-shirt and boxers. They smell like Archer. I'm pretty sure I'm blushing from head to toe at the thought of the clothes I'm wearing being up against his skin. Stopping, I breathe in his scent, avoiding the moment when I'll have to emerge from this room and face him.

My purse is across the room, so I grab yesterday's clothes and shove them inside, thankful that I had my large work bag and not a tiny purse for going out. Shoes in hand, because there's no way I'm putting them on with this outfit, I put my hand on the doorknob. Deep cleansing breath, Hollie.

I open the door and step out into a long hallway lined with art and photos. There are pictures of what is obviously a young Archer on the wall with an older man and woman. I can only assume they are his parents. Like everyone else, I know his parents died when he was younger, but not much else about them. My heart aches for the pain that young Archer in the photos is going to have to endure. He still has that same mischievous smile, though he likes to hide it.

There are noises far off to my left, so I head in that direction and go down the opulent staircase. This house is absolutely amazing. There are huge vaulted ceilings, but somehow with all that space, it doesn't feel cold. It's cozy and warm and feels like a home. I wonder if this is where he lived with his parents. I tiptoe into the kitchen and stop, frozen in my tracks.

Archer is at the stove with his back to me. His thick brown locks are still damp from his shower. He's dressed in a pair of gray slacks that somehow perfectly frame his ass and a white button-down shirt. It's obvious his clothes are made for him. They are tight enough to enhance his obviously firm physique, but loose enough to allow him movement. He's taking advantage of that by flipping something on the stove.

I clear my throat before softly saying, "Good Morning."

Archer spins around as if I've caught him off guard. With a heated look in his eyes that will fuel my nighttime fantasies for weeks to come, he looks me over from the top of my head down his own t-shirt and boxers, all the way to my bare toes before landing on my face.

"You're alive." His mouth ticks up and forms that smile I just observed on his younger self. On adult Archer, it isn't just mischievous, it's downright sinful. He looks like he's about to devour me whole.

"Thanks to you. Look, I'm so sorry about last night, I'm so embarrassed. Thank you for taking care of me. I can't even remember anything after we left the bar."

As he listens to my stuttering thanks and apologies, his face hardens back up. This is better. This is the Archer I'm used to dealing with. I can handle bosshole Archer. I'm not sure what to do with playful Archer.

"You can't do that again, Hollie. What if I'm not there to save you next time?"

"I know, I never do that, I promise. The night kinda got away from me. Are... are you going to fire me?" I can hear the crack in my voice and make a vow to myself that I'm going to try to be less pathetic.

His features soften a bit and he runs his hand over his face in a gesture I now recognize he uses in frustration.

"No, Hollie, I'm not going to fire you. You need to be more careful. You're a brilliant assistant. I'd hate to have to replace you," he adds sarcastically.

My face breaks out into a smile. He thinks I'm a brilliant assistant? This is news to me. He never gives me any hint of whether or not I'm doing a good job. I guess if he hasn't fired me yet, I should take it as a confirmation that he's happy with my performance.

Plating the eggs he's been working on, he slides a plate across the counter at me and points at the barstool.

"Sit. Eat." If the man hadn't taken care of me last night, I'd have something to say about him ordering me around like a dog. I decide to keep my mouth shut and hop up onto the barstool. I eye the eggs a bit skeptically before taking a small bite, surprised they're actually edible.

"These are actually pretty good," I say, before taking another bite.

He lets out a chuckle at that and looks at me while taking a bite of his own eggs. "What? You don't think I can cook?"

"I assumed you didn't. Don't guys like you not cook? I mean, we get takeout for lunch every day."

"Guys like me?"

"Oh, you know," I say, gesturing around the large expanse of the kitchen, "rich guys. I'm sure you could have a private chef on retainer or something. I'm lucky if my roommate bakes me a cookie where she doesn't mistake the salt for sugar."

He lets out a little cough, choking on the coffee he tried to swallow. "She's done that? Aren't sweet cookies like the first rule of baking?"

"You'd think. Just be happy I haven't brought any of her creations into the office. The entire floor would be out with food poisoning."

"You have my eternal gratitude." He lets out another tiny laugh. I'm starting to like that sound. If I wasn't already sitting down, I think my knees might be weak. "I'm not home enough to have a full-time cook, so I had to learn to make a few things, or I'd starve. Takeout is easier most of the time." He shrugs those broad shoulders, momentarily stretching the linen of his shirt across his taut muscles.

Dragging my eyes away from him, I shovel more eggs into my mouth. Apparently, my hangover has made me ravenous.

There's a small ding, and then Archer is putting two pieces of toast on my plate. I grab one and take a huge bite, not caring about looking like a lady right now. Toast is the perfect thing to soak up any alcohol left in my body.

"I can drop you at home before work so you can change."

"Could you take me to the office instead? I can grab my car there, head home, and come right back. That way, you won't have to go out of your way." As I'm chewing, I suddenly remember why I was so upset yesterday.

Biting on my lip briefly, I decide to bring up the topic I've been avoiding, even though I really don't want to. "I hope I didn't cause any problems with your girlfriend. I'm more than happy to apologize to her face to face. Is she here?" My eyes dart around the room, like it's possible I just missed her when I walked in and she's silently sitting in some corner, judging me.

He turns his head and raises his eyebrow at me like he's not sure if he's annoyed or amused. I'm hoping the amusement wins out.

"I guess you don't remember, but I told you last night, I don't have a girlfriend."

"But—" I try to interrupt, but he continues on like I haven't said a word.

"In fact, I haven't had an actual girlfriend since college. Julia and I went out a few times, months ago, and she was under the completely incorrect assumption that we were together. I have corrected her of that assumption. In fact, add her to the 'straight to voicemail' list."

He corrected her of that assumption? That sounds like the worst way to break up with someone ever. It would figure that this man has women all over the city thinking they're in a relationship with him. I'm sure he sleeps with women and doesn't want any strings while they want more.

Yeah, that fits in better with what I know about men like him. But I mean, who could blame them? He's one of the hottest men in Seattle and he's stupidly wealthy. Hell, he can even be a little charming when he wants to be. But he's obviously not looking for any sort of commitment. I'd do well to remember that. I won't be one of those women desperately clinging to him while he can't get away fast enough.

"Okay," I shrug, not wanting to talk any more about the women he dates, "but don't blame me if she goes barging into your office again when she can't get ahold of you."

The corners of his mouth tip down in a frown, making him look like some kind of sexy, grumpy bear. "You're right. We should probably alert security that she's not allowed up to the executive floor without permission."

He snatches his keys off the counter and heads towards the garage, leaving me to trail behind him. Not that I mind. The back of Archer is almost as hot as the front. I barely suppress a frustrated groan. This job is getting more difficult by the day. I'm still unbelievably attracted to my boss. Hell, half the time I think I'm going to jump his bones even though I've never been very assertive in physical relationships. I shouldn't want him the way I do. Even if he insists he doesn't have a girlfriend, getting involved with him would be a mistake. It's not only the fact that he's my boss and it's against the rules. Archer would use me up and leave me ruined for anyone else. That's obvious from how my body reacts to his mere presence.

I'm firm in my new resolve. No more nighttime fantasies. No more thinking about how he smells. And definitely no more almost kisses. It's fine. I can do this. What other choice do I have?

TWELVE

ARCHER

That night at the bar, and afterwards at my place, something was knocked loose in our relationship. Yes, we're still completely professional, but we're also a little more comfortable. We call each other by our first names. We make more small talk. I even occasionally say please and thank you.

Hollie is still the most amazing assistant that I've ever had. She's so efficient that I'm able to accomplish more in a day than I ever have before. The minutia has been taken off my plate. She either handles it herself or passes it off to other employees. When she first started as my assistant, she was timid, almost shy. Over the past weeks, she's grown more outgoing and confident. I'd be lying if I said it wasn't sexy as hell.

Our new, more familiar relationship has done nothing to stop my increasingly depraved thoughts of her. Ever since that night when she gave me that chaste kiss then later blurted out she'd only had sex with one man, I've been in a bit of a sexual haze. I don't know how it's possible that she's almost completely untouched. I wasn't joking when I told her it makes me want to fuck her until she can't remember his name. It definitely does. Now I can't get the image of me fucking her while she screams my name out of my mind.

Hollie was in my house for only a few brief hours and somehow, it's seemed emptier ever since she left. I never invite anyone over to my place. I don't have many friends to speak of and if I meet a woman for sex, I take her to my reserved suite at The Clarke. It's convenient and there are no awkward morning afters trying to get her to leave. I can take off and head home. It's always worked for me. Now the place seems a little colder. I swear I can still smell honeysuckle in the guest room she stayed in.

Not only has Hollie taken to running my business schedule, but she's also got my home life whipped into shape. She's taken charge of my housekeeper, gardener, shopping services, you name it. All it took was one off handed mention that I noticed my fridge wasn't stalked so the service may have not shown up and next thing I know, Hollie has them dropping groceries to my housekeeper within the hour. From then on, she's basically taken over the running of my daily life.

I'd like to say I didn't love it, but I do. Besides the fact that I now only have to concentrate on the most important work issues, I'm pretty sure it's the fact that Hollie is the one doing all these things for me. She's taking care of me. No one's even attempted to take care of me since before my parents died. Sure, I'm paying her, but I didn't ask her to insert herself so deeply into my life that I'm not sure how I'll ever get her out.

The intercom buzzes, and Hollie's voice fills the room. "Archer, Caroline DuPont is on the line for you." I straighten up in my chair and reach for the phone, quickly bringing it up to my ear.

"Go ahead, send her through."

The line clicks as the connection is made. "Mrs. DuPont, to what do I owe the pleasure?"

"Please, Mr. Clarke," she says, her voice as calm and confident as steel through the phone. "Let's cut out the pleasantries, shall we? I realize you want The Village, but you should know that I'm not going to just hand the property over to the highest bidder. I want you to present me with a proposal."

"A proposal?" I get out. My brain is still trying to catch up with what she's saying. I wasn't expecting her to run headfirst into this conversation. She's actually caught me off guard. Point one to Caroline DuPont.

"Yes, that's right. I want to know what you're going to do with The Village if you get it. If you'll be doing anything for the community or local businesses. You realize I don't need the money from this sale. I want to make sure that whoever buys my land has the best interests of the city in mind."

"Yes, I completely understand. A Clarke Hotel will bring in more dollars for local businesses and raise the profile of the entire city."

"We'll see about that." There's skepticism in her voice that's difficult to miss. It's going to be an uphill battle getting this woman to give me an inch. "I'll need you here Friday to pitch your ideas to me."

"There? In Santa Cruz?" I ask. Again, she's throwing me for a loop. I can see this woman doing battle with some of the toughest business titans in the country and still coming out unscathed.

"Yes. Will that be a problem?"

"Of course not. I'll have my assistant contact your team and set everything up. I'm looking forward to meeting you in person, Mrs. DuPont."

"Good bye, Mr. Clarke." With that, I hear a click and she's gone from the line. I place the phone back into the receiver while I try to figure out what just happened.

She wants me to give her an actual proposal presentation to buy her land. I'm not used to people caring about what happens after they sell me a property. Normally, we absorb and move on. Even though a part of me didn't quite believe it, it seems the article Hollie found is completely accurate. Caroline DuPont wants to make sure whoever buys her land means to help the community. At the very least, it has to show that the company will enrich the town. It's Monday now. That means I have four days to come up with a strategy and put together an entire proposal.

I spend the rest of the afternoon holed up in Richard's office strategizing about the upcoming meeting. I wanted to put together some kind of charity program where we donate a percentage of our profits to local charities. However, Richard pointed out to me I would need board approval for that kind of commitment. I don't have the time or inclination to go to the board for anything right now. If she really pushed me, I would go back to the board but I don't want to give them the idea that this deal isn't in the bag. They're already skittish with the amount of money we are sinking into this project.

Eventually, we come up with a loose plan. One thing we need to show are the statistics on how much money destination resorts bring into the surrounding town and businesses. There's a lot of data on that out in the world, what with most luxury resorts in the Caribbean and South Pacific being in poor countries and communities. It's not as if people in Santa Cruz are hurting for money. Not at all. But small business owners and workers may be from the less affluent surrounding areas. I decide that I'll personally commit to large donations from the Clarke Family Foundation to local charities as part of our community outreach.

When I finally make it back to my office, Hollie is still sitting at her desk, even though it's far past the time everyone else leaves for the day. I know she's been waiting for me to get back. She never leaves until I do unless I forcefully tell her to go, but even then, she wants to argue. Besides myself, I can't think of anyone with a better work ethic than this girl.

"Did you nail down a time with Mrs. DuPont?" I ask her.

"Yes, I have you scheduled for a ten a.m. brunch. I told her assistant to pick her favorite place. I figure we could use any upper hand we can get."

"Ten a.m.," I mutter underneath my breath while I think. This won't be so bad. We can go down in the morning and be back that afternoon. "Call my pilot and give him the details so he can create the flight plan. Tell him we'll be leaving Friday morning and return the same day."

"We?" she asks quietly. I bring my eyes back to hers and she arches her brow questioningly. I can see she wasn't expecting to be going with me.

"Yes. We. I have to concentrate on this meeting. You're my assistant. I'm going to need you there to handle everything else. I'll pick you up at your place Friday morning on the way to the airport."

She merely nods her head and starts jotting down notes, ever the dutiful and organized assistant. It's another two hours in my office, pulling data and organizing my notes before I'm ready to go home.

I pass Hollie's empty desk as I head towards the elevator. I sent her home about an hour ago. There wasn't anything else I needed for the evening, so one of us should get a little sleep. As expected, she fought me all the way, insisting that she stay until I was done. I had to threaten to fire her before she agreed to leave. She indulgently played along. I think we both know that I'm not going to fire her.

What would I do without her?

The thought is mildly terrifying, so I shake it off. For now, Hollie isn't going anywhere. She'll continue to bring together the disjointed pieces of my life, smoothing them out into something that looks similar to a well-oiled machine. Consequently, making me more and more dependent on her.

Between Hollie and myself, we hobble together the presentation over the next few days. It's been a week of late nights and early mornings. My caffeine consumption is through the roof, and I'm sure my doctor would freak out if he saw my current blood pressure readings. By the time Thursday afternoon rolls around, we're finishing up the last piece of the proposal in my office.

"I'll pick you up tomorrow morning at seven."

"I'll be ready. Do you need me to bring anything else besides my laptop and a backup copy of the proposal?"

"That should be it. Go ahead and take off. I'm right behind you."

Hollie gathers her things from her desk and heads towards the elevator with a quick little finger wave to me. I rub my eyes and take another sip of the coffee that's been on my desk for the better part of the afternoon. It's freezing cold, but I wasn't going to have Hollie make a brand new one when I'm about to head out. The proposal we put together is good. I wish it was great. What Caroline DuPont seems to be looking for, no one can give her except perhaps a non-profit. They certainly don't have the type of funding that they would need to purchase and develop the property. We're all businesses, we're here to make money. That means putting our shareholders' needs above the community most of the time. I'm hoping that some of the appeasements I've made, along with the high price we're willing to offer, is enough to sway her to sell to Clarke Hotels.

Unless Shaw straight up lies about what he is going to put there, I can't imagine her going with whatever he has planned, no matter the amount of money he offers. I've never seen him build anything but commercial properties and housing that looked like he bribed the building inspector to keep it propped up. There is no way that she wants that kind of thing besmirching her beautiful town. At least I'm pretty confident about that. I'll have to make sure that I point out some of Patrick Shaw's flaws to Mrs. DuPont during our meeting. It's not something I would normally stoop to, but according to Richard, he's already giving her an earful about me, so I might as well take my shot. With my head filled with thoughts of tomorrow's meeting, I head home, alone, like every other night since Hollie came to work for me.

THIRTEEN

HOLLIE

I've finished packing everything that I'll need for the day in my computer bag when I get a text from Archer alerting me he's waiting outside. I take a last glance at myself in the mirror. My hair is up in my normal work day bun and I'm wearing just enough makeup to help me project an air of confidence. I'm Hollie Simmons, assistant extraordinaire. I've got this.

I'm *not* super excited about flying in a private jet and getting to attend my first real business meeting. So, maybe one of those is slightly cooler than the other.

I'm wearing a pair of dark gray slacks along with a light gray wrap top and a pair of sensible flats. I know heels appear more professional, but if I'm going to be walking around on a tarmac and in the air, then I'd rather not be in danger of falling flat on my face.

Swinging my bag over my shoulder, I head out to the chauffeured car that Archer's hired to take us to the airport. The driver opens the door to the backseat for me and I slide in while he secures my bag in the trunk. Without a word, Archer stretches out his arm to me and hands me a cup of coffee.

"This is new," I laugh. "I'm the one that's supposed to be getting you coffee, not the other way around." I take the cup from his hands, careful not to touch him. Our relationship might be more comfortable than it was before, but there's no reason to tempt fate. I refuse to walk around all day in wet panties because I touched this man's freaking hand.

The entire way to the airport, we are both glued to our phones, answering any messages that came in last night and anything that's already made it into our inboxes this morning. I glance over at Archer and surreptitiously study his profile. If it's possible, the man's gotten even hotter over the short time I've known him.

The morning light that's spilling in through the car windows pulls out the naturally golden highlights in his hair and the sharpness of his jaw makes me want to brush my fingers along it. I've never had a jaw fetish before, but that's the type of thing Archer Clarke does to me.

Before he can catch me staring, I focus back on my phone and forward a request for some financial data over to Mr. Solomon's assistant. When we arrive at the small airfield, we're quickly let through the gates before the car pulls up alongside a small but sleek looking plane. I don't know much, but I know that I'll never have enough money to own a freaking plane. I'm going to enjoy the relatively quick trip down to Santa Cruz and back today. Getting to spend time with Archer is just a bonus. Nothing can ever happen between us for many many reasons but that doesn't mean I can't enjoy his company. I can't explain it. He's still a bosshole, but he's almost softer with me somehow. I don't understand why, but I'll take it.

I'm buckling myself into a plush leather seat when the pilot comes into the cabin and tells us that the flight to Santa Cruz will take a little less than two hours. He retreats to the front of the plane, where I'm assuming he's getting ready to take off. The flight attendant delivers me the coffee and bagel I asked for then turns to hand Archer his large coffee. One cream. One sugar. It's nice to see someone else have to fetch his coffee for once.

Archer must have caught me smiling to myself because he's asking me, "What's got you so happy over there?"

"Nothing. I'm just excited. I've never been on a private plane and I've never been to Santa Cruz."

"Don't get your hopes up too much. Our schedule is pretty tight today. It's going to be straight to the meeting and straight back to the plane. There won't be much time for sightseeing."

I shrug at him. "Doesn't matter. It's still nice to go somewhere new." I flash him a smile, take another sip of coffee, and turn back to my emails. The next two hours seem to fly by. Archer and I don't speak. We sit in companionable silence while working on our own projects.

When we're settled into the chauffeured SUV that was waiting for us when we exited the plane, I feel the notification buzz from the phone in my hand. I scan the email quickly, then turn warily to Archer. He's going to be pissed.

"That was an email from Caroline DuPont's assistant. She says that Mrs. DuPont had an emergency and has to push the meeting back to this evening."

"You've got to be fucking kidding me." Yeah, he's definitely pissed. He's facing straight forward and I can see his jaw muscle twitch. I'm sure he's grinding his teeth down to stubs right now.

"What is this, some kind of power play or something?" I ask him. I'm not sure what happened, but I hope she's not messing with us. Canceling a meeting with people from out of town thirty minutes before the designated time is a dick move. Even in my short tenure as an assistant, I've learned that much.

"I don't think so." He lets out the breath he was apparently holding and runs his fingers through the thick hair on his head. "She doesn't seem like the type to play games. She's too straightforward for that. Something must have come up for her to reschedule like this. At least she's going to meet with us tonight. We'll stay over here and leave in the morning."

"We don't have any bags with us," I point out to him. I'm not looking forward to wearing the same outfit tomorrow that I have on.

"If you need something that you don't have with you, just put it on the company card. Part of the perks of getting stuck in Santa Cruz with the boss." He flashes that panty melting, mischievous grin at me. It's a smile that

I've been seeing more and more of over the past few weeks, and I don't hate it.

"You're right, it's a total hardship," I say back to him teasingly. Archer directs the driver to take us to a hotel down on the beach. There are no Clarke Hotels here—yet, he likes to point out—so we check into a beautiful hotel that looks like the cost per evening would equal that of my weekly paycheck. The front desk attendant takes our carry-ons and tells us he'll have them waiting for us in our rooms upon our return.

"So, what's the plan?" I ask Archer. It looks like we have some time to kill. I'm hoping I can get him to let me go do a little sightseeing while we're here. I'll use my lunch hour if I have to.

Archer smiles down at me and places his hand on my lower back, steering me back out to the front of the hotel. Even though there's the cotton of my shirt between us, I can feel his fingers as if they're directly on my skin. My entire body flushes as I walk beside him. So much for dry panties.

We leave the car at the hotel and head down the street, chatting easily back and forth while his hand lies on my back the entire time. Does he even realize he's touching me?

A few minutes later, we approach the opening to what the sign proclaims is The Santa Cruz Wharf. It's basically a long pier lined with shops and restaurants, making me glad I decided on the flats this morning. I walk up to the edge of the pier and look out over the beach next to us and the ocean as it disappears into the distance.

"It's beautiful here." I'm tilting my face up, the warm sun against my skin as a breeze blows by, tugging at the strands of hair trapped up in my bun.

"Yeah. It is." Archer's voice sounds almost like a growl. I turn around and see that he's staring directly at me with one of the most intense gazes I've ever seen in his eyes. I wish I knew what he was thinking right now. Tucking the loose hair back into my updo, I leave the railing and return to his side. His hand seems to automatically fall to my lower back once again, and I let him steer me deeper into the crowd. "Come on, I want to show you this."

We browse the Made In Santa Cruz shop and everything is so cute, I want to take it all home. I'm wondering if I should get some things to take home to Violet and Bianca, but decide to just buy a UCSC Banana Slugs t-shirt. Not only is it a fun souvenir, but I'll also be able to sleep in it tonight. I'm nothing if not practical. Archer insists on paying for the shirt even though I assure him he doesn't need to. The man pays me enough where I can purchase my own souvenirs. He tells me I wouldn't have to buy something to sleep in if it wasn't for the job, so it's really a business expense. I finally relent and let him buy the damn thing.

The cashier hands the bag containing my new sleepwear to him and instead of handing it over to me, he holds onto it and uses his other hand to grab my elbow, pulling me excitedly along to the next store in a long line.

I'm not entirely sure that our plane didn't land in an alternate universe. I've never seen Archer so happy. He's smiling, laughing, and being downright playful. If I hadn't been sitting next to him the entire flight and saw him only drinking coffee, I would swear he was drunk.

He tries to buy me something in every store, but I put my foot down in a small art gallery. There is no way he's buying me a $2,000 painting. When I refuse him, I could swear he pouts a tiny bit.

"Archer, you can't justify buying me that as a company expense. What? I was in Santa Cruz and forgot to bring the artwork I normally travel with?"

He laughs and finally gives in. "Fine, no painting," he raises his hands in a sign of surrender, "but I still get to buy lunch."

"Yes, you can still buy lunch." I laugh with him. I'm having so much fun I forget that this is supposed to be work. Archer is giving off this happy and relaxed vibe that's setting me at ease too.

We take our time exploring the wharf, visiting small souvenir shops, wandering the fish market, and watching the sea lions lazily sleep on their platforms in the water. Being a sea lion never looked so good.

As I'm peering over the railing at them, Archer rests his hand on the small of my back. The man has been touching me in one way or another since we left the hotel. His hand is always either on my lower back, arm, or at my hip. I wish he knew what it was doing to me.

It's taking all of my self-control to keep me from leaning into his touch. All I want to do is press myself against his firm chest and have his arms wrap around me. Okay, so that's not *all* I want to do, but it's all I'll let myself think about right now. I might as well go into the bathroom and chuck these panties into the trash. They'll never be the same.

We eventually decide that we're hungry and Archer takes me to the Firefish Grill. We're seated at a table directly up against a floor to ceiling window that shows the Pacific Ocean stretched out into the horizon.

"This place is amazing. I can see why you want to build a hotel here. It's California but somehow feels like a small town. No wonder Caroline DuPont is so protective of it."

"It's a great town. Did you know they found an actual Megalodon tooth in the mountains above Santa Cruz in 2014? That means ten million years ago the ocean completely covered those mountains and a 60 foot long apex predator roamed the waters."

I grab a breadstick from the middle of the table and chew on it while considering what he's just revealed. This is a whole different side of Archer that I didn't even know existed. Geeking out about sharks and history? I never expected it. "Are you some kind of undercover science nerd?"

He laughs easily and shakes his head. "No, I'm just a Santa Cruz nerd." Before I can continue questioning him, our waitress appears at the side of the table. She's looking at Archer like she wants to unhinge her jaw and swallow him whole. She hasn't even bothered to look over at me yet. I clear my throat to get her attention. She begrudgingly takes her eyes off of my lunch companion and asks me what I would like. Believe me girl, I get it. The man is hot. Like red hot.

We both place our lunch orders. I get the Fisherman's Pasta with a glass of iced tea and Archer decides on the Seafood Tacos and ice water. While we wait for our food, I decide to pick our previous conversation back up. "So, why are you such a Santa Cruz nerd? I know you want this project to get off the ground, but I don't think you had to learn about Megalodon teeth in order to do it."

A stormy expression I can't quite read clouds his face as he turns his light brown eyes away from me and out to the sea. I don't know where happy, carefree Archer went, but I want him back. I want to kick myself for digging deeper into this. We were having an amazing day, enjoying each other's company. I, for one, can't remember the last time I had so much fun exploring a new place.

"I used to come here a lot," he breathes, without even taking his eyes off the water. He's speaking to me, but it feels like he's a million miles away. "My family and I used to vacation here before my parents died."

My eyes widen as soon as the understanding washes through me. This isn't about business to him. Or at least, this isn't only about business. This is personal for Archer. I'm remembering that little boy I saw in the photos hanging on his walls. I'm imagining him running around on the beach, playing in the water, exploring the wharf when it hits me. "You stayed at The Village at Santa Cruz, didn't you?"

He drags his eyes back to my face and I can see his thoughts are lost in the past. "Bingo," he says with a faint smile crossing his lips. "Richard, my uncle, and now you are the only people who know that. I don't want anyone thinking this is some kind of a sentimental flight of fancy. Yes, I've always wanted to bring Santa Cruz a Clarke Hotel, but it also makes business sense."

I'm not sure why he's trying to justify himself to me. I think it's incredibly sweet that he wants to own the piece of land he used to stay on with his family. He's going to build a high-quality resort so other families can enjoy this beautiful town as he did with his parents.

"That's wonderful, Archer." I instinctively reach across the table and cover his large hand with my smaller one. I've never heard him speak about his parents before, so I'm sure it's difficult. It's the most vulnerable I've ever seen him and all I want to do is hold him and run my fingers through his hair, comforting him. This will have to be enough. "Thank you for sharing that with me. Don't worry, your secret is safe with me."

The storm clouds that were in his face clear and he flips his hand over so that our hands are laying against each other, palm to palm. He slowly starts weaving his fingers through my own. Yup, we're holding hands. Is there someone here to take a picture? I want this moment recorded in history. Archer Clarke is holding my hand in the middle of a seafood restaurant in Santa Cruz which we got to this morning via his private jet. What the hell has happened to my life?

We're both sitting in silence, staring at each other, and holding hands. I don't say a single word. If I could avoid breathing, I would. I don't want to risk doing a single thing to ruin this moment. I'm not sure what's happening, but it's obvious that Archer feels this thing between us too. It's then that his thumb caresses my wrist, sending a shiver all the way through my body. Before I can stop myself, a low moan escapes my throat.

Horrified, I pull my hand back, almost knocking over my iced tea. I know that I'm probably blushing from my scalp all the way down to my toes, but there's nothing I can do about it. There's a teasing glint in Archer's eyes that tells me he definitely heard the noise I made. I busy myself with smoothing out my napkin in my lap, making sure that my eyes don't meet his. It feels like he can see into my soul right now and there's no way I'm prepared for that.

The waitress interrupts our awkward silence by placing down the dishes. My pasta smells amazing and I grab my fork, ready to dig in. I can't help it, I love seafood. It's a good thing I live in Seattle where I have access to a fresh supply of the stuff.

Our conversation goes back to neutral topics for the rest of the meal and I'm almost able to forget the fact that I moaned at him. Almost.

We decide to head back to the hotel. There'll be some time to get work done and then freshen up before our dinner with Mrs. DuPont later. Archer walks us through the Santa Cruz Boardwalk on the way back to our hotel and it's honestly one of the coolest places I've been. It's an old school amusement park and, according to Archer, local Santa Cruz nerd, this is the oldest amusement park in California. The boardwalk opened in 1907 and has been in continuous operation since.

Archer guides me through the crowd, occasionally stopping and pointing out something that he loved as a kid. My heart is melting in my chest. Archer Clarke loves Whack-a-Mole. Who would have guessed?

Eventually we come out the other side of the Boardwalk, but we're both now holding enormous clouds of cotton candy. Archer laughs and tries to steal some of mine, but I smack his hand away. I don't care how sexy laid-back Archer is, nobody comes between me and carnival snacks.

The sun is beating down on us by the time we make it to the hotel lobby. We ride the elevator up to the fourth floor and both head into our separate rooms with talk of texting when we're ready to go.

I want nothing more to get out of these clothes that I've been schlepping around in all day. Too bad we hadn't planned on staying here, so I have nothing to change into. Plus, while this outfit would have been appropriate for a business lunch, it's a little casual for a dinner where we're going. Maybe there's a clothing shop nearby that I could run to before our meeting.

More than ever, I want to do everything I can to make sure Archer ends up with this property. Now that I know how personal this is for him, I want to make sure that I make a good impression on Caroline DuPont. I smile to myself as a stretch out across the plush king size bed. Plus, it wouldn't hurt to knock Archer's socks off either.

FOURTEEN

ARCHER

I didn't intend to tell her about vacationing with my parents. In fact, I try to talk about my time here as little as possible. It's not that the vacations spent here were bad, it's just the opposite. They are some of the best times I have ever spent with my parents. Even after all these years, it's still hard to believe that they're truly gone and that I'm here alone.

When I was sixteen years old, I was a bit of a hellion. I'd already been kicked out of one prep school and was well on my way to getting kicked out of another. I never did anything too wild, but if there was a fight, prank, or scandal happening on campus, you could bet I was in the middle of it.

That day's suspension was courtesy of a fistfight between me and Freddy Anderson. I never liked Freddy much. Then I found out that he was secretly bullying my best friend. He's lucky a punch in the face was all he got from me.

I was waiting at home for my parents to return from the school after meeting with the principal. I swore that lady had it out for me. As the afternoon moved into evening, I knew that my parents should have been back already. I just didn't think about it too closely. I guess I figured they had stopped at the store, or maybe the meeting took longer than expected. You never think that your parents might have died in a horrible, fiery crash while you were sitting at home watching television.

A part of me seems lighter now that I've told Hollie about one of my major reasons for wanting this property. I don't share that part of myself with many people and the fact she seemed to take it all in stride, not accusing me of being a sentimental fool, makes me want to share more with her.

Showing her Santa Cruz today had been a fun and joy-filled experience. I need someone else to love this place as much as I do to help me fight to get it. It's not like spending time with Hollie is a hardship.

In fact, I haven't been that light-hearted since I was a kid. Dragging her from shop to shop, teasing her, having my hands on her, it's the most fun I've had all year. I tried not to touch her so much but couldn't stop myself. With all the people around, part of me wanted to make sure she was safe right there by my side. The other part needed to show those other poor fuckers that were walking around that she was already taken. Well, not *taken* taken.

Shit. My protests are sounding weak, even to me. This girl has me in knots.

After parting ways with Hollie this afternoon, I spent some time in my room answering emails. Caroline DuPont rescheduling our meeting threw a monkey wrench in today's schedule, but I was making it work.

The hour was quickly approaching six, so we needed to get moving if we didn't want to be late. The restaurant was only a few blocks from the hotel, so I figured we could walk since the weather today was warm and should hold throughout the evening. It's nothing like Seattle where you automatically bring an umbrella with you everywhere you go because you never know when Mother Nature will decide to rain down upon you.

I leave my room and knock on Hollie's door, directly adjacent to mine. She opens the door and I'm momentarily struck stupid. I can't get anything to pass my lips except for the sound of my ragged breathing.

She's standing in the doorway in a dress that she was definitely not wearing this afternoon. The white dress has off the shoulder sleeves that rest on her upper arms, the skirt flares out slightly before stopping to rest just above her knees. The entire dress is covered in a light floral applique.

Her blonde hair is falling down around her shoulders. I haven't seen her hair down except for that one night at the bar. Now I want to send out a memo banning updos at the office. The fading sun is filtering through the windows and giving her a golden hue. I thought she looked like an angel before. This is on a whole other level. I think she might be glowing.

I know that I'm standing here staring at her like an idiot, but I can't seem to think of anything to say. My eyes roam all over her as if they can't stop on any one detail.

She shifts uncomfortably in front of me. I've obviously been gaping too long. "There was a shop next to the hotel. I didn't want to go to dinner in what I walked around in all day," she explains to me.

"Let's go." I can tell that my voice is coming out much harsher than I mean it to by the way she gets a crease in her brow, like she can't understand why I'm being so rude. Thankfully, she doesn't put up any resistance and follows me out of the hotel.

When we're out on the street, I once again place my hand on the small of her back, guiding her down the block towards the upscale Ember restaurant, making sure she's on the inside of the sidewalk. You can never be too careful.

We arrive at the meeting to discover that Caroline DuPont is already waiting for us. We're ushered into a private dining room near the back of the eatery that's spotted with numerous fireplaces, giving the place a homey atmosphere.

Mrs. DuPont raises from her chair and quickly greets both Hollie and me. She's a rather statuesque woman in her sixties with gray hair that's so vibrant I'm not sure it isn't a dye instead of natural aging. She's dressed in a navy blue sheath dress and is drinking a martini, hard eyes assessing the two of us.

After some polite conversation and placing our orders with the waiter, it seems Caroline DuPont is ready to get down to brass tacks.

"Mr. Clarke, I appreciate you coming down here to meet me and that you've been so accommodating today. My grandson fell ill, and I needed to look after him."

"Oh, no," Hollie chimes in. "I hope he's doing better."

"Yes, he's doing much better and his mother is home with him now." She gives Hollie a small smile before turning her attention back to me. "I'll cut to the chase. I'm not sure if there is a deal to be had between us. Something should go into that space that's going to enrich Santa Cruz's residents and community. I'm highly skeptical that a resort the size you're proposing could accomplish that."

I concentrate on projecting a calm and confident facade while Hollie hands her a copy of our updated proposal. I'm so close to making this happen that I can taste it.

"If you'll join me on page—"

"I'm sorry, Mr. Clarke," she interrupts me before I can even get started. "I'm sure you put a great deal of time into this, but I can review it later." She waves the monogrammed Clarke Hotels folder at me before setting it back on the table. "I want to hear from you what your plan is, without all the numbers and business jargon."

"Of course," I say, homing in on her. "A resort the size we're proposing would be a source of employment for residents. Our guests would boost the local food and tourist economy."

"I understand that, but what will your hotel bring me that any other hotel won't? Yes, it will bring in some money to local businesses, but there's more to life than money, don't you think?"

I'm momentarily thrown off my game. I knew she wanted to have something go in that took care of the community, but I didn't think she was going to discount money all together. What does she want to put there? An animal shelter? Before I can get my thoughts in order, Hollie jumps in. "I agree with you, Mrs. DuPont. It isn't always about the money. Today was the first time I've ever been to Santa Cruz and I think I've fallen in love a little."

A flush covers her cheeks and I can see the expression on Mrs. DuPont's face soften as she listens to Hollie speak. Apparently, I'm not the only person who can fall under her spell so easily. "There'll be activities on property for our guests like snorkeling, windsurfing, boat tours, surfing lessons, you name it. We could offer a special discount to residents and workers in the city. That way, they can take part without breaking the bank. I would have loved to have something like that where my sister and I grew up."

She's looking over at Hollie while taking a thoughtful sip of her martini. Hollie and I never talked about that discount and it's not in the presentation, but if Caroline DuPont likes it, it's in. I could probably even get around having to have the board's approval for that. Finally, Mrs. DuPont says, "That's an interesting thought, Miss. Simmons. I must admit, it's not something I had considered before. It would be nice for some of our lower income residents and workers to take advantage of Santa Cruz's beauty. Not merely the affluent."

I see an opening and don't hesitate to build on Hollie's success. "We're also planning to put a program in place that will donate a percentage of the resort's proceeds to local charities that you and I can choose together. This would be an ongoing program, not a one and done. That could go a long way to helping people here."

Our food arrives, and it seems she's heard our pitch and isn't interested in discussing it any longer. We spend the rest of dinner switching between eating and light conversation. I'm not sure if that's a good thing or not but it's out of my hands at this point.

Caroline has certainly taken a liking to my assistant. The two of them are chatting like old girlfriends by the time the evening comes to a close. We're about to leave the restaurant when she puts her hand on my forearm, drawing my attention to her.

"Mr. Clarke, I want to thank you and your lovely assistant again for coming down here to meet with me. I'll take everything you said to heart and review your official proposal." God help me, but I'm feeling optimistic before she continues with, "I'm not entirely sure that a resort is the best thing for Santa Cruz, but I'll think about it. I'm sure you realize I have several other parties interested in the property and I want to hear their proposals as well."

"Of course, I wouldn't expect anything less."

"I'm sure you think I'm a sentimental old fool for guarding who I sell my land to so closely, but it's something that's dear to my heart. My husband, Charles and I, ran The Village and our children grew up there. It's an important place to me and since none of my children are interested in taking it over, I don't want to worry about running it myself."

"I completely understand," I assure her with a smile. If the woman only knew how sentimental I was about the project, she wouldn't be questioning my motives so closely. However, that's not something I'm going to spread around. Telling Hollie was probably too much. I'm certainly not going to tell a woman who could spread my less than professional interest in this property to my competitors.

"Yes, thank you. I also wanted to give you a word of warning. I'm not sure what is going on between you and Patrick Shaw, but he certainly has it in for you. Before he even heard about the property, he was already telling me how dishonest you were and how I shouldn't trust you."

My entire body turns to stone at the mention of his name. Fucking Patrick Shaw. "I can assure you, Mrs. DuPont, Mr. Shaw and I have crossed paths many times over the years and there is nothing he wouldn't say to keep me from obtaining something I want."

"If I didn't already suspect he was full of shit, I wouldn't even have told you. I didn't get to where I am in this life by blindly trusting men like Patrick Shaw. I prefer to form my own opinions."

"Of course. I'm glad to hear that."

"My team will review your proposal and I'm asking everyone to send me one last offer before I make my final decision."

"That's fine, just send Hollie—" I glance to my right where Hollie was standing a moment ago and see that she's sunk back into the chair looking a bit like a ghost. I think I should stop giving this girl wine. Though she did only have one glass this evening. "Hollie, are you alright?"

I crouch down next to her chair so that I'm eye to eye with her. She nods her head slightly. "I'm fine, just a little dizzy. It's probably the wine," she practically whispers. I brush some strands of hair that have fallen on her forehead out of the way of her face. Her skin feels a little clammy.

"Oh, you poor dear," Mrs. DuPont is on the other side of Hollie, her hand grasped between her own.

"I'm fine, you two. No need to worry about me." She gives us a smile and raises out of her chair. If I didn't study Hollie as closely as I do, I might have thought that smile was genuine. However, that smile is fake as shit.

"I'm calling a car," I say while pulling my cell out of my coat pocket to make the call.

Mrs. DuPont pulls Hollie into what I can only describe as a bear hug. I'm a little worried that she might be squeezing Hollie too tightly, but let it go.

"You take care of your girl, Archer," Mrs. DuPont says as she gets into a chauffeured car that's pulled up to the curb at the restaurant entrance.

"Honestly, I'm fine now, Mrs. DuPont. It was so lovely meeting you." I wrap my arm around Hollie and pull her close into my side. Something that Caroline DuPont said just feels right. She's my girl. I need to take care of her.

As her car pulls away from the curb, Hollie turns to me. "You don't have to call a car, Archer. I'm totally fine. It was just the wine and then standing up so quickly. I was a little dizzy, but we can walk back to the hotel."

"Forget it, angel, the car is already on its way." She gives a small harrumph and crosses her arms across her chest, letting me know she's annoyed. However, she hasn't extracted herself from my arm around her waist. Now that she doesn't seem to be in any immediate danger of passing out, I take a moment to relish her plastered to my side. She's so soft I want to rub my hand up and down her body, taking in the feel of her.

When the Town Car arrives, I open the door for Hollie, settling her into the seat and buckling the seat belt across her lap before I move to the other side of the car and slide in beside her. I give the driver the address of where we're going and sit back. It should only take us a few minutes to get there. Luckily, in Santa Cruz, most things are close together.

Hollie looks at me questioningly. "Why are we going to The Village?" I'm not surprised that she has the address memorized. She worked hard on this project.

"I want to show you something." We sit in a peaceful silence until the car pulls into a long drive and stops at the now deserted and gated property.

I grab her hand and pull her through a hole in the derelict fence, moving towards the beach where some of the original bungalows are located. "Hold on." She laughs, pulling her hand out of mine. I have an urge to snatch it back, but I'm able to control myself. Barely.

Bending down, she shows me her delicious curvy ass in that white dress and removes her shoes before stepping into the sand.

We make our way across the sand towards one of the dark smudges on the beach. As we draw closer, you can see the outline of a bungalow. I don't know exactly why I wanted to bring her here and show her this, I just did. I'm not going to think too much about it. She deserves to see what she's working on.

I spent so much time here with my parents. Happy times that I'll never forget. Telling her that my family used to stay here seems to have opened up a crack in my carefully constructed walls. I want to show her more. I want her to know me. Know Everything about me. I want to share this with her.

"Is this where you stayed when you were little? It's beautiful. It looks like a kid would have so much fun here."

Even though The Village officially closed down about six months ago, the buildings don't appear too worse for wear.

"I remember sitting there with my mom, going through shells and sea glass I collected on the beach while my dad would grill dinner." Talking about this with her doesn't leave me with the hollow feeling in my chest I usually get when thinking about all the happy times with my parents, so I decide to keep going. "My parents met here when they attended UC Santa Cruz. Even though we lived in Seattle, we always came here at least once a year. This place was special to them, especially my mom. She always seemed lighter here." I take a quick, steadying breath before I continue. "I didn't want the magic of this place to be destroyed. Other families should be able to come here and make those kinds of memories I have. It would be a tragedy if a developer got the property and built some crappy commercial buildings here."

Hollie stands next to me, both of us staring straight ahead at the darkened bungalow. I'm half expecting her to ask me why I don't tell Caroline DuPont about my history here. It's true that it would most likely give me a leg up in the bidding process, especially since she's also sentimental about this place. Instead, her fingers tentatively curl around mine. This is the first time she's gone out of her way to touch me. I want to scoop her up and kiss her breathless as a reward, but I'm almost afraid any movement will have her pulling away.

"I love it, Archer. Thank you so much for bringing me here and sharing this with me." She didn't ask, because she knows I would never use something that private as a business weapon. This is my secret. This is something that I keep close to me that is only mine.

She squeezes my hand and then drops it to step forward and get a closer look at the building. She runs her delicate fingers down the wood railings, walking gingerly on the porch like she's worried she might fall through, and then sits on a small wooden bench before turning to smile at me. "This building doesn't actually look so bad. Did you ever think of saving them instead of knocking them down? Maybe you could fix them up instead? This place is so charming. It would be a shame to lose it."

That's something I hadn't considered. I'm so used to leveling everything I buy I haven't thought about renovating. I turn in a small circle, observing the beach and the buildings scattered throughout before letting out a sigh. "We hadn't considered that. Unfortunately, there's no way I could get the board to approve it. The bungalows are low occupancy and scattered over too much space. It wouldn't make fiscal sense. It's a nice thought, though."

I move and sit on the bench next to her, staring out at the ocean. The bench is so small that our thighs are flush against each other. A shiver runs through her body and I can see goosebumps along her naked flesh. I'm not sure if it's from the desire that's growing between us or if she's simply cold. Just in case, I shrug out of my suit jacket and wrap it around her shoulders.

"I'm so happy that you got to spend time here with your parents," she says softly. "We didn't do vacations and if we did, it wouldn't have been to a place like this."

"Your parents never took you on a vacation?"

A pained laugh escapes her lips and then she goes quiet. There's a steady silence between us and just when I figure she isn't going to answer, she says, "It was only my mom. My dad didn't want anything to do with me, emotionally or financially. I've only met him a few times over the years. Even if we had extra money to go on vacation, Mom would have been too high to take us. My sister and I were already taking jobs to cover our living expenses, even before we could legally work."

What? I'm stunned for a moment. She's never spoken about her childhood before. No father, a junkie mother, and zero childhood if she was already worried about covering bills. It makes the fact that Hollie is so sweet and caring a fucking miracle. Lesser people would not have gone to college, they wouldn't have fought their way out, and they wouldn't be the best assistant an asshole CEO ever had. "I'm so sorry, Hollie. I didn't realize. Here I am talking about my happy family—"

"Oh no, Archer. I didn't tell you because I want you to feel sorry for me. Not at all." Her hair glides across her shoulders as she gently shakes her head. "I had it a lot better than some people. You shared so much about your family with me today t-that I wanted to share something with you too."

Amazing. This woman wasn't angry or bitter, but rolled with the punches life gave her. She could tell it meant something that I shared my childhood with her today. She knew and wanted to share her own childhood with me.

She leans farther into my side, letting our shoulders meet. Even though layers of clothing separate us, I swear that her body's searing mine everywhere we touch. I don't know what the fuck is happening to me, but I know I have never wanted anyone more than I want Hollie at this moment.

I cast my eyes down to her face, only to find that I'm already the focus of her gaze. It's like she's seeing completely through me, to my very soul, and she understands me. I feel like I'm going fucking insane. What the hell has this woman done to me?

I can't take it anymore. I want a taste of her. Just this once. Then it will be out of my system and I can move on with my life. Before I have time to think better of it, I bring my mouth down on hers. She lets out a little gasp against my mouth and as soon as her lips open, my tongue moves in, swiping inside, teasing her tongue with my own. It's only a moment before she's kissing me back in full force.

This isn't some soft, hesitant, getting to know you kiss. This kiss is full of hunger, yearning, and pure lust.

It's like as soon as my lips touched hers, an explosion ripped through my entire body. Every inch of my skin is on fire and I hope the flames never go out.

I wedge my hands under Hollie's gorgeous ass and give it a quick squeeze before I yank her over into my lap so that she's facing me with her legs straddling my own, my suit jacket fallen to the floor, forgotten. I massage her cheeks through the material of her dress while leaning forward and tasting the skin of her neck and chest with my tongue. Her skin tastes like peach cobbler. This fucking girl is made of summers.

When I nip her collarbone with my teeth, she lets out a low moan and arches her back. Her fingers are running through my hair and she's holding me against her as her pussy grinds directly on top of my prominent erection.

My hips instinctively push up to meet her grinding pussy, the warmth radiating from her directly onto my cock. She's incredible. I haven't even really touched her yet and I'm worried I might explode before I get my pants off. My lips return to hers and she's making these little moaning noises that go straight to my dick.

Unable to stop myself, I reach behind her and pull down the zipper on her dress while she continues to squirm in my lap. The top falls and pools at her waist, trapping her arms at her sides with the sleeves and leaving her breasts only covered in a white lace strapless bra. The fucking thing is so sheer that I can see her large rosy nipples through the fabric. They're already pulled into tight points, begging me to taste them. I don't even bother removing her bra before bringing my mouth down to latch onto the bud underneath the lace, sucking gently.

Hollie makes a high mewling sound and moves her hands from my hair down to my shoulders, holding on like she's worried I might pull away. Not fucking likely.

I take her pebbled nipple between my teeth and give it a small bite. Just enough to give her a little surprise before it melts into pleasure. She lets out a gasp and pulls my head harder to her breast.

"You like that, angel?" It seems like my girl might like a bit of pain with her pleasure, and I'm happy to oblige. I move to the other breast and give that nipple the same sharp bite. The pace of her pussy rubbing against me picks up, and she's letting out little whimpers. It's the most erotic fucking sound I've ever heard. I almost come in my pants right then.

My cock is dripping with pre-cum, and if I could see my slacks, I know they would be soaked with both of our juices. "Tell me you like it. Tell me you need it." I want to hear her say it. She's obviously horny and into it, but I'm not that big of an asshole that I don't want to make sure she won't have any regrets. We both need this so that we can move on and work together. This tension between us is too much.

"I like it, Archer. I need it. Please."

That's all I needed to hear. I lift her off my lap and stand her up in front of me. The dress that was bunched around her waist falls to the floor. She's left standing in only her matching white lace bra and panty set.

"Beautiful," I breathe and start unbuttoning my shirt as quickly as possible.

"You think I'm beautiful?" She moves her hands up to cover her stomach, suddenly shy.

"You don't think you're beautiful?" I ask as I grab a hold of her arms and put them back to her sides so I can feast on her with my eyes. Her pale skin is almost glowing in the low light of the moon. Her breasts are full and heavy and a perfect fit for my mouth, while her stomach and hips are all plush curves that I can't wait to get my hands on.

She stands in front of me, thighs clenched together, and I can see the slightly dark spot in the center of her panties, proving how much she wants me. Wants this. She's the most beautiful thing I've ever seen.

"I just didn't think *you* would think I was beautiful. I know that I'm not your type."

"Oh, and what's my type?" I've shucked off my shirt and am unbuckling my belt, my eyes never leaving her. She's standing in front of me in these innocent yet sexy as fuck bra and panties while I can see how wet she is for me. She is simultaneously the most innocent and most sexy woman I've ever met. And she thinks she's not my fucking type?

"I've seen pictures of you out with women and they don't look like me." She's lost her mind. How can she possibly think I wouldn't want her? I've wanted her since the moment I set eyes on her. Actually, even before then if you want to get technical about it.

"Take off your bra," I tell her as I'm finally divested of all my clothing except my boxer briefs. She doesn't even hesitate before doing as she's told and discarding her bra. *Good Girl.* "Now your panties." She slides them down her legs and kicks them off into the pile of her clothing that's formed on the old wooden porch.

I grab onto her hips and pull her close to me before depositing her on the bench and sinking down on my knees between her thighs. I put my hands on each of her knees and gently guide her legs farther apart until she's bearing everything to me. The small patch of blonde hair above her pussy is trimmed, allowing me to see she's dripping wet. I can't do this without having a taste of her. I've imagined her taste too many times.

I nuzzle her perfectly pink pussy, breathing in the aroma that's distinctly her. I look up into her eyes and simply tell her, "Right now, you're my type."

Her eyes widen as I practically dive into her pussy. I'm running my tongue up from her tight hole to that sensitive bundle of nerves before circling it and moving back down. Hollie is moaning and writhing against me. Her hands are in my hair again and she's pulling my face tighter into her. I smile against her pussy as, once again, my tongue barely misses the spot she is so desperate for me to touch.

"Wait, wait, Archer." I still immediately, my face pressed tightly into her core. She's changed her mind. She doesn't want this anymore. A wave of fear washes over me. If she sends me away right now, I'm not sure my blue balls will ever recover. But if that's what she wants, I have no choice. The thought of her regretting me has my stomach tightening with an emotion that I don't have the time to examine right now.

I pull back and look up at her face. Her hazel eyes have darkened and are now focused on me. There's an anxiety in the air that's surrounding her.

"What's wrong, angel?"

"I need to tell you something—"

"Hollie, is what you have to say going to affect whether you want me to eat your delicious pussy right now?" I can see her blush even in the night's darkness. She couldn't hide an emotion from me right now if she tried and I love it.

She lets out an embarrassed giggle and shakes her head no.

"Then it can wait until tomorrow." I move forward and pull her hard clit between my lips and suck it in my mouth, applying gentle pressure while flicking it with my tongue.

All thoughts of what she was about to say, gone. I'm sure she wants to tell me she's only been with one man and that it was all the way back in high school. Odds are she doesn't remember telling me that the night she stayed at my house.

Frankly, I didn't want to talk about it. The thought of her with another man's hands on her fills me with unreasonable rage. For some reason, I want to beat the shit out of the kid. I've never cared about the former partners of women I slept with before. Especially not some high school kid who probably couldn't give a woman an orgasm if his life depended on it. I wasn't joking when I told her it made me want to fuck her until she couldn't remember him. I'm going to do just that tonight.

With my tongue and lips still working over her clit, I bring up my index finger and run it through her crease, covering it in her juices, before slowly sliding it into her channel. Holy shit, she's tight. As soon as I probe the walls of her pussy, seeking her g-spot, she detonates.

She screams my name into the night, somehow covering the sounds of the waves crashing against the beach. The sound of my name on her lips as she comes for me causes another spurt of pre-cum to exit the head of my cock and coat the inside of my underwear as she shakes, her body curling into herself. My face is flooded with her sweet juices, and I move my tongue frantically, making sure not to miss a drop. I can't help it. She's the most delicious dessert I've ever tasted.

My thumb moves up to press against her clit, applying light pressure, stretching out the last waves of her orgasm. I watch as what I can only describe as pure bliss crosses her face and I want to beat my fists against my chest in satisfaction, like a Neanderthal. I gave her that pleasure. And I'll be giving her more. She opens her eyes and looks down at me with awe and all I want is to be inside her.

FIFTEEN

HOLLIE

Holy shit!

Archer Clarke just ate my pussy like it was a five-course meal. I'm trying to get my breathing under control as I come down from my orgasmic high. I've never come so hard in my life. Then again, no one has ever done that to me before.

I'm slumped on the bench against the wall of the bungalow with my legs obscenely spread open in front of me. And who is down there kneeling between my legs, licking his lips, and looking at me with a naked hunger I've never seen before but Archer Clarke?

He stands abruptly and pulls me up with him, putting his hands under my naked ass, and lifting me into the air.

I instinctively wrap my legs around his waist so I don't fall. His heavy erection presses between us and my desire ratchets up ten fold. You would think I didn't just have an orgasm two minutes ago. Now it seems like not enough and I'm desperate to get him inside of me.

I wiggle my hips until I get the underside of his cock notched between my pussy lips and rock back and forth, stroking his hard length with my pussy.

"Jesus Christ, Hollie." His voice comes out as a harsh growl that only serves to notch up my desire. His lips move to claim my own in another hungry kiss. I get a small shiver of female satisfaction that I can make him this crazy and wild with lust, even though he's doing the same thing to me. I've never been so turned on in my life.

While never breaking our kiss, he moves us over to the old wooden railing and perches my ass on it. I let out an involuntary squeal and keep my arms and legs wrapped tightly around him. Is he nuts? I'm heavy and this railing is old. The last thing I want is to be dumped over the side down to the sand.

"Archer, I'll fall," I caution.

"Do you actually think I would let you fall, angel?" He moves his lips to the pulse in my throat. I know he can feel how wildly it's beating. I loosen my death grip on him a little and let him move his mouth down to my breasts. He pays careful attention to the first one, then the other with his tongue and teeth. Nipping my skin, then running a soothing lick over it. I know that I'm moaning too loudly but can't seem to stop myself.

I reach down between our two bodies and grab the head of his cock. "Fuck!" he shouts.

At some point, he must have lost his boxers without me noticing, because there's nothing in my way of enjoying the feel of him. I glide my hand from the tip of his shaft all the way to the base and then back again. He's slick and sticky with pre-cum, and I quicken my pace until he shudders in my arms. He stills my hand, moving it away from his pulsing cock. "You've got to stop."

"Did I do something wrong?" I thought he liked it. I certainly did. He places the palm of my hand against his chest and then leans his head forward so that our foreheads are resting against each other.

"You're doing everything right, angel. But if you don't stop, this is going to be over before we start. Understand?"

Does that mean he was about to—Oh! "No, we don't want that," I say as I continue to grind my hips against him. I can hear how husky my voice sounds but can't do a damn thing about it.

"I need to get inside that hot cunt of yours, Hollie. Right now." A whimper escapes my lips. No one has ever spoken to me like that before. If I'm judging by the gush of liquid I can feel escaping my pussy, I'd say that I love it. The corner of his lips quirk up in a satisfied smile. He reaches down between my pussy lips and starts to gently rub circles around my clit.

"You like it when I talk dirty to you, don't you? Your cunt got so wet when I talked about how much I want to fuck it." Even if I wanted to respond, I wouldn't be able to because he's now pushing one of his fingers inside me. Holy shit, is that just his finger? I look down at the size of his large erection and seriously wonder if he's going to fit.

"Answer me, Hollie," he says in a low, hard voice, dragging my attention back to his face.

Yes.

No.

What was the question again?

Now he's pushing a second finger inside of me. I whimper and lock one of my hands around his forearm, making sure that he can't pull away from me. My entire body feels hot and cold at the same time. I'm worried that I'm going to fall back off the railing, but he's holding onto my hip so tightly I'm sure I'll have finger shaped bruises in the morning and I love it. "I need the words, Hollie," he says while running his lips from my neck down to my shoulder.

He's moving his index and middle fingers in and out of my pussy in a steady rhythm. How can I answer him when I can't seem to catch my breath? "Please, Archer," I gasp. Trying to concentrate on anything except my orgasm that's fast approaching seems impossible.

"Please, what, Angel? Say the words," he commands.

I'll say whatever the fuck this man wants me to say. He can't stop finger fucking me right now. "Please talk dirty to me. Please fuck me."

He makes a sound of satisfaction and moves his thumb up to my swollen clit, rubbing it back and forth firmly. "First, you need to come for me. Come for me, angel. Make that pussy gush for me."

The combination of his dirty words, fingers filling me, and the sweet torture of my clit sets me off and white lightning is flowing through my body. My eyes roll into the back of my head and I swear I lose my sight for a moment. I can't stop my body from shuddering while he continues to work me over.

"Good girl."

The praise sends a shot of warmth straight to my chest. I've never thought about being called a good girl before, but now that's all I want him to call me.

Archer plucks me off the ledge and spins me around, bending the upper half of my body over the railing. My legs are shaking and I'm not actually sure I've stopped coming yet. I hear a rustling behind me and turn my head to see him covering his rock hard erection with a condom. Thank god, he still seems to be thinking clearly because I didn't stop for one second to think about a condom. Even though I'm relieved that he's being safe with me, there's the tiniest bit of disappointment. I wanted to see what he felt like inside me, with nothing between us. But I don't want it enough to have a baby with my boss.

When he's finished sheathing himself, he steps up behind me and pushes me down farther over the wooden railing so that my ass is pushing out against him. I wiggle my ass and can hear him moan as he takes a moment to run his cock from my clit to the entrance of my pussy and back again, coating himself in my cream. He grips my hips and thrusts forward forcibly, impaling me all the way on his cock. I let out a scream that's both for the pleasure and the slight pain of being stretched wide so quickly.

"Good girl, let me fuck you right." His hand wraps around the long strands of my hair and he pulls back, forcing my face up to the night sky. I'm not sure if I'm seeing literal stars or if they're just spots in front of my vision from the intense sensations he has running through my body.

He bends over and presses his lips to mine, sweeping his tongue inside my mouth, letting me get used to the huge appendage that is now buried deep within me. He sucks my tongue into his mouth and runs his teeth across my lower lip.

I can't stay still any longer. I need him to move. My hips gyrate against him, and he quickly picks up my signal, withdrawing from inside me until only the very tip remains. With a hard thrust, he pushes all the way back inside, making me see stars. Again and again and again. He's still got my hair in his fist and his pelvic bone is slamming into my ass harder each time.

He brings his other hand to my front and grabs my tit, squeezing the entire thing roughly. I let out a sob and I'm not entirely sure if it's from the slight pain or the pleasure. I'm on complete sensory overload.

"Fuck, your pussy feels like heaven. You better be close, angel."

I nod the best I can with his hands in my hair and his pace quickening. It's not long before he loses his pace completely and starts moving erratically inside me. I don't know how it's possible, but his cock swells, growing larger inside me just before he explodes, shouting my name out to the waves.

Feeling his release coating my insides pushes me over the edge one last time and my body shudders. My pussy convulses almost violently around him as he pumps two, then three more times inside me before collapsing forward across my back.

For a few moments, neither of us says a word. All I can hear is the crashing of the waves and both of our ragged breathing. We eventually pull apart and start gathering our discarded clothing, silently pulling them back on piece by piece.

∞

Thirty minutes later, I'm tucked safely back into my lavish hotel room. Alone.

I can't believe I just fucked Archer on the porch of a derelict beach bungalow. And it was dirty, rough, and fast. I was not prepared. I honestly didn't even know that sex could be like that. It was all-consuming. I felt half out of my mind. If what we just had was sex, what the hell did I have before?

Archer played my body like an instrument he'd been training to master for years. I've never had three orgasms in the same night, let alone back to back before. He's showing me I'm capable of things I never even thought of. Part of me, that insecure bitch we all have inside, whispers to me, *he must have had a lot of practice to be that good. A lot of broken hearts in his wake. Be careful or you'll be next.*

I don't want to think about Archer's past conquests, but I can't seem to stop myself. I wonder how I stack up against the supermodels and actresses he's been out with. He probably thinks I don't even come close.

After the hottest fuck I'll probably ever have in my life, we quickly got dressed, barely saying a word to one another. I didn't know what to say. Part of me wanted to reassure him I didn't think that this meant anything. The last thing I wanted was for him to worry that I would become some psycho who would follow him around after she got one taste of him. That's not my style. I'm a big girl, I understand how men like Archer work. A quick release and then on to the next.

He didn't go completely cold on me when we were done, but he had put distance between us. He quietly helped me back into my dress and pulled the zipper up my spine, securing it back on my body. We walked back to the chauffeured car in companionable silence, but I couldn't help but notice that for the first time all day, Archer didn't have his hands on me. I felt a slight tug inside my chest. Who would have thought that I would have gotten used to him touching me in such a short amount of time? Who would have thought that I would miss it?

It was fine. I didn't expect anything from him. But when he said that *right now* I was his type, I didn't think the window for *right now* would close so quickly.

I thought about inviting him into my room for a drink and perhaps a repeat performance, but he was so quick to say goodnight and leave me in the hallway that I didn't even get a chance. So here I am, alone in my fancy hotel suite, and thinking about how he rocked my world, while he's only one wall away.

God, what if I was horrible, and he didn't like it? No way, I don't think he could fake the reactions he was having. But then again, what do I know? I'm practically a born again virgin. Or I was until tonight.

I let out a groan and bury my face in my hands. Of all the unprofessional things I've done, saying this is the worst would be an understatement. God, I hope he doesn't fire me.

I step out of the shower, pulling a towel around me, and look at myself in the fogged bathroom mirror. There are small bites on my neck and chest where Archer's teeth have left marks. I run my fingers over them, marveling at how they make my stomach clench in renewed lust. Just thinking about him leaving those marks on me for others to see has my pussy slick with need.

I should have guessed that Archer would be forceful in bed, but it still came as a slight shock. I had never even had a fantasy about rough sex before. Now I'm not sure I want to go back. If he's ruined me for other men, I'm going to be pissed. It'll be a long, horny existence without that kind of sex in my life.

I dry my hair and then slip the UCSC tee shirt I bought earlier today over my head. I can't help but smile to myself, remembering Archer's face when he opened the door and saw me tonight. He looked stunned. I was a little nervous about the dress. I would never normally wear white, it's obviously not a slimming color. But sometimes, when you're a plus size girl, you take what they have in stock. I was happy to see he obviously appreciated it.

Turning off the light, I slip between the high thread count sheets of the king-size bed. I toss and turn, trying to get comfortable, but the huge bed seems so cold and empty. I wish Archer had come back to the room with me. If his new withdrawn attitude is any indicator, this is a one-time thing, and we only had tonight. But couldn't we have made tonight last a little longer?

A few hours pass and I still haven't managed a single second of sleep. I'm staring up at the ceiling and wishing I was at home in my own bed right now. Or even better, Archer's bed.

Stop it, you silly idiot. He obviously doesn't want you there.

I'm pulled out of my thoughts by a tapping sound coming from somewhere deeper in the room. It almost sounds like a knock, but it's not coming from the room's entrance.

Tap, tap, tap.

I scramble out of the bed as quickly as I can and my legs tangle in the sheets, almost sending me face first into the ground. What the hell is that noise?

My breath catches as my eyes scan the area immediately surrounding me, looking for some kind of weapon. Oh god, what if it's a rat? I will definitely scream.

Grabbing the hotel provided curling iron from the bedside table, I slowly tiptoe deeper into the darkness. What the fuck am I going to do with a curling iron? And why the hell didn't I grab my phone flashlight? Oh, it's because I'm too scared about the possibility of meeting Remy from Ratatouille up close and personal to think straight.

Tap, tap tap.

I almost jump out of my skin because this time the sound is coming from directly next to my ear. Stumbling back a few steps, I catch myself before crashing into an end table with a lamp perched on it. I put a hand over my heart, hoping to calm down the erratic beating in my chest. There's a dim outline of a door to my right that I didn't even realize was there.

I map out the suite in my head and realize this door must be the one to Archer's adjoining room. Fireworks go off in my lower belly just thinking about him.

I'm about to open the door when I realize I'm annoyed with him. He ditches me in the hallway as soon as we get back and then comes knocking at my door in the middle of the night? We may have had a one time fling, but I am *not* a booty call. Hell no!

I unlock the door and fling it open, ready to lay into Archer when I catch sight of him. He's so large he's filling the entire doorway. The only scrap of clothing on his body is his pair of boxer briefs, and I suddenly have the urge to drop to my knees in front of him and slide them down his thighs.

Before my mind wanders too far, he lurches forward into my room. He's looking at me with those whiskey brown eyes that are simultaneously exhausted and a little wild and unfocused. His brown hair is messier than I've ever seen it, like he's been running his fingers through it for hours. It only takes him a few steps to reach my side, but he doesn't stop like I expect him to. Passing by me on my left, he stretches out his arm and hooks it around my middle. Before I know what's happening, I'm being dragged backwards.

"Archer!" I squeal, trying not to fall back onto my ass as he picks up momentum. As soon as my legs hit the mattress, he releases me and crawls into my bed, fluffing the comforter and arranging the surrounding pillows.

I don't know what he thinks he's doing and I realize I'm standing in front of him in only a T-shirt. My panties were so wet from earlier I couldn't even put those back on. I cross my arms across my chest self-consciously, hoping he doesn't notice that my nipples are hard as diamonds. "What are you doing in my bed, Archer?" My voice sounds a little high and panicked, but I honestly don't know what's going on right now. Does he think I'm at his beck and call? Like some kind of sex slave?

He's propped up on his elbow as he lifts the edge of the comforter and pats the empty sheet beside him. "Come to bed."

Is he fucking serious? He's going to order me into my own bed? I always knew he was an asshole, but this is a whole other level. Why the hell did I let him touch me tonight?

Because you've never felt pleasure like that in your entire life. Shut up.

"You can't charge in here anytime you want and demand I fuck you, Archer! I'm not a booty call!" My voice is too loud for the quiet room, but I can't help it. I'm pissed.

"No, angel. You're not a booty call," he mutters. "It would be a hell of a lot easier if you were." I'm not sure how to reply to that. I'm not even sure what it means.

He's still laying there, holding up the comforter, patiently waiting when exhaustion finally rolls over me. It's been an extremely long day, topped off with some delicious sexual escapades. I can't decode whatever he's trying to tell me right now. My shoulders sag as I crawl into the bed beside him, laying where he previously indicated but careful that none of my body brushes up against his.

I'm surprised when he lowers his head into the crook of my neck and nuzzles me, sending shivers through my body. His arm snakes forward and wraps around my middle, pulling me backwards so that our bodies are seamed together and I'm tucked in tight against him. His hard erection rubs against my cotton covered ass as I wait for him to take control like I know he will. After a few minutes, I realize that he's not planning on doing anything with that hard appendage against me.

"You're not going to fuck me again?" I ask him, more than a little disappointed.

He gives a low chuckle that I almost miss before whispering into my ear, "No angel, I'm going to hold you and we're going to go to sleep."

"Oh." What else am I supposed to say? The man has struck me speechless.

If you had asked me this morning, hell, five minutes ago, if Archer Clarke was a cuddler, I would have laughed in your stupid, stupid face. But here he is, in my room, in my bed, limbs wrapped around my body, breath on my neck. Before I know it, my breathing is synced with his and I can feel myself being drawn into sleep. My last thought before everything goes dark is that I am utterly screwed.

SIXTEEN

ARCHER

Did I mention I was fucked?

It's been a week since that night in Santa Cruz and my desire for my assistant hasn't tempered at all. In fact, I'm now practically consumed with thoughts of her. I haven't touched her silky smooth skin even once since I woke up in that bed alone the next day with only my morning wood to keep me company. She's made it quite clear through her almost complete avoidance of me that our relationship is staying professional. Apparently, as far as she's concerned, what we did was a one-time thing, just like I wanted.

Then why am I so pissed off?

The problem is that when thoughts of Hollie invade my mind, it's not only the memory of us fucking like animals outside under the stars. Nope, there's also holding her hand at the wharf. Us laughing over lunch. Her opening the door in that dress that was created in heaven just for my angel. As inexplicable as it seems... I think I've caught feelings.

Unfortunately, those feelings seem to be one-sided. She's the epitome of the consummate professional at work. Even if I try to have a friendly conversation with her, she deftly moves the topic back to something work related. It hasn't been like this between us since she first started working here. She's right in front of me but, somehow, I still miss her.

I'll admit, my ego is a bit bruised. I know what we shared was something special. She may not have much experience, but I do. The electricity between us is something rare. I've experienced nothing like it before. Hands down, it was the best sex of my life. Yet somehow, she so easily pushes it aside like it never happened.

I hadn't wanted to be cruel to her, but I distanced myself from her after we fucked. I didn't want her to think there was more to it than two people mutually enjoying each other's bodies, so I went to my room alone, trying to think of anything but Hollie Simmons. It didn't work.

By the time I had shucked my clothes off and stepped into the shower, my cock was ready to go another round with her. Instead, I jerked off thinking about coming inside Hollie's tight cunt rather than my fist.

I laid in bed restlessly for a long while before finally drifting off to a troubled sleep. I don't know if it was because I was in Santa Cruz or if it was because I had been speaking about my parents to Hollie today, but the old familiar nightmare visited me once again, causing me to awaken in a cold sweat.

If you were to ask me during the day if I was responsible for the death of my parents, I would give a resounding no. I've had years to dwell on their passing and realize that in life, anything can happen. There's no way to know if there would have been a different outcome if I hadn't gotten suspended. It was the drunk driver's fault, not mine.

Ask me the same question again in the dark and I'd have a different answer. No matter how much I try to convince myself otherwise, my subconscious knows that it's my fault. I wouldn't have those dreams if it didn't.

After another thirty restless minutes in bed, I gave up on sleeping entirely. I was exhausted and didn't want to be alone. It had only been a matter of hours since I satiated my lust with her body back on that beach, and I already missed her. This girl had torn all my resolve and bachelor ways to shreds.

I barged into her room and pulled her into the bed with me. Of course, the minute I did, I was hard all over again. My dick was a hopeless cause when it comes to Hollie. I thought that fucking her would get her out of my system. Ha! I already wanted her more than I ever had. She huffed and puffed, playing annoyed in my arms, before drifting off to sleep. I laid there and watched her features relax into a peaceful slumber before my exhaustion took over and let the darkness slowly overtake me into a dreamless sleep. I hadn't slept that well in years.

Waking up the next morning came with a crushing sense of disappointment. I was alone. Hollie had already dressed, and according to her note, was downstairs having breakfast. I had to talk myself out of barging downstairs, throwing her over my shoulder, and bringing her back to bed so that I could ravish her properly in the light of day.

The rest of the trip home was filled with an odd formality between us. It wasn't awkward or cold exactly, but it was a far cry from how we had spent the day before together. There was no teasing, laughing, or touching and damn, did I miss it.

When Monday rolled around, I thought perhaps she regretted what we had done, but I never once saw a glimpse of regret or embarrassment cross her face when she looked at me. Instead, she seemed to move forward, leaving me in her dust. It was a past event that didn't factor into the future. And that makes me want to put my fist through a wall.

She's been treating me with a cool professionalism. I'm back to being Mr. Clarke, and at this point, I'd give every last cent of my fortune to hear her say my name. I decided I could wait her out. She would realize eventually that what we had together was too good to throw away on a one-night stand, but after a week of her cold shoulder, I'm not so sure anymore.

I've spent most of my days holed up in my office with Richard, going over every detail of our Santa Cruz proposal. After some strong-arming, I got the board to agree on a price increase. We also have everything in place for not only the charity donations but the local discount program that Hollie came up with.

I was feeling optimistic, even if I didn't know what Shaw had up his sleeve. I couldn't imagine what he could offer that would make Caroline DuPont sell her family property to him. But I still don't know why the man wants it in the first place. It's probable he just hates me that much.

"This is the last set." Richard leans across my desk and hands me the final stack of papers. We've spent the last hour going through the proposal one last time. Three official copies need to be sent out. The first needs to go to Caroline DuPont and needs to be there tomorrow by 3 p.m. in order to meet her deadline. The other two copies need to be signed and go to both my legal counsel and the director of the board.

I leaf through the pages, signing and initialing where the sticky notes Richard has placed indicate. With one last flourish, I set down the pen and lean back in my chair.

Placing each copy in its pre-addressed FedEx envelope, Richard comments, "Now we just need to get these out. I hate waiting until the last day to send paperwork, but I guess it can't be helped."

"All we can do is wait. I'm just happy it's finally almost over."

"Are you still worried about Patrick Shaw swooping in with a better offer at the last minute?"

Am I still worried about Patrick Shaw? Probably not as much as I should be. Between getting the last offer prepared and my obsession with Hollie, there hasn't been much time to think of anything else. "Not really. I think I would be more concerned if it was only about the money for Caroline DuPont. Even if he comes in at the last minute with a better offer, I honestly don't think she will sell to him. I can't imagine what he would build there that she would approve of."

Nodding, Richard places the set of envelopes on my desk. "Yeah, it's about time we beat Shaw out for once. I've been getting really tired of losing out to him lately."

"You're preaching to the choir here, buddy." I laugh and come around the desk, slapping him on the back and walking him to the door. As he leaves, I glimpse Hollie working at her desk, completely focused on the computer in front of her. I can't help the smile that creeps onto my face. Even though I can't stop thinking about getting her on her back, I'm genuinely happy for the first time in a long time. The Village is practically mine and I get to spend my days in the heat of Hollie's sunshine. I quickly duck back into my office before she can catch me mooning over her like some kind of teenage Romeo. Spying the envelopes ready to go on my desk, I snatch them up and hand them over to Hollie.

"Are these it?" she asks with a gleam of excitement in her eyes. "Are you guys finally done?"

Her excitement is contagious, and I can't help but grin back at her and nod. Jumping out of her seat, she wraps her arms around me in a spontaneous hug. My body goes rigid immediately, my mind going back to that night when my hands and mouth were all over her. My body relaxes against her when she seems to realize what she's doing and quickly jumps so far back from me, I'm a little afraid she's going to fall over her chair. "That's great, Archer." She blushes. "I'm really proud of you."

I can't stop my chest puffing out like a peacock. She's proud of me. I'm not sure why, but her being proud of me feels important. I never want to let her down. I want her to be proud of me every moment of every day. I clear my throat of the sudden emotions I can't quite place that are welling up inside me. "Thanks. They need to go out in the next few hours. Priority overnight. They have to arrive by three tomorrow afternoon."

"No problem. I'll take them down to the mailroom on my way to lunch."

I nod and retreat to my office, trying to get my mind back on anything else that needs to get done today. About five minutes go by when my office door slowly opens and in walks the woman of my dirty dreams. She looks nervous as she walks up to my desk. Her cheeks are already stained with a slight smattering of pink that usually only shows up when she's embarrassed or I've been teasing her.

"So, I got you something. It's just a little thing. I was going to wait until Mrs. DuPont agreed to sell the property to you, but I guess this can be a kind of good luck present instead of a congratulation present. Not that you need the luck. I mean, you're Archer Clarke after all. But just in case, and anyway, I wanted you to have this." She's speaking so quickly that I almost can't follow her rushed words. My attention is drawn downward, and I see she's sticking out her hand, shoving a small, flat box towards me.

"You got me a present?" I'm a little off kilter from her rambling and the fact that this girl bought me, Archer Clarke, billionaire trust-fund kid, a present.

"Yes, Mr. Clarke."

"Archer," I growl at her before gingerly taking the box from her outstretched hand, purposefully brushing my fingers against hers. I've had just about enough of this Mr. Clarke bullshit.

She snatches her hand back to her side quickly and gives me a soft smile. The small white box is about six inches long and three inches across. A red ribbon wraps around the package and is tied into a neat bow. I slide the ribbon off and remove the lid. My brow furrows at what I find inside. A key.

It's definitely an older key that looks dirty and worn. It's attached to a long, diamond-shaped key chain the color of the Caribbean Sea. Then I notice the white writing stamped on the front of the key chain.

The Village at Santa Cruz
Santa Cruz, CA
Cabin 4

Holy shit! This is a key to the bungalows? I swallow down the lump of emotion in my throat. "Where did you find this?" I don't even recognize my own voice. It's deep and scratchy, sounding like I just smoked an entire pack of cigarettes in one sitting.

She still looks nervous, but the smile remains on her face. "If I told you, I'd have to kill you. I thought this was a little piece of Santa Cruz and your vacations there that you could bring home with you. Especially if Caroline DuPont was crazy enough not to sell to you. I hope you like it?"

I'm blown away. She got me a present. I can't even remember the last time anyone bought me any present, let alone something that was so personal and so utterly, *me*. My heart is pounding so hard in my chest I'll be shocked if she can't hear it too. I can almost hear the last of my walls crumbling to the ground. I think I'm falling in love with this girl.

The revelation should scare the shit out of me, but instead, does just the opposite. I'm energized, excited even. I've never been in love before, so I don't know if what I'm feeling is normal, but it feels right.

Thinking back on this week, I can't believe I let her pull away from me for so long. We should have been together this week, not playing this stupid game of chicken with each other, each hoping the other would cave first. And I know she's been waiting too. There is no way she would have gone out and gotten something like this for me if she didn't have feelings for me, right?

Before I even realize I'm doing it, I'm around the desk, pulling her into my arms and crashing my mouth down on top of her own. I put every thought and feeling I've held back from her over this past week into this kiss. It's not hurried, but it's still filled with passion and longing. I want to show her how much I've missed her. How much she means to me.

Hollie's molded to the front of my body, kissing me back with just as much intensity. Our tongues dance back and forth, teasing and stroking. I slide my hands down around her delectable ass and squeeze it hard. She gasps into my mouth and pushes back against my hand, seeking out more of my rough treatment.

I've always been more aggressive and rough in bed, but she pulls something out of me that longs to possess and dominate her. I want to make her prove that she's mine. That she can't help but react to my touch.

I walk her backwards, deeper into my office, guiding her towards the couch I keep for more casual meetings. Before I direct her to sit, I shuck up the hem of her skirt around her hips so that I can see her soft-pink panties. I moan at the wet spot clearly visible in the middle of them. This girl is always ready for me.

I roughly yank them down around her ankles. She's kicking them off as I push her down onto the couch, stretching her out. I place one of her legs up along the back of the couch and the other firmly on the floor. She's spread wide open for me, her chest rising and falling with little pants. Her eyes are on me and look glassy with desire.

"Where have you been?" I ask her, trying not to let the hurt shine through my voice. I can't even pinpoint why I'm hurt exactly.

"Right here, Archer." It's not really an answer, but I let it go. We both have our reasons to be wary of relationships. Jesus, is that what this is? A relationship? Before I can think too much about what exactly is happening between the two of us, I move my mouth to the swollen bundle of nerves between her legs. I lathe it with my flattened tongue and hear her let out a gasp followed by a satisfied moan.

I smile against her pussy then whisper, "shhhhhh!" My breath against her most intimate spot causes her to jump into the air. "You don't want everyone in the office to know that the boss is starving for your pussy, do you?"

A shudder runs through her body and I'm smiling again. I'm not sure I've ever smiled as much during sex as I do with her. It's an interesting side perk.

I turn my attention back to her pretty pussy and run my tongue along her crease, picking up any of her juices that have gathered there. She grabs my hair and pulls my face more firmly against her. My girl is feeling needy today. Who am I to deny her?

I attack her delicious folds, licking and sucking, teasing and biting. Her pussy is exquisite. I'm eating like a man that's been starved and she's my first meal in days. She tastes even better than I remember. Is it possible she's gotten sweeter in just a week?

Her thighs are now wrapped around my head, squeezing tightly. My gaze moves up her body and I can see her chest heaving, nipples clearly outlined in her shirt. Her eyes are closed, and her head is thrown back in ecstasy. She's letting out little whimpers but seems to do a good job of controlling her volume.

Without warning, I wrap my lips around her clit and I suck it into my mouth, steadily increasing the pressure while she writhes around me. I move my index finger to her opening and slowly slide it inside her. She's still so fucking tight. I think about how her tight pussy felt squeezing my cock and I nearly come in my pants.

Her eyes are wild and even though she's now looking into my eyes, I'm not sure she's actually seeing me. I continue to bat her clit back and forth with my tongue while slowly finger fucking her. "Come for me, Hollie." She whimpers and pushes her cunt against my mouth. "Come all over my face, Hollie. Right now. Come."

As if on command, her entire body shudders and seizes up. Her thighs clamp down on the sides of my head and hold my face against her. I don't stop my oral ministrations and continue to eat her through the orgasm raging through her body. When she finally comes down, her thighs relax, letting me free.

"Good girl," I tell her while undoing my belt and shoving my pants and boxers down my thighs, freeing my engorged cock, not bothering to remove them all the way. I need to be inside her tight cunt right now. I'm going to fuck my way under her skin so that there's no way she'll ever be able to ignore me for an entire week again.

I crawl up her body and latch onto her lips again, allowing her to taste how sweet she is. She needs to realize that she's mine. It seems she likes the taste of herself on my tongue because she's fiercely kissing me back while her nails dig into my back. If I didn't have my shirt on, she would be drawing blood. Perhaps some other time.

I put my hand back to her pussy, making sure that she's still wet enough for me, before wrenching my lips from hers. "Are you ready for me, angel?"

"Yes, please!"

"I told you to be quiet, angel." I reach down and grab her discarded panties off the floor. "Open," I command.

She looks at me with hesitant eyes before popping her mouth open for me. "Good girl." I gently put the panties into her mouth so that they'll muffle her cries. "Now you can scream all you want, got it?" Her eyes turn darker and her pupils are blown out as she nods enthusiastically. Damn, I'm pretty sure she was always supposed to be mine.

I don't wait a second longer before lining myself up at her entrance and thrusting my hips forward, sheathing myself in her tight, wet heat.

Hollie lets out a scream as I force my way inside her unforgivingly and I'm glad I gagged her with her panties. That would have definitely brought some attention to our impromptu liaison.

I angle my hips so that each time I'm thrusting into her, my shaft runs along her clit, giving her the friction she needs to get off. Nothing has ever felt better than her pussy clamped tightly around me. It's then that I realize I forgot a condom. Fuck. I don't even slow down my fuck stroke. In fact, the thought of taking Hollie bare makes me speed up, sending me further into my lust-filled haze. We can do this once. The odds are in our favor. There's no way I can stop now.

Hollie is underneath me, moving her hips up to meet my every thrust, panties still firmly in her mouth and it seems she's taken my permission to make as much noise as she wants to heart. The only thing I can hear is our skin slapping against each other and a high keening sound that's coming out of her.

"I'm close, angel. You better come with me."

She nods her head emphatically at me since she can't speak and moves her hands to my ass, pulling me hard, trying to force me deeper inside of her.

Her nails digging into my ass is enough to make that tingle appear at the bottom of my spine and my balls to draw up, ready to fire into her. I know I should pull out, but fuck. I just don't want to. I slam into her harder. I'm about to come and I *need* her to come with me. I move my hand between us and find her bundle of nerves, giving it a hard pinch.

That's apparently all she needed. A muffled scream escapes her and her entire body spasms, her pussy squeezing my cock so tight I see stars. I push forward as far as I can inside her before my own orgasm overtakes me and my cum is shooting inside her in strong spurts, coating her insides.

I quickly reach up and pull the panties out of her mouth so that she can easily catch her breath before sitting up and pulling her still shaking body into my arms.

I made a mistake the last time we had sex. Treating her like one of my one-night stands and removing myself from her as quickly as possible was the wrong way to handle things. I should have immediately let her know she was mine. Claimed her. I wouldn't be making that mistake again.

SEVENTEEN

HOLLIE

I guess he liked my gift.

I'm completely wrung out as Archer cuddles me against his chest on the couch that probably costs as much as six months of my mother's rent. His arms have me pulled in close while he looks down at me with an inscrutable expression on his face.

His head bends down as he places a gentle kiss on the top of my head while his hand runs up and down my back in a soothing motion that sends little chills down my spine. This isn't an Archer I've seen before. He's being tender and almost reverent with me. I'm used to cocky, sexy Archer.

I'm a little thrown as his lips move down to my neck, nipping at the sensitive spot underneath my earlobe before coming back to my mouth and claiming it once again. He's kissing me so sweetly that I almost tear up before tucking my head back underneath his chin.

"Are you alright, angel? I wasn't too rough, was I?"

I shake my head against his chest. "No, I liked it." I realize that it's true. Yeah, Archer's been rough with me, but it was something that my body has craved since the very first time he touched me. Being with him has awakened something inside me I never would have known was there.

I was a little shocked when he shoved my panties into my mouth, but more than that, I was incredibly turned on. When he was taking charge, I found his power and strength almost intoxicating. I couldn't get enough of him.

"Have dinner with me," he says, his lips buried in my hair. My head jerks back in shock. This is the exact opposite of last weekend. He had pulled away as soon as we had had sex and I had kind of expected to be sent back to my desk to work. Instead, he's asking me out to dinner? Ok, so *asking* is a bit of a stretch.

"Dinner?"

Placing a finger under my chin, he turns my face up so that he's staring directly into my eyes. He's so close to me I think I could taste him if only I reached out my tongue. "Yes, dinner. I'll pick you up at seven."

"What if I already have plans? This is a little last minute," I tease. His face darkens and his forehead scrunches up like he's deep in thought. If I didn't know better, I would think he was jealous.

"Cancel them," he says in that gruff tone when he's telling me what to do before sending my body into a state of pure bliss. Before I can argue with his highhanded attitude, he leans forward and, with his lips against my ear, whispers, "Plus, I can fuck you in an actual bed after."

I don't even think twice before giving him my answer. "Yes."

"Yes?" he asks, obviously a bit thrown that I'm agreeing so easily. Frankly, I am too. I shouldn't trust him. I know his type because I've seen men like him all my life with my mom. But something seems different about him. Like maybe he values me and even likes me a little. At that moment I realize I have feelings for Archer. I'm not exactly sure what they are, but I care for him more deeply than an employee should for her asshole boss.

For once in my life, I decide to just go with it. I'm young. I want to go out and have fun with the amazingly sexy man who's doing things to my body I never thought possible. Where's the harm in that?

I lift myself off his lap, straightening my skirt and looking around for my wayward pair of panties. I spot them half poking out from underneath the expensive couch. As I'm reaching for them, Archer swoops in front of me and scoops them off the floor, shoving them into his suit pocket.

"I'll be keeping these as collateral. Just in case you try to change your mind." He's got that mischievous little boy smile on his face that makes my insides melt, but I can't help but tease him a little either.

"They're just a pair of panties, Archer. They aren't that valuable."

"They are to me."

He says this with such an earnest expression that I'm both taken aback and slightly uncomfortable. What am I supposed to say to something like that? Is he running some kind of game on me? Maybe he has a bet that he can turn me into the prom queen. Whatever is going on, I hope I make it through the other side with my heart still intact. Something tells me it may already be too late.

Quickly slipping out the door, I leave Archer to straighten himself up, and unexpectedly crash into the soft male chest of Gilbert Clarke.

"I'm so sorry, Mr. Clarke, I didn't see you standing there." Come to think of it, he was standing a little too close to Archer's office door. I hope he didn't hear what was happening inside the office. I can feel my cheeks go rosy as I think about what he might have heard from the other side of the door.

"Not a problem, my dear. We all get distracted at times. Tell me, how are you liking it here at Clarke Hotels? Is my nephew treating you well?"

This is strange. I'm nobody to Gilbert Clarke. The man has taken zero interest in me, either personally or professionally, since I started here. He barely even looks at me. Until now, I've garnered as much attention from him as that of a potted plant. Why is he interested in my well-being suddenly?

"Everything has been great. Mr. Clarke keeps me busy, but I enjoy the work." I try to move around him to my desk so that I can get back to work, but o he's blocking my path and doesn't seem inclined to get out of the way. "Is there anything I can help you with this afternoon?" I ask, trying not to show my impatience.

"I wanted to check in and see how things were going. Remember, if you ever need any help with young Archer there. Don't be afraid to come to me. I'm sure I could help." He's giving me a tight-lipped smile that's half creepy perv, half sneer. That he thinks I would come to him for anything, let alone an issue with his nephew, is laughable. I've heard the gossip, Gilbert Clarke is kept on here as a relic of days passed. He doesn't do much of anything except gossip with the board and dine out on the company dime. I'm a bit surprised he's even here, considering it's the middle of the day and there's no board meeting. He never comes to the office unless he has to.

"I'll keep that in mind. Thank you, sir." I give him a smile, hoping that will be the end of this unsettling conversation. There's a disconcerting glint in his eyes. I think he knows that there is something going on between Archer and me.

"You do that." He bends down and lifts his briefcase from where it was leaning against my desk before heading down the hallway to the elevator. Now that I've dealt with that entirely odd interaction, I can get back to my actual work.

I grab the stack of FedEx envelopes from my outbox and head to the mailroom in the basement. I want to get these proposals out as soon as possible. After triple checking with the clerk at least three times that they would make it to their destinations by the deadline the next day, I head back to my desk to catch up on work. As

I'm answering and forwarding emails, everything finally catches up with me.

I have a date with Archer Clarke.

I want to give a little squeal of joy but contain myself like the adult woman I am. Rummaging through the bottom of my purse, I pull out my phone. I never told the girls about my rendezvous with Archer last weekend. It's not that I was trying to hide it from them exactly, I just didn't know what it meant, or if it even meant anything at all. They would have so many questions, ones I wouldn't have answers to. How could I explain something like that to them when I couldn't even explain it to myself?

However, now was not the time for discretion. I was going to need my girls tonight.

Me: You guys going to be home tonight? I need you!

Violet: What's going on? You ok?

Me: I have a date and I need help getting ready.

B: Who???

Me: ...Archer...

B: Bahahahaha I knew it! <eggplant emoji> <squirt emoji>

Me: Ewww! It's just dinner.

B: Have you seen him? There's no way it's ewww!

Me: Are you gonna help me or not?

Violet: Of course. I'll be there by the time you get home.

B: I'm already going through your closet!

Me: I'm not wearing anything crazy B!
B: Me? I'm insulted!
Violet: Don't worry, we've got your back.
Me: Thank you both! See you at home.

There will be a million questions once I get home, but it doesn't matter. I'm going to need their moral support tonight. I may not understand exactly what's going on between Archer and I but I know I want to make sure he can't take his eyes off me.

A few hours later, Bianca is putting the finishing touches on my makeup and I decide it's a good thing I asked them for help. I would have been lost. What does one wear on a date with a billionaire? Normally, I would wear jeans and a nice top for a date, but Bianca has assured me that's not good enough for tonight. Instead, I'm sporting a little black dress out of her closet. With a split neckline and a fit and flare skirt, it teeters the line of sweet and sexy. It falls a little shorter than mid-thigh on me, so I have to stop myself from continually trying to tug it down. Bianca is taller than I am, so I'm not sure how she gets away with walking around in this thing.

Violet is combing out the curls in my hair so that they fall in soft waves over my shoulders. With all the attention focused on me, it's more like I'm getting ready to go to a school formal than a date. The swatch of red across my lips is normally much bolder than I would wear, but Bianca convinced me to step out of my comfort zone. Even I have to admit, it brings out the color of my eyes and adds a glow to my pale skin. I look good if I do say so myself.

I was right about having to answer a million questions. Between my two besties, it was like I was in the middle of the Spanish Inquisition. I'm pretty sure Bianca was going to have a heart attack when I told her about sleeping with him last weekend. She's already been planning the bridesmaid dress she's going to wear at my wedding but I put the kibosh on that real fast. The fact that I was going out with Archer at all was a minor miracle. I may have admitted to myself that I have feelings for him but could he ever feel the same way about me? To let myself think he wants anything long term would be a mistake and setting myself up for disappointment. I've decided to enjoy tonight's dinner for what it is and try not to worry about anything beyond that.

As I'm slipping my ID and lipstick into my clutch, there's a sharp knock at the door. A thrill runs through my body, leaving me slightly breathless. I've forbidden my roomies from entering the living room while he's here. The last thing I need is them gawking at him.

I take a calming breath and open the door. His frame almost fills the doorway, blocking out the last remaining rays of sunlight. He's changed from the suit he was wearing at the office into a pair of dark denim jeans and a black button-down shirt with a blazer on top. The ends of his hair are still damp, indicating that he just got out of the shower. He looks good enough to eat and I plan on doing just that right after dinner.

"You look beautiful," he says. The weight of those golden-brown eyes on me is heavy as they roam over my body almost like a physical touch and I feel my cheeks heat. This man seems to have me constantly blushing. If this keeps up, I'm going to have to invest in a redness reducing foundation.

"You don't look so bad yourself." I smile up at him playfully. "I don't know where we're going, so I hope this dress is okay. Do you think I should change?"

"You're perfect. I was planning to go back to my place and cook, actually. If that's alright with you?"

He sounds a little hesitant, like he's worried that I'll balk at going to his house. Little does he know, I'm extremely relieved. I don't have to worry about dropping food in my lap in front of an entire restaurant, just him. Sure, I enjoy going to nice places once in a while, but all I care about is spending time with Archer, alone tonight. Now that I've admitted to myself that I care about him, I want to learn more about him. Spending the evening with only the two of us sounds like a good way to do that.

"Of course, that sounds great." I smile at him reassuringly. I can physically see the tension that was in his shoulders melt away.

"Wait, you cook more than just eggs?" I ask incredulously.

"Why Hollie, are you trying to say that you don't think that I have the skill set? I'm truly hurt." He places his hand over his heart like I've wounded him.

I laugh and bump into him with my hip on the way out the door. "I'll believe it when I see it, mister."

EIGHTEEN

ARCHER

The drive back to my house is filled with pleasant, light chatter between the two of us. Even though we're talking about nothing of consequence, I'm absolutely floored. She's barely spoken to me in a week if it wasn't about work. Now I have her in my car, headed to my home, and she seems... at ease. If I never see cold, professional Hollie again, it will be too soon.

Once in the kitchen, I pull out ingredients for Spaghetti Bolognese, garlic bread, and a garden salad. Sure, it's simple, but I've made this for myself enough times that I won't burn the water at least. I could have taken Hollie anywhere, to the most expensive restaurant in the city, private restaurants she would only ever experience because she was there with me. I was about to reserve a private dining room at Aerlume but changed my mind at the last minute.

I wanted Hollie to realize there was more to me than money. She's never given any indication she was overly interested in my wealth, but over time, it's like money has almost become a personality trait for me as far as women are concerned. Now, that's not to say it's entirely their fault. I didn't let any of them close enough to me to know much else. I took them out, wined and dined them, and showed them the good time my money could afford them. It was important Hollie not see me the same way those women did. I wanted more from her. I wanted all of her.

Hollie sets down her purse on the counter and hops up onto the same barstool she sat on the morning after the night she spent here weeks ago. It looks like she's found her place in my kitchen and she fits perfectly.

"You can throw something on the television in the living room while I get this together. It shouldn't take too long." I pull a bottle of rich Merlot from the wine rack, pop the cork, and pour us each a glass, placing hers on the counter in front of her.

"Why would I want to do that?" She sips her wine and shoots me a smile. "Can I help with anything? Put me to work."

"You sure? It's your night off," I tease her. "How about you put together the salad for us?"

She hops off the stool and makes her way across the kitchen to where I'm standing at the counter, chopping up some peppers for the sauce. I can't help but look at her legs encased in those knee-high boots. For a second, the only thing I can see is her laying in my bed, her boot clad legs wrapped around my waist as I'm thrusting mercilessly into her.

Now that I'm ready to chuck dinner into the trash and bend her over the kitchen island, I push the vegetables for the salad over to her and hand over a cutting board and knife. She gets to work on chopping the heads of romaine, taking her time with each precise cut, while I mentally try to school the hard length growing in my pants. There will be plenty of time for that later. Now I need to show her I'm—what? Boyfriend material?

"I know I've said this before, but I'm honestly surprised you don't have a chef," she tosses at me playfully, elbowing me in the side. I elbow her right back. Two can play this game.

"Nah," I put the water on the stove to boil for the fresh pasta I have in the fridge. "My mom always cooked here. I don't think I need one either. I've learned to make enough things to survive. Plus, takeout is only an app swipe away."

"True, you seem to have a fondness for takeout. So what? You make this for all the dates you bring over here?" Her voice is hesitant, and I detect a hint of jealousy that makes the corners of my mouth tick up in a smile I try to hide.

Setting my knife aside for a moment, I turn to face her. I'm going to take care of this right now. I can't move forward the way I want to with Hollie unless I make it clear to her that this isn't a fling for me. Any time I've slept with a woman in the past, I've never brought them to my place. I own a luxury hotel chain. I could walk into any of my hotels and get the best suite in the place. Why would I invite them into my private sanctuary? Hollie isn't like them. She isn't some random woman I'm sleeping with. I want to share things about myself with her, and that includes my home.

I patiently wait in silence for her to look up at me. Once her eyes meet mine, I grab her chin, holding her gaze with my own. "Let me be clear, angel. I've never brought a woman back to my home before. I've never just hung out with one before. And I've certainly never cooked for a woman. Do you understand what I'm saying?"

Her eyes widen in surprise. Whatever she thought I was going to say, it definitely wasn't that. Her gaze darts back and forth from one of my eyes to the other, like she's trying to get a read on me. There's no need. I'm laying it all out there for her. She finally seems satisfied and gives me a solid nod before turning back to the salad.

We work side by side in companionable silence until she circles back to our earlier conversation.

"You said your mom cooked here. This was your parents' home? You grew up here?"

"Yup, I inherited it when they died. It's a nice house and you can't beat the location, so I never had a reason to sell it."

"I have to admit, it surprised me the first time I was here. I totally expected you to have a steel and glass bachelor pad, like a penthouse apartment or something."

I chuckle at that, because the thought had crossed my mind. And honestly, if I hadn't had access to hotel suites on demand, I might have moved downtown into one of those so-called *bachelor pads*. "It's a great house, and I have a lot of wonderful memories here. Plus, I'd like to raise my family here one day too."

Where the fuck did that come from? I've never truly considered having a family before. Of course, I've thought about it in the most abstract sense, with it being the normal thing that people do, but I've certainly never planned it. As I'm questioning myself, I realize I really do want to have a family in this house. I love this place. It was filled with so much love when I was growing up and now that I've had the thought, I can't imagine having kids anywhere else.

I glance at Hollie, who is tossing the salad together in the wooden bowl I pulled down from a high shelf for her. She's beautiful standing here in my kitchen, helping me make dinner. I can practically see her standing in the same spot, cooking dinner, her belly gently swollen with our child.

Holy shit, get yourself together, man! It's way too early to be thinking anything like that. Hollie is only twenty-two. If she knew the kinds of thoughts that were floating around in my head, she would run for the hills.

"That's actually really lovely," she says. The only response I can give to that is a half-hearted grunt. My emotions are tied into a knot. I need to put thoughts of pregnant Hollie out of my head and focus on the here and now.

When the food is finished, we gather up the plates and I guide her outside to the patio. What's the use of having a house on Lake Washington if you can't eat and enjoy the view? I pull out her chair and she sits before I scoot it back in and take my seat opposite her.

"I can't believe that you get to eat like this every day. Now I'm jealous, Archer. If I had a view like this, I would eat outside for every meal. Morning coffee? Right here.

Late-night snack? Again here. You wouldn't be able to drag me away."

"I have to admit, I don't sit out here nearly enough. I'm usually too busy running from one thing to another." She gives me a little frown as she takes a bite of her salad. I think she actually feels bad for me. "Tell you what, you can come sit out here anytime you want. In fact, you can go swimming in the lake if you want or check out the hot tub on the side of the house." I'm sure I sound too eager to get her back over here, but I'm beyond caring at this point.

She lets out one of her giggles that does strange things to my chest and says, "We'll see."

She's smiling at me, eating the meal I made for her and I feel... content. "Hold on one second. I forgot something." Before she can question me, I race off to the kitchen and return shortly thereafter with a bottle of dressing just for her. I present it with a flourish and set it down on the table in front of her. "Some Green Goddess for the Goddess?"

"A little cheesy there, Archer." She laughs good-naturedly. Examining the bottle, she looks up at me questioningly. "How did you know this is my favorite dressing?"

I merely shrug my shoulders at her to show it's not a big deal. "We've been having lunch together for weeks. I notice what you order, especially if it's obnoxiously green. Plus, you like my brand of cheese." I shoot her a wink.

"I guess so," she mumbles under her breath while shaking her head. It's like she can't believe I would remember anything about her. She better get used to it, because I'm about to learn everything there is to know about Hollie Simmons.

The patio and backyard are spacious with a lawn stretching out almost all the way to the water and a dock with a few personal watercrafts tied up. I don't bother keeping a huge boat here like some of my neighbors because I don't have enough time to go out on the water. Perhaps I should take Hollie, though. I bet she would enjoy it. I can see her standing on the bough, the wind whipping through her flaxen locks, perhaps leaning against the railing in a swimsuit that shows off her incredible body. Then I could take her down to our cabin and make love to her until she's hoarse from screaming my name.

Shaking those thoughts from my head so that I can pay attention to the here and now, I take a sip of my wine, enjoying how it slides down my throat, warming my stomach and calming my nerves. I've faced off with some of the most ruthless men in the business, had my own uncle removed as CEO of my company, but none of that has come even close to the anxiety this twenty-two-year-old girl has brought up for me.

I need for her to want me. I've decided she's necessary for my existence. Having her in my home tonight has only highlighted that fact. I'm pretty sure this is where she belongs. With me. She can redecorate the whole damn place for all I care. She just needs to stay.

Hollie is looking down at the water and the boats lazily passing by. "I would have killed to have grown up somewhere like this," she says with a smile. It hurts to think she had to struggle growing up.

No child, especially not someone as sweet as Hollie, should have to endure the childhood she did. Even after my parents died and I was shipped off to Uncle Gilbert for a few years, I may not have had much love, but I was always safe and taken care of.

Settling my large hand over her much smaller one, I ask, "What was your childhood like?"

She's quiet, lost in thought. I hope I haven't brought up anything too painful, but I need to know this about her. I need to know everything so I can take care of her from now on.

Who would have thought? Archer Clarke, caregiver. This girl brings weird shit out of me.

"It was nothing like this, I can tell you that. I won't bore you with the details."

"You're not boring me, Hollie. I asked because I want to know. I want to know everything about you. That includes your childhood." Her cheeks heat with embarrassment. I am pretty sure this isn't something that she shares with many people. That makes any tidbit she'll give me that much more special.

She squirms a bit in her chair, uncomfortable, but continues forward. "It was just my mom and me for a long time. I never even met my father until I was older. Even then, we've only had a few conversations. I honestly don't want to have anything to do with him. We've lived in Milford basically my entire life and my mom never got over getting left by a rich man when she was certain that he was her meal ticket and instead she was saddled with a baby. She was always kind of bitter after that and turned to drinking. When my half-sister, Paige, came along, things only got worse. She didn't even know who

Paige's father was. She started spending less and less time at home and more time with her loser boyfriends. One of them got her hooked on heroin and that was that. I basically had to hold together our family. I worked whatever jobs I could to get money and take care of my sister.

"Paige is a junior in high school, so she's still there with my mom. I felt horrible leaving because I know they need me, but there were no opportunities there. No college and certainly no jobs that would pay me enough to send money back to them."

I'm a little stunned at what she's revealed. I already knew she didn't have the best childhood, but this is much worse than I thought. "What about your sister? Should she be there with your mom if she's always high and has sketchy guys coming over?"

Hollie lets out a deep sigh as if this very thing has been on her mind for a long, long time. Knowing her, it has.

"As soon as Mr. Moreno let us move into his property without paying rent, I tried to get Paige to come live with me. But she was a sophomore in high school and didn't want to leave her friends. Plus, I know she would feel guilty about leaving our mother even if she would never say that to me. I bring it up to her every once in a while, but it's a no go."

Dante Moreno has been footing the bill for her rent? I'll have to find some way to thank him for taking care of my girl. Normally, I would be a jealous motherfucker at the thought of another man laying eyes on Hollie, let alone taking care of her in any way. However, since it's before I knew she existed and she needed someone watching out for her, I'll let it go. That, plus the fact that I know he's been hung up on some woman for years, lets me not dwell on it.

"Hollie, I could help by sending—"

"Oh, no you don't," she interrupts, putting her hand up to stop me from continuing. "You gave me a job. You've done quite enough. The money you pay me helps immensely. I would never be able to give them the money I've been able to send if it weren't for you. That's all the help I need." I see tears gather in the corner of her eyes as she continues, "I could actually send enough money to my little sister last week so that she could buy a dress and shoes for her school dance. She's going to Homecoming because of you. Thank you."

A tear slips from her eye and runs down her cheek. I reach across the table and capture it with my thumb. Before I can stop myself, I grasp her wrist, tugging her over to me and settling her in my lap.

"No Hollie, that's all you. You take care of your mom and sister. I didn't do anything except hire an amazing assistant. It's your heart that's pure and takes care of everyone you know."

The first order of business tomorrow is getting my angel a raise. It's not like she doesn't deserve it. She's hands down the best assistant I've ever had. Plus, she obviously needs the money to take care of her family. She won't let me do anything to help directly, but she can't stop me from doing this. I'm not even going to tell her. It will be a nice surprise on her next paycheck.

Her warm body leans into me easily, molding up against my solid chest. She nuzzles my neck, shooting bolts of lightning through my body. I duck down to capture her lips with my own. She opens for me immediately, letting me explore her mouth. The kiss is softer than our previous ones, almost as if it's full of emotions neither of us wants to say out loud yet. At least I hope she has emotions for me. Her plump ass is rubbing against my lengthening cock and I'm ready for dinner to be over. Now.

I put my hands under her ass and stand, scooping her up with me. Her legs immediately wrap around my waist and she lets out a little gasp of surprise.

"Where are we going?"

"Dessert."

I push inside the French doors, not caring that I've left the remnants of our dinner out on the patio, and make my way swiftly up the stairs to my bedroom, my mouth never leaving hers. I don't bother turning on the lights. There's enough of the moon shining in my windows to highlight the bed, almost as if there's a spotlight on it. Good, I don't want to miss a moment of this.

Hollie releases her legs from their hold around my waist, and I let her slide down my body. She doesn't stop once her feet hit the floor, but continues on until she's kneeling before me, her face mere inches from the large bulge in my pants.

"What are you doing?" I ask, desire making my voice thick.

Loosening my belt, she looks up at me through her eyelashes, lips red and swollen from our earlier kisses. "I want my dessert."

A growl escapes from my mouth and I reach down to help her, impatient to have that perfect pout of hers wrapped around my cock. Once I've kicked off my pants and boxers, her hands wrap around my shaft firmly. My head falls back from the pleasure radiating from my cock through the rest of my body. I don't know how I'm going to get inside her without coming when I can barely remain standing with just her hand on me.

She leans forward, her tongue licking around the tip of my cock, collecting the drop of pre-cum that's escaped the slit. She swallows it down and brings her eyes back up to mine. Her entire body is flushed and there is a look of pure lust on her face.

"Dress," I bark out at her. She raises her hands in the air and I reach down, pulling it over her head and toss it into the corner of the room. She's kneeling before me in only her knee-high boots and a black lace bra and panty set. I almost come all over myself right then, instead I finish unbuttoning my shirt and slip it off my shoulders. I can see Hollie eyeing my chest appreciatively before lowering her mouth back to my cock once again. This time she takes the head in her mouth and gives it a gentle sucking. I groan and attempt to still my hips from thrusting into her. I want to let her take her time exploring me. For now.

Instead, I tangle my fingers in her hair, murmuring words of encouragement. She moves her mouth slowly down my shaft, pulling back after a moment, then taking more of me into her throat. Her tongue runs along the underside of my cock, sending me into a frenzy every time it hits that sensitive spot under my head. Her mouth and hand continue to run along my turgid shaft until I'm about to explode. I use my hand still buried in her hair and pull her off me, her mouth making a popping sound that releases a groan from deep within my chest.

"You have to stop, angel, or I'll come down your throat and it will be over before we make it to the bed."

This girl actually purses her lips and pouts at me. "What if I want you to come in my mouth?" She crosses her arms over her lace clad breasts, in defiance.

Her sassy mouth is my undoing. I pull her up to her feet and push her until she hits the bed frame and falls backward, sprawling across the mattress. I grab each of her legs, removing those sexy as fuck boots. Another time we'll leave them on. Tonight I want to feel her. Skin to skin. Nothing in between us. After the boots, I have her bra and panties off in short order.

Standing back, I take in the whole of her body, spread out on my bed and my mouth goes dry. The moonlight is streaming in from the window and highlights the gold in her hair. Her entire body is flushed and glowing like a goddess. I honestly can't believe she's here. I'm a lucky bastard to have an angel like her take a chance on an asshole like me. She may not have officially agreed to give me a chance yet, but she will. I'll make sure of it.

I fall to my knees in front of the bed and between her legs. I can smell how aroused she is from here. Her pussy is pink, swollen, and glistening with moisture, just waiting for me to take a taste.

I run my tongue from the bottom of her slit to the very top, collecting the juices that have gathered there. If it's possible, her taste on my tongue has made my dick even harder. I wrap my hand around my cock to keep it from going off and stopping things before they've even started and go back to enjoying her pussy. As my tongue dips into her tight hole, I hear her mewl above me as she lifts her hips, trying to get more of the pleasure my tongue offers.

"Patience, baby," I scold her. "You'll have me inside you soon enough." She makes a little sound of protest and wiggles her hips at me. I move my tongue up to her clit, laving it leisurely. Batting it slowly back and forth before sucking it into my mouth. Her hips are thrusting up into my face and she's making noises like an angry kitten.

"Please, please, please, please," escapes her lips in a whisper. I decide to take mercy on her this time and gently place her clit between my teeth while continuing to rub it with my tongue. That seems to be all she needed. She screams out my name, which almost has me coming all over the sheets, as she convulses against my face. Her fingers are digging into my hair with such force I'm a little worried she'll pull it out by the handful. She rides through the last few waves of her orgasm as I collect as much of her sweet juices into my mouth as possible.

I need to show her she belongs to me so I'm not wearing a fucking condom. I need to be inside of her with nothing between us, claiming her. This afternoon was an accident, but it won't be tonight. If she insists on using one, then that's her choice. But if I'm right, she wants this as much as I do.

I move to position Hollie in the very center of the bed while she catches her breath. I stretch and settle on top of her before claiming her lips once again, feeding all the passion inside me into the kiss, wanting her to know how she makes me feel.

"I'm not using a condom, angel. I'm clean, I promise, but I need to paint your pussy in my cum." My mouth is on her neck as I breathe in her scent before nipping at her pulse, praying she won't tell me no.

"I'm clean, too, and I'm on the pill." There's a disappointment that runs through me that I don't have time to examine. Kids aren't in my immediate plans, but if I was going to have them with anyone, it would be with Hollie.

I push her legs wider apart, settling between them, letting my cock slide back and forth through her crease. She lets out a whimper when my cock hits her engorged clit, still sensitive from her latest orgasm.

Her nails dig into my shoulders as she gazes at me pleadingly. "More, Archer. I need more."

"Tell me what you need," I say while continuing to tease her with my cock, the head grazing across her hole, never quite putting it where she needs it.

She's panting now, arching up into me, leaving scratches along my shoulder and back, giving me pain that's grounding me in this moment with her. "I need you inside me. I need you to fuck me."

That's it, I'm done for. Holding back any longer isn't an option. I notch the head of my cock into her entrance and pause for a moment before I push into her slowly. She's still incredibly tight, and it feels like my cock is being strangled. My forehead breaks out in sweat as I work my cock back and forth, slowly sinking deeper inside of her, inch by agonizingly sweet inch.

Hollie's heels are digging into my ass, urging me on, and it's all I can do to stop myself from slamming into her, taking her like a wild animal. There'll be plenty of time for that later.

When I'm finally seated all the way inside her, I let out a groan and lower my forehead until it rests against hers. "You're fucking perfect, baby."

"If I didn't know better, I'd think you might like me a little." She grins before pulling me against her lips again.

Like her a little? That might be the understatement of the century.

I begin moving inside her, keeping my pace slow and steady, letting the pressure and pleasure build for us both. Hollie's head is tossed back and her mouth is open as she lets out little moans that send shockwaves straight to my cock.

Sex has never been like this with anyone but Hollie. Yes, it's physically the best sex I've ever had, but it's also the only sex where I've felt a connection. It's like more than just our bodies being connected. Maybe it's our souls as well. The warm look in her eyes says that she feels this too, and I pray that I'm not just kidding myself.

"Please, more," she begs me. Who am I to deny my angel anything? Quickening my pace makes her whimper beneath me, increasing in volume. I move my hand down between us and find her swollen clit, working it back and forth as I continue pumping my cock inside her while she clings to me.

That familiar tingle starts at my spine and my balls pull up tightly. I know that I'm about to explode, but I need her to come for me first. I redouble my efforts on her clit and suck one of her nipples into my mouth, giving it a quick nip and tug. That's enough to send her over the edge and she lets out an unintelligible scream while shaking below me.

Her pussy convulses, and that's enough to bring me over with her. I throw my head back and let out a roar as load after load of cum moves up my cock and bursts out of my head, burying itself all the way into Hollie's womb. My stomach muscles are cramping up and my arms are shaking.

Before I can completely collapse on top of her, I roll off and onto my side, pulling her against my body and holding her through the shaking aftermath of both our orgasms. I bury my head into her honeysuckle hair and tell her what a good girl she is, how amazing she feels in my arms, how I want her in my bed every night. Things I should absolutely not be saying to my twenty-two-year-old assistant. But I don't give a fuck.

As soon as her body shakes cease, I drag myself out of the bed and head into my en suite bathroom. I take a moment to clean myself off, then grab a warm washcloth for Hollie. Once I re-enter the bedroom, I see that she's sitting up with the sheet pulled up to her chin, suddenly shy.

"Give me the sheet, angel," I say, holding out my hand for it. She gives out a huff, but puts the corner into my hand. I pull the sheet down to the bottom of the bed. She lets out a squeal and tries covering herself with her arms. "It's too late, angel," I chuckle. "I've already seen all of you... tasted all of you." That makes her blush a cute shade of pink I haven't seen before. Making Hollie blush may be my new favorite hobby. "Open your legs for me."

"What?" she squeaks out. I climb into the bed next to her and gather her in my arms, kissing the corner of her mouth.

"Let me clean you up, baby."

"I can do it myself."

I frown down at her. She better get used to me taking care of her real quick because the need inside me is overwhelming. Ignoring her weak protests, I bring the warm cloth between her legs, cleaning off the remnants of our lovemaking so she can sleep comfortably. Once I'm done, I toss the cloth back towards the bathroom. I pull her closer to my chest and bring the covers over top of us.

Her hand instinctively covers my heart as she tucks her head under my chin while my arms encircle her. I'm drifting off when a thought suddenly occurs to me.

"No leaving, Hollie."

"What?" she asks sleepily. Apparently, she's already halfway to dreamland.

"I don't want to wake up with you gone like I did last time. No leaving." I grip her chin so that I can make sure she's looking directly into my eyes. I want her to see the sincerity in them. "You got it?"

"Yeah, I got it," she whispers.

I release her face and relax against the pillows. My bed has never felt more comfortable and I have the distinct impression that it's because of the angel that I'm holding in my arms.

NINETEEN

HOLLIE

Morning sun pours over my face, gently pulling me from my bone-weary sleep. The bed is so soft that it's like I'm floating on a cloud, yet still somehow weighted down. It's then that I realize Archer has both his arm and leg across the entirety of my body, holding me in place.

I maneuver my body so that we're face to face, careful not to disrupt his slumber. He looks so relaxed in sleep. More like the man I've come to know over the past few weeks than the ruthless businessman I first met. I reach out and brush back a lock of hair that's fallen across his forehead, making him appear younger than his years.

A smile crosses my lips as I remember last night's activities. After we made love the first time and fell asleep, it wasn't long before Archer was waking me up so that we could do it all over again. He didn't get any complaints on my end. In fact, the next two times were initiated by me. Even though my body is deeply satisfied, I'm exhausted and I seem to ache in places that I didn't even know existed. Who needs the gym when you have Archer Clarke?

I grab my phone and see that it's already past eight. We're going to be late. Like, really late. I jump out of bed, no longer concerned about waking the sleeping giant, while I gather my clothes that are strewn around the room. I can hear Archer yawn and stretch behind me before giving a little growl.

"I told you not to leave," he says, as if I'm across town somewhere and not right in front of his eyes.

"I didn't leave, but if we don't start moving, we're going to be late to work. Very late. Plus, I need to get home and change." I fish one of my boots out from under the chair in the corner of the room and plop all the articles of clothing I've collected onto the seat.

"Come here, Hollie," he says, reaching a hand towards me. He hasn't moved a muscle yet to get out of bed and get ready for work. I approach him hesitantly, torn between hurrying to get to the office and crawling back into bed with him.

It's then that I notice I've been traipsing around naked, so I practically dive back into bed next to him, pulling the covers up around me. Sure, he may have seen every inch of me last night, but that doesn't mean I'm ready to be out walking around in all my naked glory in the sunlight.

Laughing, he gathers me into his arms and buries his nose in my hair. He sure likes to smell me a lot. "We're both going to be late. I'm sure the boss will give you a pass this once."

All at once, I'm drowning in him. His lips on mine, gentle yet persistent, his body surrounding me. The scent on his skin is a mixture of the two of us and what we shared last night. His hands are all over my body, stroking and caressing me, teasing me to the point of no return.

Before things get completely out of hand, I pull away from him slightly. "We have to get going, Archer. It's going to look suspicious if we're both late."

"So what? I'm the boss. We can do whatever we want." This man can be exasperating.

"Actually, no you can't. Remember the no-fraternization clause you so kindly pointed out to me? You could get removed as CEO and I could lose my job. There's no reason to let this—" I gesture wildly between the two of us, "—thing between us cause problems." He doesn't answer me, and I can't quite read his expression. I'm assuming he understands what's at risk here, so I push forward. "Besides, we have a ton to do today and you have that charity dinner tonight for Seattle schools. I had an intern pick up your suit. It's hanging in the closet in your office."

He sighs and pulls himself out of the bed. "Fine, I'll behave. But only if you agree to go with me to the dinner tonight."

"What? Why?" I ask.

"Because I want you to, that's why." He comes around the bed, not at all embarrassed by his own nudity. And why should he be? The man looks like hot sex on a stick. In fact, I'm half tempted to say the hell with work and dive back on top of that glorious cock.

"You know we can't, Archer. We could get in trouble."

"You let me worry about that."

I study him skeptically. The thought of not worrying about it, of letting him handle this thing for a while, is tempting.

"I don't have anything to wear to a fancy dinner like that, Archer." Bringing the subject back around to tonight's event.

At that, he smiles. "Again, let me worry about that. Now hurry," he gives my ass cheek a sharp whack and points me towards the bathroom, "get a quick shower and then I'll drop you at home so that you can change and grab your car."

At this point, why even argue? If I'm honest, I don't even really want to. Spending time on Archer's arm sounds like a great way to spend an evening, if you ask me. If he says not to worry about it, I won't. It's not like he's going to risk it all and lose his company over me. He'll make sure that I don't lose my job. He did say that I was the best assistant that he ever had. And frankly, I don't know who else would put up with his grumpy ass.

He doesn't join me in the shower, and I'm a little disappointed—shower sex has always intrigued me. But if he got in here with me, we would never make it to the office. Thirty minutes later, he's leaning over the console of his car in front of my house and giving me a kiss that leaves my head spinning.

I pull away and exit the car a little unsteadily. Bending down to wave goodbye, he shoots me a knowing wink. Fortunately, I make it all the way inside and out of his sight before collapsing against the wall sucking in some much needed oxygen.

Holy shit. I'm pretty sure I'm in love with him. What the hell am I'm going to do? I can't imagine a man like him would want anything long term with a woman like me. I'm not sophisticated. Hell, I'm barely educated. Sure, he said he wants to take me out, not caring if people see us together, but we never spoke about what that means for us. Are we dating? Am I his girlfriend? How long before he gets tired of messing around with the girl from the wrong side of the tracks and moves on to someone in his league?

One thing is for sure, if I ever want there to be anything between Archer and me more than a fling, I need to tell him the truth I've been avoiding.

At first, it didn't matter. I wasn't anything more to him than one of a long line of assistants. Nothing about me or my past would have directly affected him. Now, I'm not just his employee and I know it's going to seem like I'm trying to hide something when he finds out. I tried to tell him that night in Santa Cruz, but he brushed me off and told me he didn't want to hear it.

I need to tell him. Tonight.

With a plan and strengthened resolve, I head back to my bedroom. The house is unusually quiet for this time of morning. Usually, the place is full of the noise of three women getting ready for work and classes. The shower should be going. I should hear Violet's hair dryer in the distance while Bianca scrambles for something in the kitchen worth eating on the go. Instead, it's filled with silence and the house seems empty. I poke my head first into Violet's room and then Bianca's. Both of their beds don't appear to have been slept in.

Guilt washes over me. I've been so wrapped up in work and Archer that I've barely spent any time with either of them.

That's it. Tomorrow I'm making dinner and we're having a girls' night. I need to catch them up on last night's date. More importantly, I need to find out what's going on in their lives. Violet's been even quieter than usual and I'm worried something is going on with her. I don't want to pry, but I want her to know that I'm here for her if she wants to talk.

As I'm getting changed, my phone rings and Paige's picture pops up. My sister has never been a morning person, so her calling me this early is unusual. Oh well, it's not like the boss is going to say anything about me being a few minutes later than I already am. A huge grin overtakes my face as I accept the call.

"Good morning, sunshine. What can I do for you today?" I ask while rummaging through my closet until I spy a blue blouse that goes with the pants I've already set aside.

"Hey, Hollie. I'm sorry for calling so early. I wasn't sure if I should call you or not—"

"You should always call me, Paige."

"Well, I don't know if it's a big deal or not, but I haven't seen Mom in almost four days. I keep checking the apartment to make sure she hasn't come home while I'm at school and left again, but nothing's been touched. She disappears a lot, but this is a long time even for her."

"I'm sure she's fine." The response comes out of my mouth without me even having to think about it. This is my job, to make sure Paige is taken care of, that she doesn't worry. That she concentrates on being a kid. Why the hell didn't I make her come live with me? I collapse onto my bed and let out a sigh. "Hey, why don't I come drive down there tomorrow and bring you back up here with me for a while? She'll turn up eventually and then you can go back."

"You know I can't do that. I have school and my job. I can't just take off to Seattle—"

"Fine. Fine. You win. I understand, you can't come stay with me, but first thing tomorrow I'm driving over there. We'll check out her usual haunts, and I'll make sure you have everything you need. Plus, we can have some sister time."

"You don't mind?" Paige is a tough girl, but this would be hard for anyone to deal with. She would never ask me to come be with her just because she was upset or scared. She puts on a good front, but she's worried about Mom. No matter what she's done, she's ours. I hope Mom gets it together one day, but I'm honestly not holding my breath. As long as I can eventually get Paige out of her whirlwind relatively unscathed, I'll be happy.

"Of course not," I say lightly, like it's totally normal for someone's mother to disappear for four days without a word. "I've been meaning to come for a visit, anyway."

"Have I told you today that you're the best sister, Hollie?"

"Not yet, but there's still time." I laugh. We chat for a few more minutes, her trying to get some comfort and reassurance, me trying to smooth things over and pretend like this is no big deal. There go my plans to have dinner with my roommates. Knowing those two, they wouldn't let me stay here with them even if I asked. They would make sure my butt was headed over to Milford ASAP.

After getting off the phone, I finish dressing and head over to the office. Archer is already on the phone in his office when I make it upstairs. On my desk, front and center, is a bagel with cream cheese and a latte from the artisan coffee place down the street, which makes me break out into a smile. I bet I'm the first assistant that's gotten coffee *from* Archer Clarke.

I spend the rest of the morning trying to concentrate on work while Archer's voice drifts out of his office, sending chills throughout my entire body. Scenes of last night play repeatedly in my head. My panties are completely soaked through. I should have brought an extra pair with me.

A quickie in his office couldn't hurt, right? *Bad Hollie.*

"Miss. Hollie Simmons?"

I look up and spot a currier who has approached my desk without me noticing. "Yes, that's me."

"Great, sign here, please."

I take the stylus and sign the electronic tablet before he hands me the fanciest two boxes I've ever seen in person. Honestly, they look like they belong in a Christmas movie. Both boxes are white, one rather flat and square, while the other is smaller and more rectangular. Both boxes are adorned with beautiful gold ribbons made of a cloth with almost real looking golden strands woven throughout.

There's no card attached to either one, but they couldn't be from anyone except Archer. Who else in my life would know where you could order something like this, let alone afford it? I glance behind me and see that he's still on his conference call.

I lift the top off the larger box and nearly drop the lid. The inside is all tissue paper and iridescent white and pink sequins. I pull the material out of the box and reveal a one shouldered mini-dress complete with a blush-colored bow over the shoulder.

Carefully setting the dress aside, I pick up the second box and pull off the lid. Settled gently inside is a beautiful pair of Badgley Mischka nude kitten heels covered in rhinestones.

I glance at the sizes on both and they are on point. How he figured that out, I don't know. I don't think that I would ever pick out either of these items for myself. They both scream "look at me." I'm usually much more comfortable in a little black dress blending into the background. Not only are these beautiful and expensive, but Archer got them for me.

Frankly, I can't wait for him to see me in this dress. I place everything back in their designated boxes and store them under my desk. I don't need anyone coming by and asking uncomfortable questions I'm not prepared to answer.

The intercom on my desk buzzes alerting me Archer needs something.

"Yes?"

"Miss. Simmons, will you come into my office a moment, please?"

"Of course." I switch off the intercom and grab my notepad and pen to take notes. Are we already back to Miss. Simmons? There's a drop of fear in the pit of my stomach. Has he decided that last night was a mistake? Then why send me the dress? Now that I've finally admitted to myself that I'm in love with him, the thought of him rejecting me makes me want to curl up in the corner of the office in the fetal position. Steeling myself for whatever he has to dish out, I head into his office.

"Close the door behind you," he says as I pass over the threshold. With a gulp, I pull the door closed and make my way over to his desk. He's gazing at me with an expression that I can't figure out. Suddenly, he pushes back his chair and makes it over to me in three long strides, pulling me into his arms, his lips capturing mine in a searing kiss. My body sags against him in relief and I return his kiss with my own.

"I didn't have time to say good morning," he whispers in my ear once he's done devouring me. I'm not sure if it's the relief that nothing's changed since this morning or the fact he's now got me turned on beyond belief, but I'm absolutely giddy.

"I'm pretty sure you said that to me this morning at your place," I tease him, not bothering to pull away from him. It feels too good to be wrapped in his arms. If I could be anywhere in the world right now, I wouldn't choose anywhere else.

He takes his time, gently stroking a path up and down my spine, giving me goosebumps even through my blouse. I take the time to enjoy this moment of him holding me like I'm something precious before I lean back and catch his eyes on me.

"I got the dress."

"Oh, yeah?" he asks, his face lighting up. "Do you like it? If you don't, I can get you something else."

"No, it's perfect," I reassure him. "How did you know my sizes?"

At that, he looks sheepish and pushes a lock of my hair that's escaped my sensible work bun back behind my ear. "I might have taken a peek at your clothes from last night while you were in the shower."

"Smart. Sneaky, but smart." I lightly slap his arm. "Have you heard from Caroline DuPont yet?"

Archer releases me and takes a step back. It looks like he's back to business mode, which is probably a good thing. A few more minutes engulfed in him and I would be panting with need.

"Not yet, but her team would probably contact Richard first. We still have plenty of time if you want to spend the afternoon doing anything else..." He raises a devilish eyebrow at me that shows we're not *completely* back in business mode.

"Oh, no you don't," I tell him, heading back to my desk. "I've got a ton of things to do today, plus I have to go home and get ready for the dinner tonight."

His arm snakes around my waist from behind and he draws me up against him before I can make it out the door. His hard dick is pressing against my back and it takes every ounce of self-control I have not to push him to the ground and straddle him in the middle of the office.

"Why don't you go home for the rest of the day? Consider it flex time since you have to work tonight."

I give out a laugh at that. "Somehow, I don't think it's going to feel much like work." Turning, I plant a quick kiss on his lips. "Besides, don't you need me here?"

"You've already spent more time than your fair share working on the proposal, and there's nothing that can't wait until Monday. We probably won't even hear from Mrs. DuPont today. Go home, relax, and take your time getting ready. I'll pick you up at six."

"Who am I to argue with the boss when he wants to give me time off?" My hands slip inside his suit jacket and begin wandering his muscular back. I really should get going before things get out of hand.

After one last, passionate kiss to tide us over, I pack up my desk, grabbing my brand new dress and shoes, before heading home.

Tonight feels like the start of something. Something bigger than either he or I alone. It feels like the start of us.

TWENTY

ARCHER

Knowing that Hollie is gone seems to make the rest of my day drag exponentially more than it would otherwise. She's right, there's always plenty of work that needs to get done around here, but I wanted her to have some time to get ready for this evening. Besides, I know for a fact that she didn't get much sleep last night.

Waking up with her beside me this morning filled me with a deep sense of contentment I didn't know I needed. As the sun was rising in the sky, I watched her sleep next to me, her head on my chest with her fist tucked underneath her chin like a child's.

I've never met a woman like Hollie before. Certainly not one that makes me feel the way she does. I've never been particularly interested in other women beyond the time we spent together in the bedroom. With Hollie, I want to know everything about her. I want to know her dreams and make them happen, her fears and vanquish them. I'm ready to go all in with her and I never thought that was possible for me.

I'm getting ready to leave and head home to shower and change when Richard comes bursting into my office without knocking. There's an air of chaotic energy around him, his face a particularly unappealing shade of scarlet.

"What's wrong, Richard?" I set the papers I was collecting back onto the surface of my desk, bracing for whatever bad news he's about to dump on me.

"It's over. It's all fucking over," he huffs out, pacing in front of my desk.

"What's over?" I ask, my eyes tracking his movements, back and forth, back and forth.

"The goddamn Santa Cruz deal, that's what!"

"What the fuck are you talking about?"

"Caroline DuPont's people never got our proposal."

A quick glance at my wristwatch shows me it's already almost 4 p.m. Long past the deadline.

"That's not possible." I reach down to pick up the receiver of my desk phone, but Richard puts his hand on mine to stop me. It's not like I would know who to call, anyway. That's what I have Hollie for.

"I'm sorry, Archer. I've already spoken to her people. They never received it. All the copies were delivered on time to their destinations, but not hers. I had my assistant call FedEx and they can't even find an envelope originating from us going anywhere in California. How did you send them out?"

"I gave them all to Hollie to send out yesterday. All the others made it to where they were supposed to go, so she must have sent them." I sit back in my chair and cover my face with my hands. What an absolute shit show.

How could something like this happen? If I hadn't been so caught up with thoughts about Hollie today, I would have remembered to check they were all delivered. Hell, Hollie would have been sitting right out there at her desk checking without me even having to ask. Instead, I sent her home so she can get ready for me to show her off tonight.

"Here's what you needs to do," he says, "you're going to call Caroline DuPont. Explain to her that there was some kind of mail mix-up, see if she's willing to take the offer from us past the deadline. It might be helpful if we bring a signed copy to her tonight. That's not a bad idea actually, I can get the plane on standby and—"

"No."

"Excuse me?" Richard looks up at me incredulously, like I've sprouted a second head.

"No," I say again. This time with a sense of finality. I don't want to go running down to Santa Cruz tonight for a business deal. I want to take Hollie to the charity dinner and spend the entire night with her. And later I want to make her scream my name.

Yes, I'm upset about the proposal not getting in but... it's not the end of the world. I can't believe I ever thought it would be.

I'll call Caroline DuPont tomorrow and see if there is something we can work out. We've developed a mutual respect for one another, and my proposal has to be one of the few that may truly benefit Santa Cruz. There's a good chance we can still do business together. And if not? My eye catches on the worn key with the teal diamond key chain that's been sitting tucked under my monitor all day. If not, then that would be alright too.

This project was—no, still is—important to me. But I'm not only looking to the past anymore. I had wonderful times in Santa Cruz and even if I never own a hotel in the entire city, there is nothing that can change that. Nothing can take away the memories of those carefree days I spent as a child with my parents sitting on the bungalow porch.

I pick up the key, feeling the weight in my hand. That's what Hollie was trying to tell me when she gave me this. Even if I buy the land and put a Clarke Hotel there, it won't make my time there any more special. It was wonderful, but it's in the past. I have to concentrate on creating new memories.

Sure, if I can't get Mrs. DuPont to take the late offer, the board won't be thrilled, but they'll get over it. They were never totally sold on the idea of having a Santa Cruz resort, anyway. No matter which way my conversation goes with Caroline DuPont tomorrow, everything will be fine. Plus, I'll have Hollie by my side.

"Richard," I sigh, raising out of my chair, gathering my things. "Go home and tell Flora I said hi. There's nothing else we can do tonight. I'll call Caroline tomorrow and see what I can work out."

"Who are you and what have you done with Archer?"

"Funny. I just don't see it as anything that needs to ruin our Friday night. It's nothing that can't be handled later."

Richard practically chokes on what I can only assume is his own saliva. "Wasn't it you who told me a few weeks ago that a Friday night was no reason not to work?"

"Things have changed." I laugh and head out the door, leaving Richard where he's sitting.

"Things have changed?"

I stop in the doorway and glance back at him. "You know, Richard, we really have to work on you repeating everything I say." I give him a smile so he knows I'm joking.

"I wouldn't keep doing it if you said something that made a bit of damn sense!" His grumbling follows me all the way down the hallway to the elevator, and the smile never leaves my face.

I can't keep my eyes off her goddamn legs.

Hollie is sitting next to me in the chauffeured town car I hired for the evening. I didn't want to have to navigate the crush of cars that will be at the venue downtown.

She's dressed in both the dress and heels I got for her. First thing in the morning, I'm sending my personal shopper at Neiman Marcus a bonus. All I did was give her Hollie's sizes and a quick description of her and this is what she came up with. She looks like something out of a wet dream.

The skirt is short. So short, in fact, I almost sent her back inside as soon as the door opened. If I can't get my eyes off her thick thighs, every other man in the place won't be able to either.

Tonight is about showing the world that Hollie belongs to me and no one else, even if she doesn't realize it yet. The dress's single shoulder perfectly shows off the elegant line of her neck.

The irrational, primitive part of me wants to bite the delicate skin the dress is so perfectly framing, piercing her with my teeth, leaving no doubt to anyone we come upon tonight who she belongs to. I don't think she would particularly appreciate it, so I manage to rein myself in. Barely.

The car pulls up to the front of Seattle's Natural History Museum, which is the setting for tonight's event. The crème de la crème of Seattle society will be here. All the movers and shakers in both local politics and industry gather this evening to congratulate each other on writing checks to Seattle's public schools.

Don't get me wrong, I love being able to give to charity. I make sure that my company does so generously every year. But if there was a way I could mail in the check and not have to dress up and pretend that I can tolerate these people, I would take the out in a second.

The crowd of photographers and journalists milling around the front of the building can be daunting for someone new to this scene, like my girl. I could have the driver circle around to the side of the building and let us off where there's always a side entrance for those looking to avoid the red carpet. However, the exposure would be good not only for our company but the charity as well.

Plus, there's the added bonus of getting to claim Hollie in front of everyone. I give it five minutes before our pictures are plastered all over Instagram and Twitter. I make a calculated decision to not mention that fact to Hollie.

She's looking out the window at the crush of photographers and I can tell by the way she's wringing her hands in her lap that she's nervous. I grab her hand and pull it to my lips. She watches me with wide eyes as I place a kiss on the center of her palm before returning her hand back to her lap.

"I've got you, angel."

Our driver opens her door, drawing her attention away from me. As soon as I climb out of the back seat, the lights flash. I join Hollie on the other side of the car, settling my hand into the small of her back and guiding her forward with me through the throngs of reporters. Her smaller body is trembling, but when I peer down at her face, it's the picture of serenity. She's got a decent public poker face. That's going to serve her well hanging around me. And I plan on having her around me a lot.

We make it to the step and repeat that's setup for more formal photographs and wait our turn to walk the red carpet.

As we hit the first photo mark, I angle her towards the camera and wrap my arm fully around her waist, drawing her into my side. Anyone looking at us will know immediately we're an item with me draped possessively over her. But just in case...

I grab her chin and pull her face up towards mine, her eyes asking me what I'm up to. I claim her lips in a searing kiss for all to see. She doesn't hesitate to melt into me. She's right where she belongs, and she knows it.

I pull away from her and note the glassy look in her eyes before all the other sights and sounds filter back into my vision. Cameras are flashing like crazy and people are yelling questions at us.

"Archer, who's your date? Is it serious?"

"Miss, what's your name? How long have you been dating Archer Clarke?"

"Over here! Can we get another kiss?"

Having accomplished my goal of metaphorically pissing on her, we make our way inside the museum without paying the paparazzi any more mind.

"What the hell was that, Archer?" she asks me under her breath. "Is it always like this when you go somewhere?"

"Not always, mostly it's at big events like this." I brush off the crush outside and guide her farther into the building. "Come on, let's get a drink."

We're only stopped a handful of times on our way to the bar. Everyone from business associates to distant acquaintances seems to want a moment of my time this evening. I introduce Hollie to each and every one of them, keeping her planted firmly to my side the entire time. She's gracious and charms every person she meets just like I knew she would.

By the time we each have a drink in hand, the evening's activities are under way. There's a silent auction to one side of the grand hall where you can bid on anything from spending the day teaching a class to a ride on one of Seattle's wealthiest angel investor's private jets.

"What do you want to bid on?" I ask while guiding her down the line of items. Her eyes are bright and roving over the goods. Whatever she wants, I'll bid on it. Hell, if I have to, I'll grab it off the table and make a run for the doors. This girl can have anything she wants.

"Oh, I couldn't..." she trails off, looking around.

"What, why not?" I'm a bit puzzled by her hesitance. Perhaps she hasn't found anything that she wants yet.

"Archer," she says, lowering her voice so that only I can hear her, "I can't afford any of these things. Even if I could, I wouldn't know what to do with..." reaching to grab the closest bidding sheet she reads off the top, "six sessions with Seattle's premier life coach?"

I want to let out a laugh at the thought I would actually let her pay for anything, but Hollie has a lot of pride, and that would most likely not go over well. Instead, I draw her forward so her chest is pressed against mine. I try to ignore the fact I can feel her tits pressed against my upper abdomen. Instead, I lean down and brush my lips against hers in a kiss that's almost a caress. I pull away and let my chin rest upon the crown of her head, breathing in her distinctive scent that always makes my pulse quicken.

"Angel, we're bidding with the company money. That's the whole reason we're here. And if we're going to bid on something anyway, it might as well be something you want."

She leans back in my arms and smiles sweetly. "Then let's bid on that one." She points to something on the table we passed a few items ago. I release her and step closer to see what she's picked out.

"You want a box of Gurkha His Majesty's Reserve cigars?" I lift my eyebrow pointedly at her. "That's funny. I've never noticed you smoking cigars before."

"Fine." She crosses her arms over her chest and gives me my favorite disgruntled expression. "I thought you would like them. I don't need any of this stuff."

"Of course you don't *need* any of this. You're supposed to get something you *want*. Besides, if you don't bid on something, I'll be forced to go home empty-handed and no money will go to the schools. But I guess if you can live with that..."

"Fine." She gives a harrumph and continues walking down the tables, looking over what's being offered, with me dutifully following behind her. If anyone were watching us and thought it was humorous that Archer Clarke was following around a girl fresh out of college like a lovesick puppy, I've got news for them. I couldn't give a fuck. I'd follow her to hell and back.

"This one." She grabs a pen from the table and starts scribbling the Clarke Hotel information on the bid sheet. I lean over her shoulder to see which item finally caught her attention.

"A trip for two to a Château on a lake in Alberta?"

"It sounds beautiful. I wonder who I'll take with me."

My head jerks back to her and before I can protest about her going on a romantic getaway with anyone who isn't me, I notice the sparkle in her eye. Instead, I pinch her ass as discreetly as I can in a room full of people. "Don't even think about it, angel."

We make our way through throngs of reporters to find our name cards on one of the large tables covered in expensive china and elegant floral centerpieces. Hollie's hand is securely in mine when she pulls back slightly, missing a step. I stop and wrap an arm around her, noticing that her entire body's gone still as a board. Her eyes are so large they look like they're about to fall out of her head and I can feel her begin to tremble. I turn to see where she's looking when I spot a familiar but wholly unwelcome sight.

"Archer, my boy. I didn't expect to see you here this evening."

Patrick Shaw is standing directly in our path wearing a suit that's as expensive as my own, but he's nowhere close to pulling it off like I do. I only try mildly to suppress my eye roll. He is the last thing I want to deal with tonight.

"Hey there, Archer. You're looking rather well. It's been a while," Selene Shaw says to me suggestively, leaning forward allowing me a glimpse down her dress. A shudder runs through my body. I can't believe I put my dick in that, even if it was to fuck with Patrick. She's draped in a piece of fabric that could be called a dress by only the loosest of definitions. Her breasts are hanging out of the snug neckline and her face is plastered with about an inch of makeup.

I can see now that every woman in my past was just me wasting time until my angel came along. If it's possible, Hollie tenses up beside me even more than she was before. She's got a death grip on my elbow and she's squeezing into my side like she hopes she can disappear inside of me.

"I was sorry to hear about your offer not getting to Caroline DuPont on time. I wonder what could have happened." Hollie lets out a quiet gasp at my side. I hadn't had time to talk to her about the fact that the proposal had gone missing. I knew she would be upset, and I didn't want to worry her. Enjoying our evening together was tonight's top priority.

Shaw has a smile on his face that's nothing short of triumphant. I don't know how the fuck he knows the bid didn't get there today, but I don't have time to figure it out right now. I'll have Richard start on an official inquiry to who has been leaking information to Patrick Shaw on Monday, but right now I want to get Hollie out of here. There's definitely something wrong with her. I'm going to insist that she see a doctor first thing in the morning.

"If you'll excuse us, we have somewhere we need to be," I say, trying to move past the wall of bullshit that's stationed itself in front of us.

His smile turns downright evil as his eyes move from me over to Hollie at my side. Every protective instinct inside of me rises to the forefront. If he doesn't stop looking at her in the next three seconds, he's going to end up in the hospital.

"Of course. And how are you doing, Hollie, my darling?" My head physically jerks back like I've been slapped. How does he know her name? When I find out whoever has been giving information to Shaw, I'm going to kill them. I recognize that I've threatened violence, even if it was internally, twice in the past ten seconds. I'm worried that this might become par for the course where Hollie is involved.

"Fine," she says in almost a whisper.

"Frankly Archer, when I heard that you'd hired my very own daughter as your personal assistant, I figured you were either incredibly cunning or monumentally stupid." He raises one of his eyebrows up to his receding hairline, like he's waiting for me to say something.

It feels like I've just received a punch to the gut. All the air escapes my body in a rush and I want to hunch over with my hands on my knees, gulping in all the oxygen in the room. Instead, I barely maintain my upright position and direct my next question straight to Hollie. "Daughter?" I wait not so patiently for her denial.

"Archer, I—"

"Oh, I see, you didn't know." Shaw clasps his hands together in a show of mock sympathy. "I guess we're going to go with monumentally stupid then. Hollie dear, you're a chip right off the old block. I hope you understand. It's just business, after all." He lets out a laugh that sounds like it might verge on manic while pulling Selene closer into his side. I guess he really is still pissed off about our hook-up. "I hope you both have a lovely evening."

With that, he whisks his wife away from us, leaving Hollie and I in a stunned silence. The confrontation with Shaw was short and didn't draw too much attention. Still, there are a few people nearby that are eyeing us with curiosity. As quickly as possible, I guide Hollie through a closed door that leads us to a hallway cast in shadow. It's obviously some place that's off-limits to guests and attendees, but it will afford us the privacy we need for this.

"You're Patrick Shaw's daughter? Your last name is Simmons," I state the obvious.

"It's my mother's last name. I never had his. I told you I barely knew my father. He's only bothered to see me a handful of times over the years."

"And you didn't think even once this was information I might want to know, Hollie?" My voice comes out in a harsh whisper. I don't bother to temper the anger that's seeping out of my pores.

"I'm so sorry, Archer. I tried to tell you, really I did. The first few times you brought him up, I didn't think it mattered if you knew or not. It's not like I have anything to do with him, plus you were just my boss. It didn't matter who my father was. Why would it?"

"You thought it didn't fucking matter? I told you how many times he came swooping in at the last minute to take properties out from under me with proprietary information, and you think it didn't fucking matter that you were his goddamn daughter?"

There's an icy feeling in my stomach as my brain connects the dots one by one.

Hollie gets hired and suddenly Patrick Shaw knows about the property I'm bidding on in Santa Cruz, a project that's very close and personal to me. Now, with no rhyme or reason, my final proposal for said property suddenly disappears into thin air. A proposal that I handed to Hollie to mail out with a strict deadline.

"What about Santa Cruz?" I ask, barely keeping my emotions in check. She wouldn't do this, wouldn't sabotage my chances of making this happen. She knows what this would mean to me... because I told her. I told her everything.

I think I'm going to throw up.

"I don't even know what you're talking about." There's a pleading tone to her voice that makes me want to wrap her in my arms and tell her everything is going to be okay but I won't fall for her lies again. "He said the proposal didn't get to Caroline, but how can that be? I mailed them myself."

"Exactly. You mailed them all yourself." I take three steps backwards, out of the area immediately surrounding her. I need space to think. It's impossible to make sense of anything when she's so close.

"I was going to tell you, Archer, I swear I was. Once we became... more. I tried to tell you that night in Santa Cruz, but you told me it could wait."

"You obviously didn't try very hard, did you?" Willing a mask of indifference to cover my face, I slip myself back into ruthless business mode.

"I'm so sorry, Archer. I should have told you about Shaw, but I promise you I don't know anything about the proposal going missing. Please, you have to believe me!"

"You really had me fooled. I've got to hand it to you. Your acting skills are superb. Is that what you really majored in? I mean, who knows with you? It could be anything."

Hollie had access to everything. All our company's files and contacts. There was nothing I held back from her and she's going to use that information to destroy us. Destroy me.

There's a pain in my chest that feels suspiciously like my heart shattering into a million pieces. I barely resist the urge to bring my hand up and rub at it. I want to hurt her as much as she's hurting me right now. She doesn't actually give a shit about me, but at least I can bring her down a few pegs.

"I almost believed your little inexperienced college girl act. I have to hand it to you, I never would have taken you for the type of person who would get ahead by lying on her back. You know what you weren't faking, though?" I lean in next to her ear, making sure that she can hear every word. "How I make you come, angel. Just like every other gold-digging piece of trash that's graced my bed and I've tossed aside like the trash you are. Not even you are that good of an actress."

Her face looks absolutely stricken. Good. It's what she deserves. I can see her eyes watering. Is this Jezebel actually going to cry? My very first instinct is to comfort her like the fucking fool that I am. I can't handle any of this right now. Not here. I need to get out of here before I make an even bigger idiot of myself than I already have.

"I assume this goes without saying, but I'm going to spell it out for you, just in case. You're fired, Hollie. I'll have my new assistant mail you the things from your desk. If you even *think* about stepping foot on Clarke Hotel property again, I'll have you prosecuted for trespassing."

A small sob escapes her lips and five minutes ago, the sound would have brought me to my knees, ready to slay dragons for her. Instead, it just makes me sick to my stomach. Without another word, I push past her, out the door and back into the grand hall. The noise of raucous party guests fills my ears as I make my way to the bar. No one is paying any attention to me or the fact my entire world has come crashing down around me.

TWENTY-ONE

HOLLIE

I don't remember how I got home. Thank God for human autopilot and rideshare apps. Archer made it quite clear that I wouldn't be getting a ride home from him.

I should have told him, I know that. I really was going to tell him tonight.

Yeah, it all sounds pretty lame to me too.

The moment I spotted my father moving towards us in the crowd, I knew it was going to be bad. When his eyes met mine, I could see a glimmer of contempt. The strange thing was, there was no surprise in his expression. It was like he expected to find me there.

The first time Archer mentioned Patrick Shaw to me, I was genuinely shocked. It had never occurred to me he would have any kind of business dealings with my father. There was no way that I was going to tell him that Shaw was my father. He obviously had contempt for the man—not that I could blame him—and I hadn't been working there very long. Why would I want to risk my job over a man that merely gave me half my DNA? It's not like we hung out at his company picnic and had long meaningful chats on the phone or anything. I figured I could ignore the whole thing.

Then the trip to Santa Cruz happened. I started to care about him that day. Then, well, that night. I obviously was going to tell him. I didn't want to trick him into sleeping with me while having this enormous secret. He deserved my honesty. When he brushed me off, I was all too happy to go right along with it. I could always tell him later.

Obviously, later had come and gone. The entire thing had blown up spectacularly right in my face, and it was nobody's fault but my own.

Now I'm sitting on my ratty old couch in a dress that probably costs an entire one of my paychecks and crying all my expertly applied makeup down my face.

I'm so wrapped up in my misery that I don't even hear the front door open and close again. I only realize I'm no longer alone when a figure settles onto the couch next to me and gathers me up in her arms, holding me tight.

"Oh, Hollie, what happened?" Bianca asks, rocking me back and forth. The warmth and love in her voice sets me off on another crying jag.

She patiently waits for me to get myself together enough to speak, which is honestly some kind of miracle with her. Usually, she'd steamroll right over me to find out what was wrong and who she would have to fight for my honor.

"I got fired." Is all I manage to get out before I'm drawn back into my cloud of self-loathing.

"Wait, he dated you, then *fired* you?" She looks around the room briefly before asking, "Is Violet home?"

I shake my head, keeping my face buried in her shoulder. It feels like the world is falling to dust around me and I can't bear to look at it.

"Okay, hold on, I'll text her and get us set up." She leaves me on the couch and returns with water, wine, a box of tissues, and cheese. So much cheese. Did we have all this in the house? I grab a handful of gouda and shove it in my mouth before following it with a healthy swig of the white wine she's poured for me. If ever there was a time to eat my feelings, this would be it.

I'm starting in on my second glass when Violet rushes into the house.

"How is she doing? What happened?" The questions are directed towards Bianca and not me, which is a good thing, since I'm honestly not sure how I'm going to get through the explanation.

"She's moved on from uncontrollable sobs to crying in between handfuls of cheese, so I would say that's an improvement." Bianca eyes Violet somewhat suspiciously before she asks, "Where were you? The campus is twenty minutes away, and you got here in like five."

Violet looks down at her shoes and my eyes narrow in on her. She only does that when she lies.

"I was around the corner. I have a new study group and one girl lives a few blocks away."

I'm expecting Bianca to call her out on the obvious fabrication, but she brings the subject back to me. "That's good. I was waiting for you to get here before I started the interrogation."

Violet settles in beside me and starts rubbing my back in soothing circular motions. "What's going on, Hollie? You can tell us."

"He found out about my father." Both my friends let out simultaneous sounds of sympathy and understanding.

"But I thought you were going to tell him anyway," Violet inquires cautiously, like I might explode at any second. She wouldn't be wrong. My chest feels hollow. I'm sure you could fit a bomb in the space where my heart used to be.

"I was, I swear. I was going to tell him tonight after the dinner. But," I take a breath to steady myself so that I can get the actual words out, "We ran into Patrick there."

"Holy shit," Bianca mumbles, while Violet merely lets out a tiny gasp. "Don't tell me he actually bothered to speak to you. Frankly, I'm surprised he even remembers what you look like."

She's not wrong. I prayed that he'd walk right by without even noticing me. Some prayers just go unanswered.

"Oh, he recognized me alright. In fact, he didn't even seem surprised to see me there, which is crazy. He also insinuated I was working for him, like some kind of corporate spy or something."

"You've got to be kidding me. Archer actually believed that shit?"

"Yup, hook, line and sinker. He pulled me into some hallway and fired my sorry ass. I'm pretty sure that means I won't be seeing him anymore."

Violet hugs me tighter while tears spill down my cheeks. I'm sure I look like a well-dressed clown right now, but I couldn't care less. "Didn't you tell him how you don't even really know your dad?"

"I tried!" The exclamation comes out of my mouth as a half moaning, half sobbing sound. "He wouldn't even listen to me. He couldn't get away from me fast enough."

The heavy despair in the pit of my stomach is slowly being joined by another emotion, annoyance verging on anger.

"That really sucks," Violet says.

"You're right, it does. After everything we've been through, he wouldn't even give me three minutes to explain."

"He's an asshole," Bianca chimes in supportively. Except that he's not an asshole. Not really. Sure, he has asshole qualities. He's a workaholic and a perfectionist, not only for himself but for everyone around him. Still, once you get past that hardened, ruthless businessman facade, there beats the heart of a man that's looking for someone to love and love him in return. To capture that feeling of family from his youth.

"I'm in love with him," I whisper. "I'd barely even admitted it to myself, but I love him and he can't stand to be in the same room with me. Now, what am I supposed to do?"

"If it's meant to be, it will work itself out. Otherwise, he's not worthy of your love and you'll find someone who is. You can chalk this up to experience," Violet says sweetly.

At that Bianca lets out a little snort, "You can do so much better, Hollie. The man you love is an asshole who wouldn't even listen to you. You're going to be fine and someday you'll run into Archer Clarke on the street on the way home from your high-paying executive job with your gorgeous husband and two point five beautiful children while he'll be old and alone with only his billions to keep him company. We should feel sorry for *him,* really." She tips the bottle, emptying the last bit of wine straight into my glass, like the loyal friend she is.

"I wouldn't go that far." I toss back the last mouthful of wine, though my mood hasn't improved with the alcohol. "Can we watch something? I can't talk about him anymore right now. But it has to have zero romance in it. None."

After I change out of the dress that I swear to my friends I'm going to burn while secretly knowing I'll keep it and hold it while I cry for years to come, we decide to go with Disney's Inside Out. It has the no romance requirement plus the nostalgia factor of our youth built right in. Besides, I'm experiencing a deep affinity with both Sadness and Anger tonight.

I'm trying to concentrate on the movie and not my poor broken heart when Bianca calls Violet into the kitchen to help her with something, followed by a harried conversation whispered back and forth. What are they up to? I head into the kitchen and see them standing behind the island, both huddled over Bianca's phone.

"What are you looking at?" I ask. They both jump about a foot in the air when they hear my voice. Did they think they were being stealthy?

My two best friends exchange a look that comes off as both pitying and pleading all at once. What the hell is going on?

"Just tell me already."

Bianca tentatively holds her phone out to me so that I can grab it from her. Twitter is open, and a picture is pulled up showing Archer dressed to the nines and looking as attractive as ever. But the picture isn't only of Archer. Julia Kellogg, his ex, is draped all over him, smiling straight into the camera. He's wearing a black suit with a red tie that looks suspiciously like what he was wearing earlier.

"When is this from?" The question comes out in a shaky whisper. I already know the answer. I just need confirmation.

There's silence in the kitchen until Violet takes pity on me. "It's from tonight. You don't know what's going on in that picture, Holls. It could be anything. It was probably a photo op."

"So, he dumped me, fired me, then stuck around to take photos with his ex?" His expression in the photo looks completely blank so I can't tell what he's thinking. If he's upset about what happened moments before this picture was taken or if he wanted her on his arm, I can't tell.

Who am I kidding? Archer Clarke doesn't do anything he doesn't want to do. Including taking pictures with beautiful women he used to fuck.

Violet comes around the island and pulls me into a hug that I can't bring myself to return. I can feel stinging in my eyes, but I won't let myself cry. I've cried enough over him. It was one thing when I was crying because I lost the man I love. A man I thought deserved my love. At least I know now that he's exactly the kind of man I always suspected he was.

I knew this was always going to be temporary; a man like Archer Clarke would never commit to one woman and settle down. Especially not a no name girl from the wrong side of the tracks. I'd seen it again and again. Hell, even my own father was that way. I told myself to protect my heart, that this would happen. But like an idiot, I let myself fall for him, anyway. He was able to discard me and then move right on to the next woman within the hour. That's how much I meant to him.

I pull out of Violet's arms and take a deep, calming breath.

"I'll be fine, you guys. Thanks for telling me. I'd much rather know than walk around mooning over him like an idiot. I'm going to head to bed. Thanks for everything tonight."

I can tell they want to talk more about the photo, but I don't have it in me. I head to my bedroom and stretch out on my bed. Sure, I can't hide from my problems, like the fact that I'm unemployed and my heart is currently laying in a thousand pieces in some empty museum hallway, but that doesn't mean I can't hide under my blankets and sleep for the next 10 hours. If only I had known it would be a scant few hours before my world was flipped on its head for the second time in the past twenty-four hours.

TWENTY-TWO

ARCHER

After I left Hollie alone in that hallway, I made my way to the bar and took an immediate shot of bourbon, hoping it could dull some of the pain in my chest. I was surrounded by people trying to make small talk and journalists taking photos. I lasted another twenty minutes and if you asked me to recount them, you would be out of luck.

There was no way I could go home. The memory of her would be too strong there. God, was it only last night she was in my bed? I knew my sheets would still smell like her. That the towel she used to dry off her body after her morning shower was still hanging in my bathroom. I'll have to call the cleaning service and have them send someone to de-Holliefy my house so that I can get my home back to normal. I snort to myself at the thought. Like going back to normal is even possible.

Instead, I head straight to The Clarke, and post up there for the night. Sitting out on the balcony of my reserved suite, I toss back drink after drink, letting the brown liquid burn down my throat, warming me from the inside out as I sit in the frigid night air.

I honestly can't believe I fell for her bullshit. She had me wrapped so tightly around her finger I almost let the most important deal of my life slip through my fingers. Until Hollie came along, that had been the only thing that truly mattered to me. Then she walked into my office all young and innocent, smelling like summer. I thought as long as she was by my side, it didn't matter. She understood me. Maybe I could someday recreate the happiness of my youth with her.

What bullshit.

The thing that's really devastating is the fact I'm head over heels in love with her. It has to be love. Otherwise, it wouldn't feel like my heart is bleeding out inside my chest cavity right now. When I thought I'd been falling in love with her, it had already been too late. I was utterly fucked.

I have to get my life back on track. A life that no longer involves Hollie Simmons or Shaw or whoever the fuck she is. I toss back another gulp of bourbon and set the glass aside so I can peel off my suit jacket. It must be fifty-five degrees out here at most, but I'm sweating bullets.

It's 2 a.m. when I stagger my way back inside the suite and tear off the remains of my rumpled suit before crashing face first onto the California king bed. I know trying to sleep will be an exercise in futility, but I figure I might as well give it a go. It can't possibly hurt as badly when I'm sleeping, can it?

By the time the sun is shining through the hotel windows, I haven't gotten a moment's rest. It's Saturday and I don't have a single thing that has to be done. To be honest, I had hoped I'd spend the day in bed with Hollie, but I quickly push that thought out of my head. Instead, I decide I should go into the office. I need to speak to Caroline DuPont anyway. Perhaps if I do a little groveling, she'll accept our late offer. I'm not exactly hopeful, but I didn't get where I am by giving up. This may have temporarily derailed me, but I can get back on track. I just need to focus.

I call down to the concierge and order some coffee to be sent up before I jump into the shower. The water is so hot that it seers my skin while still relaxing my tense back and shoulder muscles. When I finally get out and dry off, my skin looks red and raw.

By the time I make it out of the bathroom with a towel wrapped around my waist, a silver room service tray holding a carafe of coffee, along with containers for cream and sugar, are sitting on the small kitchen table.

Once I've finished my first cup of coffee and started into my second, I reluctantly pull last night's suit back on, thankful I have a spare in the office. Deciding I might as well get the groveling over with in the privacy of my hotel room, I pull up Caroline DuPont's contact information and wait for her to answer my call.

"Mr. Clarke, I thought I might hear from you." Her tone doesn't sound irritated *per se,* but she doesn't exactly sound pleased to hear from me either. Then again, I am calling her on a Saturday morning.

"I'm so sorry to bother you during your weekend, Mrs. DuPont. Unfortunately, I found out that there was a problem with the courier yesterday and our proposal has been delayed."

There is silence on the other end of the line, so I decide to continue.

"I wanted you to know that Clarke Hotels doesn't make a habit of this kind of thing—"

"I should hope not," she huffs across the line.

"Would you be open to accepting a proposal from us past the deadline? I realize it's not standard business practice, but I believe ours will be the best you receive, not just financially but with your outlined stipulations. I'm sure there's something that we could work out."

I rub my hand over my face, trying to bring down my blood pressure a few notches. Caroline DuPont wasn't exactly my biggest fan even before I missed the deadline. Another thing I have to thank Patrick Shaw for. If he thought I was a pain in the ass before, he doesn't know the hell he's brought down upon himself.

"This is highly unusual, Mr. Clarke. All the other interested parties submitted their proposals on time. You're the only one that seems to think it's alright to disrespect my deadline."

"That's not it at all. I can promise you. You'll find that I don't play those kinds of games." I'm pretty sure I'm going to have to lay it out for her. She's not buying my brand of bullshit. "To be quite honest with you, we think there was a problem with the employee that was supposed to send it out. That's not an excuse, it's an explanation. Now that I'm aware of the issue, I can assure you something like that will never happen again."

There's a tense silence between the two of us for another few heartbeats before she continues in a considerably lighter tone, surprising me.

"Hiring an employee like that should make me question your judgment. However, I got to meet your lovely assistant, Hollie. Now that one's a keeper and the person you should entrust such an important task to."

I almost choke. It's all I can do to not sputter into the phone. My hand is squeezing the delicate device too tightly, I can hear the plastic creek under the pressure. I have to make a conscious effort to loosen my grip before I have to get a replacement.

"Yes, I'll definitely have to keep that in mind in the future." There's no way I'm telling her that Hollie is the employee in question. She seems to have some affection for my former assistant. Of fucking course.

"You know, you're really going to have to give that young lady a raise."

The last thing I want to do is talk about Hollie but I'm curious why she would have such a ridiculous notion.

"And why is that?" I ask.

She lets out a chuckle that I can barely hear over the miles that separate us before continuing. "I'll be honest with you, Mr. Clarke... I decided to sell the property to you after I spoke to Hollie earlier in the week."

"Excuse me?" the question comes out in a little squeak that would have wounded my male pride if I had any left at this point. "You spoke to my Hollie?"

She doesn't even bother to hold back her laugh this time around. "She called me a few days after our meeting and asked about obtaining some of the old Village memorabilia I have sitting around. Wouldn't tell me what exactly it was for, but I figured if there was someone that wanted to keep something of the old place, they probably deserved to be entrusted with the whole thing. Few people care about preserving the past anymore and if either your company or even Hollie in particular wants to do so, with something so small as even a room key, then I think they're the right people to protect my city."

Well, fuck. I wondered where Hollie found that key. She had gone straight to the woman herself. She did that for me. But why? She had no reason to do something like that for me when she was only trying to get close enough to me to fuck up this deal for her father.

Now I find out, because of that one kind gesture she made for me, I'm going to get the property I've had my eye on for months. Years, if I'm honest. What am I supposed to do with that kind of information? The Village was all I ever wanted until I thought I had Hollie. Then all I wanted was her. At least I'll get out of this with one of them.

"You're sure?"

"Don't try to talk me out of it. Yes, I'm sure. Unless whatever you send me is outrageous, you officially have a site for your next Clarke Hotel. Just do me proud Mr. Clarke... or I'll come back and haunt you."

Laughter bursts forth from my chest. When this woman isn't actively hating my guts, she's rather amusing. "I'll keep that in mind, but I think we've got a lot of years to come before I have to worry about that problem."

"Flatterer."

An idea is circling my head, one that was planted there by my wayward assistant and is being stoked by Caroline DuPont herself. It's not what I presented to the board, but the past day has been such an emotional shit show that I don't care. This is what I want. If I have to use my own money, then I will.

"Mrs. DuPont, I have an idea I want to run by you."

By the time I make it to the office, it's already past eleven. I'm ready to put on a clean suit and get to work on the new proposal for the Santa Cruz project. It's nice to not have the pressure of competition at this point if I believe Caroline DuPont. And surprisingly, I do.

The elevator bell dings and expels me onto the executive floor. The place is dead, as it should be on a Saturday morning. I glance to my right and notice that Richard's office is closed up tight, which is an immense relief. I'm dreading the moment I have to tell him we need to find me a new personal assistant. As soon as he finds out I was fucking her, he's going to kill me. Once he discovers that she's Patrick Shaw's daughter, he'll probably dismember my body and make sure that no trace of me is ever found.

Maybe I can tell him she won the lottery.

As I make my way down the hall, I notice that there is a light on in my office. That's odd. It was off last night when I left and even if it wasn't, security would have turned it off for me on their rounds.

I slow my pace as I get closer and see that the door isn't pulled completely closed. There's definitely somebody inside. I can hear them speaking. For a second, I think about summoning security up from the lobby, but anyone in the building must have had to pass them already, which means they belong here. Not in *my* office, but in the building, at the very least. As soon as I'm close enough to make out their words clearly, I stop and ease back into the shadows.

"He has no fucking clue, that little shithead. He's never even suspected me. I'm telling you, the kid is fucking oblivious to what happens right under his nose. I mean, I'm using his own fucking phone to call you in case he looks at phone records, which he never does."

Uncle Gilbert's voice is clear as day, but I don't know why he would be in my office or who he's talking to. It's a good ten seconds before he continues the conversation, so I'm guessing he's on the phone with someone.

"Just remember that you promised me the full hundred thousand for this one. My creditors aren't exactly the most patient men, if you know what I mean."

What the fuck is he talking about? Who is paying this idiot a hundred thousand dollars for anything? He's lucky he can tie his own shoes. The only reason that Clarke Hotels still exists is because I took it out of his greedy little hands. I inch closer and peer inside the cracked open door.

Gilbert Clarke is sitting at my desk, leaning back with his hands behind his head and his feet up on my mahogany desk. He looks like he owns the place. Pissed off doesn't even begin to cover what I'm feeling right now.

I'm also thoroughly confused. I should have had another cup of coffee this morning.

"It was one of the easiest things I've ever done. That slut was in his office fucking him, and all I had to do was snatch the envelope for the DuPont woman and toss it into my briefcase. Neither of them even knew it was missing."

The mention of Caroline DuPont makes my ears perk up as I attempt to put together the pieces from his side of the conversation.

"It was fucking beautiful. Not only do we get to ruin Archer's pet project, but we pin the entire thing on his little assistant. When I told you her name and you said she was your daughter, I couldn't fucking believe it. It's goddamn perfect. Osman has been sniffing around the board members, looking for whoever's been talking to you. Now, with little Hollie getting the blame, it will be back to business as usual and we're completely covered. The entire thing was a work of art. I wish I could have been there to see the look on his face when you outed her as your daughter."

My blood runs cold and the ache that's been in my chest since last night takes that moment to turn into a stabbing pain. He's talking about Hollie. He pinned it on her? All at once, I realize what happened. As soon as I handed Hollie the envelopes containing the proposals, we had locked ourselves away in my office and I had fucked her like it was my job.

Apparently, Gilbert took that moment of distraction to snatch the envelope from Hollie's desk and get rid of it.

Holy shit. He's talking to Patrick Shaw. They planned this entire thing. Just the two of them. And from the sounds of it, this isn't the first time they exchanged company information.

There's silence in the office, probably because Patrick Shaw doesn't know how to shut his mouth. This time when I grab my phone, I don't hesitate to call security up from downstairs. The conversation trails to an end and I hear the handset hit the cradle. I have to get in there now. I can't wait around for security to show up.

Pushing through the partially opened door, I take in the sight of this parasite sitting in my chair, feet *still* on my mahogany desk, and attempting to light a goddamn cigar.

"Archer!" He jumps up and shoves the cigar into his pocket. He has the good grace to look a little sheepish, but it's obvious that he doesn't realize that I overheard his entire conversation. "I'm sorry about using your office, but I didn't think you would be in on a Saturday. I had to make some calls in privacy, you understand." It's not a question but a statement.

My body is so tight with tension that it feels like I might unload like a spring at any second. I keep up my calm and cool demeanor even though I'm anything but.

"Really? What kind of call do you need so much privacy for?"

"Just checking in with some of the board members." He gives me a look that's both sympathetic and pitying at the same time. "I wanted to see what they were thinking after the Santa Cruz property fell through. We put a lot of time into making that happen. I wanted to make sure they were all as confident in you as I am, my boy."

A sardonic smile creeps up on my lips. "Oh, don't worry, we didn't lose the Santa Cruz property."

Gilbert looks like he's about to drop dead of a heart attack. I'm not even concerned. His mouth is moving, but he doesn't seem to be able to get any words out.

"That's right, I spoke to Caroline DuPont myself this morning. She's selling the property to us, and it's all thanks to Hollie."

At that, he finally finds his voice.

"But she's Patrick Shaw's daughter!"

My face turns to stone, and I give him a look that tells him I know everything. "How would you know that? I only found out last night and I haven't told a soul."

"Well, I—"

"Forget it, Gilbert. I heard your entire conversation with Shaw just now. I know everything. Giving Patrick Shaw information, corporate espionage, framing Hollie. Everything. What I don't understand is why you would do something like this."

"Why I would do this?" he snarls at me, spittle escaping his mouth. The two burley security guards come barreling into the room, but Gilbert's anger is so acute and focused on me he doesn't seem to notice the new audience. "Of course you would ask that. You're so self-centered you don't see anything else. You took *my* company from me. Some snot-nosed kid comes in and thinks that he can just take my job away? It's bullshit!"

"If I had left you in charge, there wouldn't be anything left." My voice is cold as ice. I always knew it had been hard for him, but I didn't think that he resented, no hated, me this much. Enough to sabotage our family's business.

He carries on like I haven't said a thing. "I got a pittance when your parents died and they cut my salary back to basically nothing when I was pushed onto the board. You owe me!" He's screaming now and I'm completely and absolutely done with him. My parents left him a pittance? Wouldn't he rather have his brother back than any amount of money in the world? I know I would. I'm beyond disgusted as I instruct the security guards to escort him out of the building and confiscate his access card.

He pulls out of their grasp and heads to the door with his head held high, like it was his idea to leave.

"Oh, Uncle Gilbert," I call after him. He pauses for a moment and looks back at me. "You can expect a visit from the cops. Corporate espionage is a federal crime, after all." Face ghostly white, he scurries out of my office, the two security officers trailing behind him.

Feeling like I've just done another triathlon, I collapse back onto the couch. The same couch I had Hollie spread open wide on. Could that really only have been two days ago?

Happiness moves through my body, filling up every empty part of me. Hollie didn't do it. She was just as loyal as she said she was. Then, my mood plummets down further than before, if it were possible.

The things I said to her.

I didn't believe her.

I didn't give her a chance to explain.

The devastated look on her face when I fired her.

There's that stabbing pain again. She's never going to forgive me and there's a voice in the back of my head that says she shouldn't. I should have trusted her. I always knew deep down she was trustworthy, but the shock of finding out like that and the fact we had just lost the deal clouded my better judgment.

Sure, she kept the fact she was Patrick Shaw's daughter from me. But now that I'm not being burned by searing betrayal, I can better understand her actions. We barely knew each other, and we've only started sleeping together recently. Why would she tell me who her father is? If I'm honest with myself, I remember her trying to stop me and tell me something in Santa Cruz. Fuck, who am I kidding? I remember every single moment of that night. I thought she was going to tell me she was inexperienced, and I didn't give a fuck about that. If I had listened, trusted her, this entire situation could have been avoided.

Maybe if I'm lucky, she'll take pity on me and forgive me. All I can do is try. What other option do I have? Live my life without her? Not fucking likely.

TWENTY-THREE

HOLLIE

"Paige!"

I wrap my arms around my little sister protectively and squeeze a little too tight. Her small body is shaking in my arms and if I could transfer some of my strength to her through this hug, I would.

I glance around the small room that smells strongly of antiseptic and has machines shoved into every corner. A steady stream of whirls and beeps fill the space as they all do whatever their jobs are.

Looking past my sister, I spy the slight form huddled under blankets on the bed. A sigh escapes my lungs and I'm not sure if it's one of frustration or relief. Probably both.

From the moment my phone woke me from my dreamless sleep at 3 a.m., I've been in survival mode, focusing all my energy on putting one foot in front of the other. I haven't let myself feel any complex emotions. If I did, I would break down entirely and be no good to anyone.

The second my weary eyes saw Paige's picture lighting up my phone, I knew something was terribly wrong. There was no good reason Paige would call me at that time of morning. I answered, bracing for the worst, and that's basically what I got.

"What happened?" I ask, while extracting myself from our hug and drift across the room to the occupied hospital bed where it's obvious Mom is asleep.

Her skin looks like it's almost gray and the lines on her face are more pronounced than I've ever seen them before.

My mother was considered a real beauty in her youth. Men clambered after her everywhere she went. After she got deep into the alcohol and drugs, her good looks had faded and were replaced with someone that looked like life had been rough on her. The last time I visited was only three months ago, and it looks like she's aged ten years since then.

"I'm not exactly sure." Paige's voice is a little shaky as tries to hold back tears. She's one of the strongest people I know, even at her age, but this is a hard blow. "I got a call from the hospital that she was here. I guess she overdosed, probably on heroin. Apparently, somebody dumped her on the sidewalk outside and then drove off."

"Jeff." I mutter the name like a curse. I guess I should just be thankful he even bothered to drive her to the hospital and didn't let her die in some shitty drug den God only knows where.

She shrugs, looking much younger than her sixteen years. "I had to call one of my friends to bring me over here because the buses don't run that late. I told her she didn't need to stay with me and sent her back home."

My breath hitches in my throat. She needs a car. I left her here with an unreliable mother and no car. My eyes close as the guilt washes over me. I tried to take care of both of them the best I could, but it obviously hasn't been enough. A change has to happen here, quick.

Now, Paige needs to be my top priority and, as luck would have it, I have no job or boyfriend tying me down.

"I'm so sorry you had to deal with this all on your own. I should have been here for you. For both of you." A tear slides down my cheek and I quickly wipe it away.

"Don't, Hollie. You do everything for us. We wouldn't make it... *I* wouldn't make it if it wasn't for you. I'm still glad you're here though." She gives a humorless laugh and settles into the chair next to the bed.

I reach down and grab Mom's hand. It's so cold that if the heart monitor wasn't steadily beeping away next to me, I would think she was dead. I hear a noise to my right and for the first time I notice that there's a curtain separating Mom's bed from another one. It's a tight fit with all of us in here, and if the other occupant had anyone visiting them, we would positively spill out into the hallway. But when you're poor, beggars can't be choosers.

"Has the doctor been in yet?" I ask quietly, trying not to disturb our roommate.

"Just some nurses. They told me a few things, but honestly, I didn't really understand what they were talking about. I know they gave her Naloxone and they think that she's going to be okay, but they won't tell me when she'll wake up."

Instead of waiting around for someone to stop by and explain what's going on, I make my way to the nurses' station to see what information I can get. I don't know what we're going to do. Even before I got fired, there was no way we could afford a hospital stay. Who knows how long they'll want to keep her here? I put together a rough estimate in my head and the sum is staggering. The sad thing is that I'm probably still way below what it will actually end up costing.

The nurse at the desk assures me she'll have the doctor come speak to us as soon as possible and I make my way back to the room. By the time I return, Paige is passed out in the chair next to the bed.

Poor kid probably didn't get any sleep at all last night. Not that I did either. I was worried I might fall asleep on the four-hour drive here. Instead, I was in my own personal hell, sponsored by Toyota. Being trapped in a tiny car with nobody for company except my own thoughts is a circle of hell that I don't remember Dante discussing.

If I wasn't freaking out about Mom being in the hospital, then I couldn't stop seeing the expression on Archer's face when he fired me. His eyes were so cold it was as if he had never seen me before. I'm still hurt. Devastated, really. But I'm also pissed. We could have been great together, but he wouldn't listen to a simple explanation. He wouldn't give me five minutes of his time after everything we'd been through. It was like he was just looking for an excuse to get rid of me. He took a knife and swiftly carved me out of his life, both personally and professionally.

It's another hour before a severe looking older man in scrubs and a white coat enters the room. The doctor appears to be in his sixties and his expression says that those years weren't very enjoyable. When he finally spots me leaning against the wall across the room, I can feel the disapproval coming off of him in waves.

"You're Mrs. Simmons's next of kin?"

"It's Miss and yes, I'm her daughter, Hollie. It's nice to meet you. What can you tell me about my mom?"

"She is extremely lucky." The look in his eyes says he isn't necessarily happy about it. I bristle and pull away from the wall. "It appears to have started with a heroin overdose," he rifles through the notes on his clipboard, "but that triggered a minor heart attack. Then there is the fact that she was dumped out of a moving car, so she has several bruises and abrasions, but nothing's broken." My entire body stiffens. No one had said anything about a heart attack. This is worse than I thought, much worse.

"Do you know when she'll wake up or when we'll be able to take her out of here?"

"When she can leave? That will depend entirely upon when she wakes up, which could happen any time. She'll probably only need to remain another twenty-four hours for observation after that."

I let out a sigh of relief. If she wakes up soon, that will only be two days in the hospital. There's still no way in hell that I can afford it, but it's a lot better than a week.

"Listen," he says, "we'll get her on her feet and out of here, but if something doesn't change, she's going to be right back in this bed or worse. She needs to get into a detox and rehab program if you want to have any chance of turning this around."

I want to fault him for delivering that kind of news so callously, but it was the cold, hard truth. Every word. I've known for a long time that at any moment she could be gone forever, but what could I do?

"Do you have any information on those programs? Something provided by the state maybe?" I ask hopefully.

I can see his gaze soften the tiniest bit. Maybe he can feel a little bit of sympathy after all.

"If you go downstairs, there are case managers that should be able to help with that. But to be honest with you, there is a waiting list a mile long for those facilities. If you combine her cardiac issues with the drug use, I don't know how long she has to wait."

My hands are shaking when the doctor leaves us. I'm at a complete loss. I always have a plan, a solution, but right now... I just want to lie down and cry. I can feel the full weight of the world on my shoulders and I have what's possibly the most insane thought that's ever been thought.

I wish Archer was here.

Well, I've finally cracked under the pressure. I don't know if it's my brain or my heart thinking such traitorous thoughts, but either way, they're wrong. I don't wish he was here. If I ever thought I could count on him for anything, he proved me wrong last night. I'm disposable, like every other woman is to every other man of his social standing. I should have listened to my mother.

Now I *know* I've lost it.

Paige has her bright eyes locked on me and I can tell she's waiting for my plan. How I'm going to fix this. So I say the only thing that I can. "Don't worry, I'll take care of everything." She doesn't look like she believes me and frankly, I don't believe me either.

I collapse into the chair next to her and take her hand in my own, giving it a squeeze to tell her I love her.

"I'm going to move back to Milford."

"What?!"

I shush her before the person on the other side of the thin curtain complains. "Look Paige, if Mom is going to go to rehab then you have to stay with someone. I know you don't want to leave your friends and school and have to start over in Seattle. Plus, if I'm here, then I can help with Mom when she comes home. It makes the most sense."

"But what about your friends and your job?"

I give her a sad smile. "I'm going to miss Violet and B like crazy, but they're only a four-hour drive away. Plus, they'll have a spare bedroom now so I can stay over sometimes. As for my job—" There's no way I'm telling her I got fired. She'll freak out and want me to tell her what happened "—I was thinking about making a change, anyway. My boss was an asshole."

She lets out a laugh and then wraps her arm around my shoulders, giving me a side hug. "I don't want you moving here for me, but I won't lie. I've really missed you."

"I've missed you too, Paige."

Before long, I decide to send her home with my car so that she can get some sleep. Mom hasn't woken up yet, so there's no need for both of us to sit here. I glance at my phone and almost subconsciously note that Archer hasn't tried to get in touch with me. I'm not really surprised but my foolish heart had hoped. It's nearing the end of the day and I want to see if there's anyone in the case management office. The sooner I can try to get some information on the rehab programs, the better. Besides, I need to get a payment plan in place.

The case management office is really just a drab windowless room in the basement that houses four desks with one person clacking away at her computer. After the gruff middle-aged woman piles me up with pamphlets on local state run rehab programs, I broach the subject that makes me want to run screaming out of the building and never look back.

"I was wondering if you have some sort of payment plan for my mom's stay here." The woman gives me a small sympathetic smile and turns back to her computer screen.

"I'll need her name, date of birth, and social security number if you have it," she says while typing furiously on the keyboard in front of her. I rattle the information off to her sans the social—I mean really, who knows someone else's social security number?—and wait for her to work her computer magic. She stops typing and looks back up at me with wide eyes. "Actually, Miss. Simmons, you have a zero balance. It appears her bill has been taken care of."

"What?" I must not have heard her right, or maybe she's looking at the wrong account. Yes, it's got to be the wrong account. "That's Simmons with two Ms," I say, correcting the common mistake.

"I've got her information right here and her billing is being handled by a third party."

I'm stunned for a moment but manage to ask, "Can you tell me who's taking care of it?"

She's shaking her head before I even finish the question. "Per HIPAA, since you're neither the patient nor the person who has paid the bills, I can't release that information to you." She rattles that explanation off at me like she gives it several times a day.

I decide to drop it for now. They'll figure out eventually that we owe them. Who ever heard of a hospital that forgot to get their money? As I'm approaching my mom's room, I see an orderly has her on a gurney and is pushing her down the hallway towards me. Panic sharpens all my senses. I was only gone for twenty minutes. What happened?

"Excuse me, where are you taking my mother?"

The orderly looks up and gives me a smile. He seems to be about my age and doesn't appear to be in any kind of hurry, so I relax a bit, figuring that he's not rushing her into emergency surgery or something, so she must be okay.

"Regina Simmons is your mom?" he asks, waiting for my nod of confirmation before continuing. "I've got an order here that she needs to change rooms."

"Let me grab my purse and I'll go with you." People get shuffled around in hospitals all the time, so it doesn't even occur to me that there's a problem until we enter her new room three floors up.

This room looks like it belongs in a hotel, not a hospital. The walls are covered with a welcoming geometric wallpaper and there is a sitting area that contains a couch, chairs, and a coffee table. The room is lit by lamps and not harsh fluorescent lights. There's one hospital bed, and it's covered with blankets and pillows that look much more comfortable than the ones downstairs.

"I'm sorry, there's been a mistake," I tell the orderly as a woman walks in and helps him transfer my mom to the much nicer hospital bed.

He grabs his clipboard from where it's lying on the edge of the gurney and looks over whatever notes he has. "Nope, says right here, Regina Simmons needs to be moved to room 513."

"But there's no way we can afford this," I try to explain, but this guy doesn't seem to care.

"You'll have to take it up with the duty nurse. The orders came from there, sorry." He shrugs and scurries out of the room with the other orderly while I tentatively take my place in a leather chair next to her bed.

Who the hell can afford a room like this? The amount of money these cost must be obscene. Now that I'm finally sitting in a chair that's not hard plastic, my lack of sleep catches up with me and it's not long before my eyes are lured closed and I sink into the darkness.

TWENTY-FOUR

ARCHER

I decide not to call her. What I have to say needs to be said in person. No mere text or phone call can convey to her how much I've epically fucked up.

I don't even realize I've neglected to change my clothes until I show up on Hollie's doorstep thirty minutes later. I don't see her little Camry parked in the driveway and take that as a bad sign. The car is so old it's practically a death trap. I make a mental note to call a dealership and get her the safest car on the market. Even if she doesn't forgive me, at least I'll know that she's safe driving around the city.

I call out her name as I pound my fist against the door. I probably should have stopped and gotten her flowers or something, but she's not the type of person to be swayed by such frivolous things. If I'm wrong and she wants flowers, then I'll buy them for her every day for the rest of her life. I'll buy her the whole fucking store if that will make her happy and give me a second chance.

I knock again when nobody comes to the door. Unfortunately, I didn't account for what I would do if she wasn't home. I needed to get here and make things right or else I would regret it forever. The longer I left things like this between us, the more likely she was to close off from me permanently and that wasn't an acceptable outcome.

After waiting five minutes, I reluctantly accept that nobody is home and weigh my options. I could either call her or go home and try again later. I don't know where else she might be besides the office and I just came from there. Instead, I decide to take a seat on the cold cement of her front porch and lean back against the blue house siding. She has to come home at some point, I can wait her out.

I try to use this time to come up with exactly what I'm going to say to her but everything seems to fall short. It's going to be a miracle if she gives me another chance. My back is hunched and my eyes are down, contemplating a bleak future without her when my thoughts are interrupted by an angry female voice.

"Hey, Vi? Did you order a sad pathetic billionaire because there seems to be one on our porch?"

My head snaps up and I immediately take in the sight of two women standing in front of me, hands on hips, and giving me matching death stares. The one that just spoke is tall with darker features and long brown hair. I immediately peg her as Dante Moreno's daughter. There is a definite resemblance. The other woman is standing at her side, eyeing me warily with her black hair pulled back into a ponytail. They both appear to be about the same age as Hollie.

"No, I didn't. I think we better return it back to where it came from."

I slowly rise to my feet and make a futile effort at straightening my suit in an attempt at being semi-presentable. Stretching my hand out to the young Miss. Moreno, "Hi. Archer Clarke. Nice to meet you."

She eyes my hand like it's covered in spiders. Instead of shaking it, she merely says, "Bianca Moreno. And this is Violet Daniels." She indicates the woman next to her, who is eyeing me up and down curiously. I get the impression that Violet might be an old soul and the more reasonable of the two to deal with.

She doesn't bother to shake my hand either, just gives me a jerky nod and keeps a close eye on me like she expects me to do something crazy at any moment. So much for my theory on her being the easier of the two. Since neither is interested, I drop my hand back to my side and take a step back, giving them space.

They are obviously Hollie's two roommates and just as obviously not a fan of mine. Not that I can blame them.

"I'm looking for Hollie," I stupidly let them know, as if there is any other reason I would be sitting here on their front stoop in the middle of the day.

"I figured," Bianca says, not bothering to hide her dislike of me. At least Hollie has some solid friends to stand up for her. "She's not here, and I don't think she would appreciate coming home and finding you here. I think you should go."

"Look, I realize she hates me right now, and she has every right to. I deserve it." My best course of action here is honesty. I can tell they won't put up with anything less when it comes to their friend. "I fucked up. I know that and I want—*need*—to fix it. If she'll just hear me out."

"Like you heard her out?" Violet asks me coolly. Her eyes are a striking shade of blue and are locked on me, cataloging every move I make.

"Believe me, no one is more angry at me than I am. I can promise you that. She was set up. I should have believed her."

"Set up?" Bianca asks.

"By both my uncle and her father. They were trying to sabotage my deal and framed Hollie for it to draw the attention away from themselves. The only reason I even figured it out was because I walked in on my uncle on the phone with Patrick Shaw an hour ago. I need to talk to her. Please." I can't remember the last time I said please to someone. It was probably Hollie.

Some of the fight seems to go out of the both of them and I'm a little surprised that they seem to believe me.

"That motherfucker," Bianca mumbles under her breath while Violet stands there shaking her head. "I knew that man was a piece of shit, but I didn't think he would bother framing her for something. I mean, honestly, I didn't even think she was on his radar enough for him to do it."

That confirms what Hollie was saying about him not being a part of her life. Not that I needed the confirmation. I believed her about everything the moment I heard my uncle on the phone.

"Why don't we go inside?" Violet asks, moving past me. I follow behind her into the entryway and watch as they set down their bags. Bianca points me towards the couch in the living room where I take a seat, my ass grateful to be sitting on something other than the concrete I've been on for the past few hours.

Instead of sitting, they both take up positions of power by standing directly in front of me. Smart girls. I'm glad Hollie's friends are just as clever and sensible as she is.

I sit patiently, waiting for them to begin. I'm very obviously not the one running the show here.

"How about you tell us about this?" Bianca reaches across the coffee table and hands me her phone. It's open on a picture of me and Julia Kellogg. I can tell it's from last night because I have on the same suit that I'm wearing right now. However, it looks exponentially crisper in the photo. Julia's arm is wrapped around my waist and she's giving the camera a lascivious smile. My body language is stiff with my arms at my sides and my gaze is somewhere off in the distance. Unsurprisingly, I have zero recollection of this moment. Everything after my confrontation with Hollie is a blur.

"What is this?" I ask, handing the phone back to her.

"I asked you first," she replies saucily, but then continues without letting me get a word in. "Hollie comes home telling us how horrible she feels about what she did and that her boss and *lover* won't even give her the time of day to let her explain. Then we find a picture with you and your ex splashed all around the internet that was taken maybe two hours after you broke her heart."

"I broke her heart?" I'm both hopeful that she might care enough about me to have a broken heart and horrified that I'm the man that caused it.

She rolls her eyes, not bothering to respond to that.

"I'll be honest with you, I was only at the dinner another twenty minutes after Hollie left. I don't even remember taking that picture. She must have come up to me and posed for the cameras. I don't care about Julia. At all. I never have. I promise you that Hollie is the only woman I've ever loved."

"You love her?" Violet jumps into the conversation. I didn't mean to tell these girls before I even told Hollie, but I don't have much of a choice. I need to get through these two if I want to see her anytime soon.

"Yes, I do. Please don't say anything to her. I haven't even told her yet. I hoped it might help when I'm pleading for forgiveness."

Violet relaxes a little, but Bianca still looks like a snake coiled to strike.

"I know it's a cliche, but if you hurt her, more than you already have, I'll kill you. Remember that my father owns a construction company. We could dump your body into a pit and put a building right on top of it. No one would ever find you. Just remember that."

Okay, this one's a little frightening, but I have to respect how much she cares about her friend. "If I hurt her, I'll jump in there myself, I swear."

Bianca seems appeased when she says, "I wasn't lying when I said she wasn't home. She's not here."

"Do you know when she'll be back?"

"A couple of days? I'm honestly not sure."

"Days?" I ask, panic rising inside me. That's too long to go without fixing things between us.

Violet and Bianca exchange a look that I can't quite interpret. This time, it's Violet that turns to me. "I don't know what she's told you about her family, but she got a phone call early this morning from her sister. Her mom overdosed, and she's in the hospital. She took off back to Milford to be with them."

Fuck. She needed me, but I was drinking myself stupid on the balcony of a hotel room. If I hadn't been such an asshole, she would have been with me when her sister called this morning. I could have taken her back home. Helped her. Maybe I still can.

I try to shove my mind back into my no-nonsense business mode when I demand, "Tell me everything."

I need all the facts of the situation so that I can tackle this new problem. They tell me everything they know and I take down all the information. The two of them provide Hollie's mom's name, her address, and the hospital she's being treated at. I'm not sure why these two are being so accommodating, but I won't look a gift horse in the mouth.

I may not have been able to be with her last night, but I'll be damned if I let her handle this thing on her own. Even if she doesn't forgive me, the least I can do is help her with this.

After leaving Hollie's house and her still slightly suspicious roommates, I make the drive back to my house. I need to take a shower, finally change out of this suit, and pack a bag for a few days. While I'm in my bedroom gathering some essentials, I form a loose plan of what I can do to help.

I have some calls to make, but I can do that from the road. I'd hire a driver to make things easier, but I don't think they would drive fast enough for my current degree of desperation. Even though the Maserati is by far my fastest car, I decide to take the Corvette. Hollie mentioned she wanted to go for a drive in it once and I'll use anything I can at this point to give me an advantage. I toss my duffel bag in the tiny back seat and hit the road. The GPS says that the trip will take about four hours. I bet I can make it in three.

TWENTY-FIVE

HOLLIE

"Hollie?" a worn, scratchy voice calls out to me as I slowly climb my way out of a restless sleep.

I jump out of the chair that's way too comfortable to belong in a hospital and rush over to the bed.

"Mom? Can you hear me?" I grab her hand and see that her eyes are open but unfocused.

"I have ears don't I?" I don't know why I thought a drug overdose, a heart attack, and a stay in the hospital would soften her up some, but I was obviously wrong.

I hit the call button to alert the nurse that Mom's awake enough to harass me.

"Do you remember what happened?" I ask her, wondering if she even knows where she is or why she's here.

"Not really. Why aren't you in Seattle?" She pauses a moment to peer around the room. It doesn't look like any hospital room I've ever been in, but the bed and gown are a dead giveaway. "Where are we?"

"You're in the hospital," I answer her. "You overdosed yesterday. Then had a heart attack," I add.

"I don't know what kind of hospital you've got me in but I don't need to be here," she huffs out. "I'm fine. We can get out of here." I should have expected this. She never has made the right decision. Now she wants to get out of the hospital before she's been cleared.

She looks so small in that big hospital bed, especially with all the tubes and wires hooked up to her. I'm a little surprised she hasn't started shaking or throwing up from withdrawals, but I'm sure that will come upon us shortly. That's something neither one of us is looking forward to. I'll have to get used to it if I'm going to move back here and help take care of her and Paige.

I'm about to argue with her about staying in bed when a tall woman in a white coat walks into the room, giving the open door a courtesy knock. She's around my mother's age and has an air of authority around her. She's obviously someone that knows what she's doing and is confident in her abilities.

"Regina, I see you're awake. That's some good news." She grabs the chart at the end of the bed and starts making notes.

"Excuse me," I interrupt, "what happened to the other doctor?"

She looks up at me with a smile before answering. "Ms. Simmons has been transferred into my care. I'm Doctor Duma. Now let's see what we can do to get you out of here and back on your feet as quickly as possible."

A new doctor? I don't know what the hell is going on in this place, but I don't have the energy to ask any longer. I'm so stressed and confused, I decide I'm just going to go along with the program. Why bother fighting about billing, a private room, or a new doctor when no one is listening to me anyway?

Mom perks up at the idea of getting out of the hospital and she sits up in her bed, trying to scoot to the edge. "Listen Doc, there's nothing wrong with me. I can get out of here now. I'm perfectly fine."

Dr. Duma gives my mom a frown and reviews the chart once again. "Actually, you should be here for another two days so that we can monitor that heart arrhythmia that you had. After that, someone from the rehab will be here to collect you."

At the mention of rehab, she starts protesting loudly. I let out a sigh of frustration. I had meant to gently break the idea of going to rehab to her because I figured she would freak out. Not only does my mom not care to fix her drug and alcohol problems, but she doesn't think she has a problem in the first place.

"Mom!" I snap sharply, bringing their attention to me. "You overdosed on heroin and had a fucking heart attack. Your loser boyfriend dumped you out of his car on the curb in front of the hospital. Don't you think it's time to get your shit together? Paige was all alone. Something could have happened to her."

I see a flash of fear and remorse in her eyes before it's replaced once again with defiance. I don't know if it was for Paige or herself, but at least she still has some emotions buried deep down. "Watch your mouth, Hollie. I'm still your mother and I don't need to go to rehab. Occasionally I like to party. So what? It's not like I have an actual problem. I'll slow down some."

I can't help but toss my hands in the air. The woman is completely delusional, not that I expected anything more from her. "It's more than that Mom, you almost *died*. You need to go to rehab. Please. If not for yourself or for me, then at least for Paige. She's still in high school. She needs you."

Mom looks like she's about to continue protesting when Doctor Duma interrupts this awkward family interaction that she's unwillingly become a party to. "They're scheduled to have someone here to accompany you to their facility in southern California the day after tomorrow, so you'll need to make your decision quickly."

"There must be some mistake. I don't have a rehab lined up yet. I need to make some calls and see if I can get her into some sort of state program. If you have any recommendations for that, I'd be grateful to hear them."

She looks at the notes once again before continuing with a frown of confusion. "It says right here that she has a room reserved at Bridges in California and when I spoke to Mr. Clarke, he mentioned that she already had a place to go."

If I was attached to the same sensors as my mother right now, I'm pretty sure they would have recorded the moment that my heart stopped. A few seconds later, it kicks back into motion, beating furiously in my chest, trying to make up for the beats that it missed.

"Mr. Clarke?" I ask, just in case I'm having auditory hallucinations now.

"Yes, Archer Clarke. I spoke to him on the phone earlier today before your mother was transferred to me. Is something wrong?"

It all makes sense. The billing that's being taken care of by a third party, the fancy private room, a new doctor, and now a rehab facility lined up. I should have realized sooner. This has Archer written all over it. That I didn't see it earlier is a testament to how distraught I've been over the past day. God, could it have only been twenty-four hours since my disastrous date with him?

Why would he do this? He doesn't owe me anything. He's already made it clear that he never wanted to see me again. Hell, he even threatened to have me arrested. How did he even find out I'm here? I don't know whether to laugh in disbelief or cry because I fucking miss him. But it seems my body has already made its choice when I feel a tear slip down my cheek and land on my shirt.

"But, why?" I ask the doctor, hoping she'll have some insight for me. She spoke to him, after all. I glance at my phone and don't see any missed texts or calls. He didn't even bother speaking to me before he did any of this.

"I'm sorry, Miss. Simmons, you'll have to ask him. He only told me you're both to receive anything that you want and the best care and treatments that we can provide."

Maybe I'm not really here. It's possible I'm a few floors below locked in the psychiatric ward because I feel like I'm in crazy town right now.

"Isn't that your boss?" Mom asks, her voice dripping with venom and loathing.

"If you'll excuse me, I have to see other patients. I'll be by later to check in with you." Doctor Duma places Mom's chart back into the holder at the end of the bed and exits the room, leaving me to face off against my mother.

"Mom, he isn't even my boss anymore," I try to explain.

"I should have known there was no way you were making all that money by being some man's personal assistant. What a fucking slut."

"Mom!" The fact that she's calling me names doesn't hurt. She's called me much worse before, and she's not even wrong about my relationship with my boss, so there's no use denying it. For a little while, I was more than his assistant. "You don't understand. Hell, *I* don't understand. There's no reason for him to do this. He hates me. I don't even work for him anymore. I already told Paige I'm moving back here to help and be with her while you're in rehab."

"No."

The word is said so harshly behind me, I spin around, almost losing my balance. In the doorway is the object of our current argument himself, Archer Clarke. Even though his clothes are rumpled and it doesn't seem like he's shaved or even slept, he still looks better than any man I've ever seen.

Hell, has he gotten even more handsome since last night?

"Are you trying to leave me, angel?" I almost burst into tears at hearing him call me angel again. Almost.

Instead, I remind myself of how cruelly he spoke to me last night before he cast me aside like I always knew that he would.

"Don't call me that," I snap, letting the hurt that's inside me seep out into the room. "It's not like there's anything keeping me in Seattle. I don't have a job or anything." He physically flinches, and I'm not sure if it's because of my tone or the words I spit at him.

"This is the boss?" Mom asks, reminding me she's in the room with us. She lets out a sharp, humorless laugh. "It fucking figures. Just look at him."

His eyes leave my face for a moment to flick over to my mother, but quickly return right back to me like she's of no consequence. "Can I speak to you in private, please?"

"The last time we spoke in private, you wouldn't even listen to me. Why should I even bother?" I cross my arms over my chest and I know I appear defensive, but frankly, I'm scared. Scared, he'll say something to break my heart all over again. Scared, he'll say something and draw me back in just to leave me ruined.

His eyes have turned imploring as he asks, "Please, Hollie? For just a minute. If you don't like what I have to say, then I swear I'll leave and never come back. I'm only asking you to hear me out."

"No." My spine strengthens with new resolve. "I don't have time for this. I don't have time for *you*. It would be best if you leave. Go back to Seattle. It's where you belong."

His shoulders seem to slump a bit, but his eyes stay glued to my face. "I know that you're not ready to listen to me yet and that's all right. I fucked up. You'll never know how sorry I am for the things I said to you. Since you obviously want me gone, I'll leave this room, but I'm not going anywhere." He points out to the hallway. "I'll be right out there when you need me."

"Don't hold your breath," I mutter while he turns and heads back out the door.

The next day is filled with doctors, tests, and the ever looming presence of Archer. Every time I leave Mom's room, I see him sitting in the small waiting area near the nurses' station. He's always either typing away on his phone, speaking with the caseworker, or staring simply at the entrance to our room. He doesn't try to come speak to me. He's just... there.

When I finally realize he has every intention of sitting there until I come and speak to him, I'm done. I have enough to deal with without him sitting there as a constant reminder of what I lost and what I could have again if I could just forget how poorly he treated me.

I make sure Mom's situated before heading out to the waiting area. As usual, he's sitting in the chair that's become his in my mind. I'm not sure the man's even gone to the restroom since I banished him from the room. He just always seems to be there. His face is decidedly scruffier than it was yesterday and his eyes look bloodshot.

I stand in front of him with my arms crossed protectively over my chest. His golden-brown eyes search my own and I'm both devastated and elated by the glimmer of hope I see in them.

"We need to talk," I bite out.

"Great." He gives me a smile and raises out of the chair before following me down the long empty hallway. It's evening now and there aren't as many people around, but there are still enough. I decide to search for a place where we can have some privacy.

Archer grabs my hand and my first instinct is to squeeze it more tightly to reassure myself that he's really here. Instead, I jerk my hand out of his grasp. He looks down at me with a frown but says nothing and doesn't try to recapture my hand. I pop my head into room after room until I find one that's apparently unoccupied. I usher him inside and leave the door cracked open behind us because I can't trust myself to be behind closed doors with him.

Maybe this wasn't such a good idea. The rooms on this floor are huge, but standing beside him, it feels like it's the size of a broom closet. It's hard to think when he's standing so close to me and I need to have my wits about me for this conversation, so I take a step backwards, adding to the space between us.

His frown deepens, but he doesn't do anything to close the distance.

"You need to leave my family and me alone. I don't want any of this. The doctor, the bills, the rehab. I don't know why you're doing it, but you need to stop." He takes another step closer to me and I don't back away this time, not wanting to give him an inch.

"I'm doing this because it's my job, Hollie. It's my job to take care of you and make sure you're alright." He stops and shakes his head. "No actually, that's not right. It's not my job. It's what I want to do. I want to spend every moment taking care of you, making sure that you're safe and happy."

They're pretty words and I want to believe them, but I can't. Not after everything that's happened. "I don't need you to take care of me, Archer. This is my family. I've been taking care of them for a long time without any help from you or anyone else."

"I know you have, angel, and you're amazing at it. But don't you understand? You're my family now. You're the only family that I have left, and that makes your mom and Paige my family too. I want to take care of all of you."

I suck in a breath as my eyes fill with tears. There's nothing more I'd rather do than believe him. It would be so much easier to let him help me, let him carry some of this weight. Instead, I stand there, silently looking at him and trying to hold back my tears.

"You can't move back here." His tone of voice says he's upset and his fists are clenched at his sides.

"Archer, I don't have a job. My sister needs me, and my mom obviously needs help, so I'm going to be here. I don't understand what's happening. How did you even find out I was here?"

"I went by your house and spoke to your roommates."
I'll kill them both.

He must be able to read the look on my face because the next words out of his mouth are, "Don't be upset with them. I basically threatened to camp out on your porch like a bum if they didn't help me get in contact with you."

"Why were you at my house?" I whisper.

"Because I'm a fucking idiot, Hollie." Well, I can't argue that point. He moves towards me and I take a matching step back. I can't let him touch me. If I do, I will give in to him in a matter of moments. "I'm so fucking sorry. I should have listened to you and I should have believed you. There's no excuse good enough, but I was just so stunned. I could have never imagined that Patrick Shaw was your father. You never mentioned him and we had just lost the Santa Cruz deal. The proposal never made it to Caroline DuPont, and you were the last person to have it. Add that to what Patrick said at the dinner and I jumped to all the wrong conclusions." Well, shit. I was the person who sent out the proposal's. No wonder he thought I had something to do with it going missing.

"I would never do that, I swear—" He shushes me and continues.

"I know it wasn't you, angel. None of this was your fault. I found out my uncle and your dad have been working together for years from the sound of it. They've been working behind the scenes to mess things up for me and the company for a long time. I should have known, I should have seen it. But I was so goddamn scared of how totally in fucking love with you I was that I freaked out. I was ready to give up Santa Cruz, to give up everything really, as long as I had you."

There's blood rushing in my ears as I study those whiskey-colored eyes that have captured me since the moment we first met. There's nothing but pure sincerity in them and maybe something else. Something that looks a lot like love.

"You loved me?"

"Love." He corrects and reaches out to grab my chin, pinning his gaze to mine. "I love you, Hollie. I can't live without you. You have to take me back because you've completely ruined me. I could never want anyone else. I need you with me, by my side, in my bed. Please, say you'll forgive me."

He looks completely distraught, and I get the feeling that the past few days have been as difficult for him as they have been for me. It's like an immense weight has been lifted off my shoulders, letting me breathe for the first time in days. He loves me. He actually loves me. There's no way he would lie about something like that. I'm about to jump into his arms but stop myself. "What about Julia?"

He pulls me into his arms, placing the sweetest kiss on my forehead, and I can't help but let out a sigh. It's been a horrible few days and I've missed him so damn much.

"Bianca showed me the picture. Honestly, I don't even remember taking it. She must have come up to me and posed. Once I left you last night, I was a total mess. I left about twenty minutes later and don't remember a moment of that time. Let me show you something." He reaches into his pocket, digging out his phone and after a few swipes, he hands it over to me. "These are the picture you should be looking at." He's on an image search for his name and there are rows and rows of pictures... of me. Well, of the two of us together. Most of them are from our walk down the red carpet, but there are a few candids thrown in too. In every single one, Archer is gazing down at me, adoration shining through his features. It's exactly the opposite of how he looked in the picture with Julia. I scan the captions.

Who is Archer Clarke's new girlfriend?

Archer and mystery girl.

Is Archer Clarke finally in love?

There are tears in my eyes when I look back up at him, handing his phone back.

"I couldn't even go home that night," he says. "My house, my bed, it was all empty without you. I stayed at the hotel and spent the night nursing my broken heart."

"You didn't get back together with her?"

"I thought I made myself clear, angel. I don't want anyone but you. Ever."

Without needing to hear any more, I move to my tiptoes and I seal my lips against his. He doesn't move for about three seconds, like he's waiting to see if I'm sure, then he moves in, forcing his tongue between my lips, taking what he needs from our kiss.

The moment is absolutely surreal. I never thought I'd see Archer again, let alone have his mouth on mine like he owns it. And he does own it. He really does.

The kiss is hot and animalistic. We're both pouring the pain and longing we've felt over the last few days into it. The kiss is both needy and healing, smoothing those sharp edges of the broken pieces inside me so that they fit perfectly against his own.

TWENTY-SIX

ARCHER

My chest aches, but this time it isn't from the pain of a broken and bleeding heart. It's because it feels so full. I have Hollie back in my arms, right where she belongs. My lips leave hers and I pepper kisses down the length of her neck and over her chest. My moves are frantic, like I can't stop at any one place on her body in my rush to taste all of her. She lets out a moan while clutching the back of my head, threading her fingers through my hair, urging me to continue.

I groan and start walking her backwards, further into the room, until she bumps up against the hospital bed. I leave her for a moment to dash across the room and shut the door. When I turn back to her, she's already whipping her top over her head, leaving her standing in only a bra.

I reach for the waist of her jeans and pop open the button before yanking them down her legs, along with her panties. She kicks them off while my mouth and hands attack her tits. Her nipples are already hard peaks as I drag my teeth across the lacy material that's still covering them. Her body gives a jolt and arches into my mouth.

My hands move to her sweet pussy and I dip a finger between her folds, running from her entrance up to her clit and back again. I let out a low growl when I feel the amount of moisture waiting there.

"You're so fucking wet. Is all this for me, angel?"

"Always," she lets out on a sigh and pushes her hips up, trying to get me to touch her where she needs it the most.

I grip her waist and pop her up onto the bed, leaning her back. She watches me with heavy-lidded eyes while I scramble to undo my belt and shove my pants and boxers down to right below my ass. I don't have the patience to fully remove them before I settle back against her. Those gorgeous thighs open for me. I take my hard cock in hand and line it up with her waiting entrance as her hands grip my shoulders, pulling me closer. With a quick and forceful thrust, I'm seated all the way inside her.

She lets out a scream that I quickly muffle with my mouth on top of her own. She's so tight and wet I'm worried my knees are going to fail me and let me topple to the ground. Nothing's ever felt as exquisite as Hollie's pussy, and I'm already looking forward to the years I'll get to spend with them both.

Bringing my thoughts of the future back to the here and now, I pull out almost completely before thrusting back in again, building up a steady rhythm while Hollie moans beneath me. Her legs are wrapped around my waist and she's meeting my every drive, urging me on. When her nails dig into my ass, I almost lose it. I'm rutting into her like an animal, my thrusts so forceful that the bed is scooting across the floor with each one.

"I'm sorry, angel. I'll make love to you next time. Right now, I need you."

"Yes," she whimpers, "Harder."

My speed picks up even more and soon we're both moaning and moving against each other uncontrollably, our bodies covered in a thin layer of sweat. I look down between us and can see my cock moving inside her, claiming her. Watching the physical representation of our soul-searing emotional connection turns me on even more, if that were possible. With a tingle at my spine, I know my orgasm is fast approaching and I need to make sure she goes over the edge with me. Reaching between our gyrating bodies, I press my thumb firmly against her clit and hear her desperately cry out my name. I keep up a steady pressure and move my thumb in slow circles before changing and moving it in the other direction. She's gasping and I can tell she's just as close as I am.

"Come for me, angel. You need to come on my cock, and I want that sweet pussy to milk me dry."

I give her clit one last hard pinch that sends her tumbling into bliss, capturing her lips with mine once again to muffle her screams. Her pussy clamps down on my cock so tightly that I'm barely able to pull out and push back in. It's only another two thrusts before I'm giving my own shout of pleasure and spilling my seed inside of her, coating her walls in my cum.

I'm still seated inside her while we try to catch our breaths. I don't want to pull out yet and lose this connection. The fact that I almost lost her once has me reluctant to let her out of my arms. Instead, I pull her more closely against my chest and gently stroke her hair, almost in awe of this woman who is mine.

"Does this mean you forgive me?" I ask.

She chuckles and snuggles against my chest. "I don't know. You've got an awful lot of making up to do." I know she's teasing me by the tone of her voice and the fact that her tongue is tracing circles around my nipple. Even if she wasn't, I'm going to spend the rest of my goddamn life making it up to her.

"It would be my pleasure, angel."

"Why do you always call me angel?"

I'm quite a moment, choosing my words carefully before answering.

"Because you look like one." I run my fingers through the golden strands of her hair once again and bend down to gently kiss her forehead. "But it's more than that. You're my own personal angel. You're as close to heaven as a bastard like me will ever get. Every moment we spend together makes me believe that you were created for me. You saved me, angel."

She burrows deeper into my arms, hiding her head in the crook of my neck.

"You saved me too."

I must have done something right in a past life because, for some unknown reason, my angel has forgiven me. I wasn't sure she would, and that anxiety had been eating away at me throughout the entire trip to the hospital in Milford.

As it turned out, I should have hired a driver. Once I started making my calls to the hospital and arranging the rehab for Hollie's mom, the number of calls started snowballing, and I was making call after call. Eventually, I had to pull over to a rest stop so that I could finish making arrangements. Even with hands free calling, I was worried I'd careen off the road with how frayed my nerves were. It had delayed me a few hours, but it had all been worth it when I finally got here and Regina was already in her new room and seen by the doctor. It took a bit of doing, finding a first class doctor in this area with privileges at the small hospital, but it had finally come together. Freda Duma is one of the best doctors within 100 miles.

I overheard the things that Hollie's mother was saying to her and wanted to set the woman straight, but first I had to concentrate on making sure Hollie knew I loved her and needed her. I don't regret any of the arrangements I've made for this woman, but only because she's Hollie's mother. Whether she deserves another chance to be in her daughter's life remains to be seen, and I'm going to make sure she knows that. The choice is ultimately Hollie's, of course, but she's mine now and I protect what's mine even if it's from her own family.

She's mine.

I'm hers.

The thought brings a smile to my face. If anyone was looking at me right now, they would think I'd completely lost my mind. I'm grinning like a fool.

Entering Regina's room, I take a seat next to her bed. She's looking at me with eyes that are the same green and gold as Hollie's, but lack her warmth or spark of joy. By her dour expression, I'd say she's lost all of her love for life. I wish her daughters were enough for her to get her life together, but they obviously aren't. Because of that, my Hollie has had an incredible burden sitting on her shoulders for years.

"Listen Regina, we need to talk," I jump in, wanting to have this conversation before Hollie gets back from the cafeteria.

"The fancy billionaire wants to talk to little old me. I'm honored."

I sigh and rub my eyes that are bone tired from lack of sleep. Add to that the incredible orgasm I had twenty minutes ago, and I just want to drag Hollie back to the closest bed, wrap her in my arms, and sleep for the next ten hours. I decide the best course of action is to ignore her tone and soldier on with what I have to say.

"This stops now, Regina. No more depending on Hollie for everything. She's been taking care of you for far too long. You're the parent and you need to step up and be there for her."

"You don't know what the fuck you're talking about. I've always been there for my daughter. It's her piece of shit father that's never been there. I raised that girl. You don't get to speak to me like that." There's a fire in her eyes that reminds me of Hollie when she gets worked up, but on Regina it looks slightly unhinged.

I'm not sure if it's the alcohol or the drugs, but her body is craving something. Her hands are shaking and she tries to hold them steady in her lap and her right foot won't stop jiggling. It looks like she's about ready to crawl out of her skin. Too bad for her, it's just started.

"She doesn't need you and she doesn't need her father. She has me now. I'm going to be her family, and I won't allow you to take advantage of her anymore. I'll handle all your expenses, including the hospital stay. The only thing you have to do is go to rehab. Stay there for the entire program, get clean, come home and you can be a part of your daughters' lives."

"Who the fuck do you think you are? Hollie won't listen to this shit. She won't abandon me just because you've told her to. I've been with her for her entire life. I'm her mother. She needs me."

"I do need you, Mom." I look over to where Hollie is standing. The light from the hallway is spilling in behind her, outlining her silhouette, and giving her a golden shine. My chest seizes up with emotion. She truly is an angel, and she's all mine. I can't believe I came so close to losing her. "But Archer is right. I'm tired of this, not just for me, but for Paige too. You leave her alone for days at a time, you have drugs in the apartment. What if the police showed up and thought they were hers? Or one of your druggie friends came to steal your stash? Both Paige and I work to pay *your* bills. Things have to change."

"What are you saying, Hollie?" Her mom asks, her voice now sounding small. I don't think she's used to Hollie standing up for herself. It's like the wind has been taken out of her sails and all the fight in her is gone. It seems like she used up her last bit of defiance on me and she can't bear to face her daughter.

Hollie moves farther into the room and sidles up to me, resting her ass on the arm of the chair.

Close, but not close enough.

I pull her down into my lap where she belongs. She acts like she's going to pull away, but I grasp her hips and give them a squeeze, silently telling her to stay put. She better get used to sitting on my lap because I need to have her close. She rests against me and my quickly hardening length settles between her ass cheeks. I almost let out a groan, but I need to focus and present a united front to her mother, showing that we both mean business. I hadn't meant for Hollie to overhear this conversation, but the fact that she's on board makes it that much easier.

"Go to the rehab, Mom." She looks back at me nervously before settling her eyes back on her mother, who is now a few shades lighter than she was before. "I wouldn't normally take a handout—"

"It's not a handout," I growl in her ear. Doesn't she know that everything I have is now hers? It's hers in spirit now and it's only a matter of time before it's hers legally as well.

"—but," she continues, giving me a sharp look that causes me to shut my mouth, "this is for your own good. We could never afford to get you to a rehab facility, so if Archer is so generously going to help us, then we're going to accept. I don't want you to die. And I'll be paying him back for whatever he spends."

The fuck she will.

I squeeze her hips again, this time letting her know I'm protesting her statement without words.

"Mom, if you don't go, if you don't get clean, I'll never let you see Paige again. And I won't want to see you either." There's a hitch in her voice and without seeing her face, I recognize that she's holding back tears.

I decide now is the time for me to jump in before Hollie has a full on meltdown. "I'll leave both you and Bridges with all of my contact information, so if you need anything, you'll be able to get in touch with me. We want to support you in this. Your daughters deserve to have their mother in their lives. You need to make yourself worthy of them."

Regina looks defeated. I don't know if she's really on board with what we've proposed or if she just doesn't want to have this conversation anymore. "Fine. I'll go. But it's only for you and Paige. I don't need to be there. If this is what you need to understand that I'm fine, then I'll go."

Hollie's entire body relaxes in my lap like she'd been holding herself together long enough to say what she needed to say to her mom. She looks like she could use some sleep. We both could.

"Thank you, Mom. I can't even tell you what this means to me."

About thirty minutes later, an orderly comes in and takes Regina out for some tests, giving me a few moments alone with my girl. I settle onto the couch in the room and gather Hollie against my side. I pull her head to my chest and stroke her back, hoping to soothe her to sleep. She hasn't gotten much over the past few days.

"Thank you."

Her words are so soft and low I almost miss them. I give her a squeeze and ask, "For what?"

She pulls out of my arms and I'm about to snatch her back to me when she climbs into my lap, straddling me so that we're face to face, noses almost touching.

"For everything, Archer. For everything. I promise I'll pay you back as soon as I find a job—"

"You have a job," I interrupt. "And you're not paying me back."

"I appreciate that," she says slowly. "I'm going to need to find something in Milford, though. I don't think there's much demand for a CEO's assistant or even a marketing—"

"What are you talking about?" My body has stiffened to where it feels like my muscles might pop. Does she still think she's moving here and leaving me? She's out of her goddamn mind.

"Archer, I'm going to need to stay and take care of my sister. Then, once my mom is out of rehab, she's going to need help. I can't abandon them."

"We won't abandon them, angel. Your sister will come to Seattle. She can move in with us. She'll have access to the best schools there. We'll cross the bridge of your mom when we get to it. If she has to move in with us too, then that's fine. We have plenty of room."

"Move in with *us*? You want me to move in with you?" She's looking at me with trepidation and maybe a bit of hope.

"Yes, move in with *us*. Do you really think I'm going to let you move here now that I've got you? If that's too fast for you—"

"No, it's not too fast," she quickly adds. She places her hand on my chest, and I know she can feel my speeding heart. "I want you to be sure. I would hate it if you regretted moving me and my sister in. Regretted... me."

I place my lips on her forehead, giving her a gentle kiss. "I could never regret you, Hollie. You're my perfect match. Without you, I'd be a lonely, grumpy bastard."

A giggle escapes her lips. "You're not so bad once you let someone get to know the real you." She scoots closer to me, resting her head on my chest while wrapping her arms and legs around me. A feeling of contentment settles over my entire being. This girl is all I'll ever need. For a moment I picture her standing in our kitchen, her stomach swollen with our child, the proof of our love and my never ending desire for her.

In the quiet of the room, I hold her, our breaths slowly syncing up with one another. However, my brain is working at light speed. My entire life is re-shuffling itself, making her and our future family my number one priority.

"I love you, angel," I whisper against her head, sure she's finally fallen asleep.

"I love you more."

Impossible.

EPILOGUE

THREE MONTHS LATER

HOLLIE

It's unseasonably warm for this time of year in Santa Cruz. The waves are crashing against the sand and the gentle breeze swirls my skirt around my thighs. I send a smile to my boyfriend, who's standing on the beach in front of a crowd of locals, thanking them for joining us for today's groundbreaking.

I reach down and grab my sister's hand, giving it a squeeze. I'm glad she's here with me. With us. It's been a long three months getting here. When I told Paige that she was moving to Seattle to live with Archer and I, she was less than pleased. Actually, she threw a fit that would rival even the moodiest of teenagers.

I knew she didn't want to move and leave behind her school and friends. I really did understand. But this was the best move for her. Especially since Mom checked herself out of rehab after only three weeks and we haven't heard from her since. It took a while, but she's finally adjusting.

It doesn't help that she has my boyfriend wrapped around her little finger. Archer is the protective older brother she never had, but if push comes to shove, he folds like a house of cards for her. Plus, he gifted her a Mercedes for her birthday. I had a few choice words for him in private about that one. He calmly explained to me it was the safest car on the market and then handed me the keys for my own. The man is incorrigible.

The crowd claps around me, pulling me out of my daydreams. Throngs of people in front of me part as Archer wades through them in my direction. Once he reaches me, he snakes an arm around my back and pulls me close before taking my lips in a kiss that sets all of my nerve endings on fire.

It's always like this with him. I thought after we had been together a few times, the desire I had for him would dim a bit. I was wrong. It seems to grow each day like a wild flower seeking the sun. Thankfully, he seems to be in the same boat as me.

"Hi, angel." He pulls back and smiles at the watching crowd with me firmly tucked into his side.

"Hey," I answer in a breathy whisper.

"You know this is all because of you, don't you?"

A blush stains my cheeks. "Please, this was all you. I might have helped a tiny bit." I hold up my hand, my index finger and thumb spaced maybe an inch apart, showing to him how little I know I've done.

Of course, when I found out that Caroline DuPont had agreed to sell to him even though he missed the deadline, I was thrilled. This was all he ever wanted.

When he told me it was because I had called her and asked about hotel memorabilia, I was stunned. Who would have thought that such a little thing would have had such a far-reaching effect? She had wanted someone to buy the land that would respect the city and the history of the place. I guess wanting that hotel key showed her I, and by extension Archer, were the best people for the job. She wasn't wrong.

Archer and I walk hand in hand across the sand towards our friends gathered near the new mockup for The Clarke, Santa Cruz.

The image doesn't much resemble the one I first saw in the office. Even though he couldn't preserve them all, Archer saved six bungalows from demolition. They'll be renovated to give occupants a private luxury experience. Subsequently, the main hotel has shrunk, but he doesn't care. Some of the board members had a minor conniption that they couldn't pack more guests in, but after Archer exposed Gilbert Clarke's misdeeds to the board and booted him, they weren't in the mood to make waves.

"Nice job, billionaire." Bianca gives him a playful punch in the arm once we reach our group of friends. Archer flew out everyone for today's groundbreaking, including Bianca, Violet, and Dante Moreno. Looking around me, my heart's filled with love like it never has been before. I'm here with my friends, my sister, and the love of my life. I honestly never thought that I would have so much.

"Thanks, Bianca," he says with a grin.

There's a band that's started playing and hors d'oeuvre are being passed around by well-dressed waiters. Now that the ceremony is over, it's time for the party to begin.

Richard Osman and his wife Flora approach. He shakes Archer's hand while Flora gives him a hug.

"I never doubted you, kid."

"Of course not. All those times you stormed into my office, pacing and complaining, really showed me the faith you had." He laughs good-naturedly.

Since we got back from Milford and Paige and I moved in with Archer, things have been less stressful at the office. Archer has taken a step back, and while he's still as serious about the business as ever, he also delegated things that weren't essential for him to handle. The lower stress has extended to Richard and Flora's mentioned several times how grateful she is for the new, less stressful pace.

Archer's told me many times that I don't have to work but we both knew that wouldn't happen. I wouldn't be some kept woman. Besides, I enjoyed going into the office every day, seeing the friends I'd made and being productive. Because of the no fraternization rule, I moved down to the marketing department. After working for the CEO, it was a change, and I found that only focusing on marketing was a bit boring for me. I was used to having my fingers in so many pies and all different aspects of the business that it was too slow paced.

Besides, Archer was calling me up to his office so often that I wasn't very productive. It seems he didn't like me working on another floor, and I couldn't say that I blamed him. After about two weeks, he went to the board, had the policy changed, and rehired me as his personal assistant. Now, I get to work with my sexy boyfriend every day and I truly enjoy what I'm doing.

As the afternoon wears on, there's a chill in the air and I guess I should be at least thankful that it was warmer for part of the day. Archer is chatting with an investor but is maintaining his firm grip on my hand.

"I've got a surprise for you," he leans down and whispers into my ear as the other man wanders to another group of attendees.

I eye him skeptically. "What kind of surprise?"

"A good one." The devilish grin he gives me makes my knees weak and my panties wet as he pulls me away from the crowd towards the rows of empty bungalows. Before I know it, we're standing in front of the building where we first made love all those months ago.

Today, the porch isn't dark and dilapidated. It's overflowing with flowers of every kind and color. The porch railing is dotted with candles that are flickering in the late afternoon breeze. I don't even notice that I've stopped in my tracks until Archer gives my hand a little tug to get me moving again. I obediently follow along, stunned at the sight. He guides me up the short steps and it's then that I see a table with a bottle of champagne.

"What's going on?" I ask, turning in a full circle so I can take it all in. There are even flowers hanging from the rafters overhead. "How did you do this?"

"I might have had a little help from our friends," he admits.

"It's beautiful."

Before I can ask him what exactly is going on, he sinks to one knee and I let out a shocked gasp. He isn't doing what I think he's doing, is he?

"Hollie, I didn't realize how much I needed you in my life until you showed up in it. I was a lonely, grumpy bastard that had little in life to be happy about. You've changed everything. You've changed me. I don't want to live another day without knowing you're going to be my wife, to be the person I spend the rest of my life with and create a family with. I want babies that look exactly like their momma to keep me in line and fill my life with joy. Even if you say no, I'll still love you until the day I die. You're it for me. My one. Will you marry me?"

I'm stunned. I should say yes. I want to say yes. But I can't seem to move. Archer Clarke, billionaire playboy, wants to marry me? The girl from the wrong side of the tracks? He's mentioned getting married before like it was a foregone conclusion for us, but I still always had a niggling doubt that it would happen.

My sudden bout of muteness is making him look nervous and his body is shifting a bit on his knee. "Are you going to answer me, angel?"

"Yes!" The word flies out of my mouth and before I realize it, I'm kneeling on the porch as well, covering his face in kisses. "Yes. Yes. Yes. Of course I'll marry you!"

"Thank God," he grumbles. Like there was ever a doubt.

There's the sound of cheers and applause behind me and I turn to see our group of friends gathered, watching the spectacle.

"You're sure?" I ask quietly so that only he can hear.

The heat in his eyes warms me from the inside out. He says he'll love me until the day he dies. Well, I'll love him beyond that. How could I not? He's perfect, and he's made all the things I never even dared to dream come true.

"I've never been more sure of anything in my entire life. You're mine, forever."

"Forever."

We seal our promise with a soul shattering kiss and somehow I know it will only get better from here.

EXTENDED EPILOGUE

SIX YEARS LATER

ARCHER

"Adam, don't dump water on your brother." Adam looks over at me with his eyes that match my own and drops the bucket he was hauling over to his unsuspecting brother, who's busy in the sand.

"Sorry, daddy!" he yells before running up to Dylan and collapsing into the sand next to his younger brother. I chuckle under my breath. If there's trouble to be had, Adam will find it.

I'm sitting in the sand on a beach towel in my trunks, watching my two boys finally playing together nicely.

Adam's dark hair and brown eyes show that he's clearly my child, while Dylan's light hair and green-gold eyes make him a miniature version of Hollie. We named Adam after my father and it's days like these that I feel closest to him and my mother.

We're in Santa Cruz for our annual vacation at The Clarke, Santa Cruz and we're staying in one of the renovated bungalows, as usual.

The past six years have been the best of my life, but the times we spend here are my favorite. I love relaxing in the sun and sand and watching my children grow. I know from experience that I'm giving them memories that will last a lifetime. If my parents were here today, they would be overjoyed that we're carrying on this tradition that meant so much to them.

When Adam was one, Hollie suggested we come here for a week to spend time together and frankly, I'm not sure why I hadn't thought of it myself. Over the years, that week extended to two, and we started sharing the time here with our friends and family. Paige usually comes down and stays with us for at least a few days depending on her schedule and the boys love spending time with their aunt.

I rise from my towel, dusting sand off my ass and head over to the boys, scooping Dylan up into my arms. He squeals and wraps his tiny hands around my neck, and I plop a big wet kiss on his cheek, which makes him laugh harder. At three years old, he's a happy-go-lucky kid and I hope he stays that way forever.

"Daddy, stop!"

"Come on guys," I say, grabbing Adam's hand, "let's go check out the waves."

"Yay!" Adam pulls his hand out of mine and takes off towards where the waves are crashing against the sand. I let him go since I'm only steps behind him and he knows not to get in past his knees. He's five and fearless.

We spend the next twenty minutes playing in the waves, splashing each other and lifting them into my arms when a larger wave comes in, threatening to knock them both over. I treasure this time with them.

Over the past five years, I've slowed down with my responsibilities at work. I'm still the CEO and I'm proud of everything that we do. I've just gotten exponentially better at delegating. As Hollie always likes to remind me, I have a great team and I should let them do their jobs. They've done nothing but prove her right time and time again. I even work from home a few days a week now.

"Guys! I'm back!" My head turns and my eyes settle on the love of my life. Hollie's approaching the bungalow with several shopping bags in her hands. Her hair falls around her shoulders in curls and her loose-fitting dress catches in the gentle breeze. The light material molds around her protruding stomach, showing off the medium-sized bump that contains our daughter.

"Mom! You shouldn't carry that!" Adam yells while racing across the sand. I laugh, bringing Dylan with me to greet her. Hollie gently rolls her eyes at Adam and gives me a pointed look that says, *this is your fault.*

"I'm fine honey. These bags only have clothes for your sister in them," she explains, while Adam takes them out of her hands. He's very protective of his mother and it's only gotten worse in the six months that she's been pregnant. He might have gotten that from me. I have a feeling he's going to be just as protective of his little sister when she arrives.

"Welcome back, angel," I say before giving her a kiss and settling Dylan on my hip. "How's Caroline?"

Caroline DuPont has become almost a surrogate mother to Hollie over the years. I'll be forever grateful to her for that since we haven't seen neither hide nor hair of Regina in three years. One day she showed up at our offices, drunk and high, demanding money. She didn't even care about seeing her daughter, all she wanted was cash. With Hollie's blessing, I sent her on her way and it's been radio silence from her ever since.

"She's great. She's almost as bad as I am with all the girls' clothes. I mean, I was bad with the boys, but there's something about all the little dresses that makes me lose my mind. I swore I blacked out and woke up outside with all these bags." She laughs as Adam carries her haul up the steps and inside the bungalow.

"How are you feeling?" I ask. I know she was kidding about blacking out, but she's been out for a few hours. Fatigue sneaks up on her when she's pregnant. "Do you still want to go out to dinner? We could always have something here."

"Oh, no you don't, mister. Dante and Violet are going to watch the kids in their bungalow, and I get you all to myself tonight." Her eyes heat and wander the expanse of my exposed chest, and I know she can't wait to get me alone. Pregnancy makes Hollie even hornier than usual, and I'm a man that's happy to accommodate his wife.

I set Dylan down and send him inside after his brother, then take Hollie in my arms, holding her tightly against me. I push my nose into the hair at the top of her head, breathing her in. She still smells like honeysuckle and summer just the way she did when she walked into my office all those years ago. If I had known that day how things would have turned out, I wouldn't have spent all that time resisting her, trying to keep things professional between us. I would have gotten down on one knee and given her a ring instead of a job.

I didn't realize how empty and lonely those years were between my parents' deaths and finding Hollie. I was a man solely going through the motions, trying to build an empire as a monument to the life that I once had but was gone. It took Hollie coming into my life to realize that my past was important, but what was more important was my future and my own family.

I kiss the top of Hollie's head. "I love you, angel. Thank you."

"Thank me for what?"

"For our family." She pulls away from me and looks into my eyes. Hers are watering, and I know she's about to burst into tears. Her emotions are always on a roller coaster ride when she's pregnant.

"Thank *you*, Archer. I don't know where I would be without you. Without our boys and our baby girl." She settles her hand on her protruding stomach, and I drop to my knees in the sand and snuggle into it.

"We're waiting for you, baby girl. Only three months left," I whisper before placing a gentle kiss against her stomach.

"Daddy's talking to da baby!" Dylan yells from the open doorway before rushing over to his mother and me, his brother hot on his heels.

They stop short of crashing into Hollie, knowing how important it is to be gentle with her. They both place their hands on Hollie's stomach, fascinated that their little sister could be inside.

"Hurry up, baby," Adam says, "we want to meet you."

"Mom, will the baby come tonight?" Dylan asks.

"Nope sweetheart, we've got a while longer than that. We'll be back home before the baby comes." He looks disappointed for a minute before tugging on my trunks, demanding to be picked up. I raise him up and tuck Hollie into my side before the four, soon to be five, of us make our way back to the bungalow. My entire world is right here in my arms, and I couldn't be happier.

Thank you for reading *Unprofessionally Yours*!

Check out Violet and Dante's story, *Made To Be Yours*, available in 2022.

I hope that you enjoyed Hollie and Archer's story as much as I enjoyed writing it. If you enjoyed this book, please take a moment to leave a review. As an independent author, nothing helps us more than your reviews, good or bad. I can't tell you how much I would appreciate it.

Sign-up for my newsletter at evesterlingbooks.com to be the first to know about new releases and bonus content!

ALL ABOUT EVE

Eve Sterling was born and raised in the Los Angeles area where she now resides after a brief detour to the San Francisco Bay Area. After climbing the corporate ladder for many years, she decided to take a break and pursue her lifelong passion for writing. When Eve is not coming up with more book ideas than she could possibly ever write she enjoys reading, binge watching shows with friends, and hanging out with her two dogs.

Contact me on social media!

Facebook: www.facebook.com/evesterlingauthor

Instagram: www.instagram.com/evesterlingbooks

Twitter: twitter.com/evesterlingbook

Website: www.evesterlingbooks.com

Email: evesterlingauthor@gmail.com

Printed in Great Britain
by Amazon

24451243R00182